Karen King is a bestselling author of fiction for both adults and children and has also written numerous short stories for women's magazines. *The Cornish Hotel by the Sea* was an international bestseller, reaching the top one hundred in the Kindle charts in both the UK and Australia.

Karen is a member of the Romantic Novelists' Association, the Society of Authors and the Society of Women Writers and Journalists. She lives in Spain with her husband Dave and their two cats, Tizzy and Marmaduke.

By Karen King

Romance titles
I do – or do I?
The Millonaire Plan
Never Say Forever
The Cornish Hotel by the Sea
The Bridesmaid's Dilemma
Snowy Nights at the Lonely Hearts Hotel
The Year of Starting Over
Single All the Way
One Summer in Cornwall
The Best Christmas Ever

Thriller titles
The Stranger in My Bed
The Perfect Stepmother

The Best Christmas Ever

Karen King

ACCENT

First published in paperback in 2021 by Headline Accent
An imprint of HEADLINE PUBLISHING GROUP

1

Cataloguing in Publication Data is available from the British Library

ISBN 978 1 4722 7873 9

Typeset in 11.25/15.25 pt Bembo by Jouve (UK), Milton Keynes
Printed and bound in Great Britain by Clays Ltd, Elcograf S.p.A.

HEADLINE PUBLISHING GROUP
An Hachette UK Company
Carmelite House
50 Victoria Embankment
London
EC4Y 0DZ

www.headline.co.uk
www.hachette.co.uk

For my readers. Thank you for the love and support.
May this Christmas be your best Christmas ever. xx

Chapter One

Friday, eight days before Christmas

Well, that was school finished for a couple of weeks, Lexi Forde thought as she started up her car. She loved her job as a primary school teacher at Rudcup Primary but it was very demanding and, whilst the run-up to Christmas was rewarding and fun, it was crazily busy. She was glad to have a couple of weeks off now and was looking forward to catching up with her family down in Devon.

This is going to be the best Christmas ever! My first one with Ben, and the whole Forde family together again.

She waved to some pupils she passed walking up the hill with their parents, then turned right to head for the shopping centre. She wanted to get some new Christmas lights so that she could put up the tree at the weekend, and buy a couple more presents for her boyfriend, Ben. She'd already bought him a Ferrari drive experience – she knew he would love that – and a retro arcade machine, which her best friend, Fern, was keeping in her spare bedroom so that Ben didn't stumble across it.

There wasn't much room to hide anything in their one-bedroom flat. And she had just finished the Christmas jumper she'd secretly been knitting while he was working late. She wasn't sure if Christmas jumpers were Ben's thing, but all her family would be wearing one so she hoped he would join in the festive spirit and don it for the day.

This Christmas was going to be so special, her elder brother, Jay, and his family were coming over for a visit. She hadn't seen Jay since he went to work in Canada five years ago or met his wife, Sonia, and their three-year-old son, Toby. They'd video called, of course, which was great, but it wasn't the same as seeing them in the flesh. Her younger brother, Ryan, would be there too, with his girlfriend, Nell. And Granny Mabe, who had moved in with Lexi's parents a few years ago when Grandpa Huey had died. Luckily, Lexi's parents' sprawling four-bedroom detached house, with the garage conversion for Granny Mabe, was big enough to put them all up. It would be a fun-filled Christmas and Lexi was longing to see them all again. Especially after last year when she couldn't travel to Devon because of the Covid restrictions. Unfortunately, Ben didn't finish work until midday on Christmas Eve and he had to return the day after Boxing Day, but at least they would all be together for Christmas Day.

'You go down at the weekend and spend some time with your family, Lex, I can come down on Christmas Eve,' Ben had urged her as soon as he'd heard that there was going to be a gathering of the Forde clan.

Although she was tempted, Lexi was a bit worried that Ben might be too tired to drive down on Christmas Eve and would go to his mum's for Christmas instead. He'd actually suggested this, but as it would be their first Christmas together, she didn't want to spend it apart. So, she'd told him she wanted them to go down together and didn't mind just having a couple of days with her family. She wanted Ben to experience a Forde Christmas. All her family were as crazy about Christmas as she was and, once the whole Forde tribe got together, the festivities really started. She knew that her parents would go overboard with the decorations, as usual, covering the outside of the house and the tree in the front garden with twinkling lights. There would be a Christmas tree in every room and in the porch, and Dad would have fetched his collection of inflatable snowmen, Santas and reindeer and placed them all over the house. Christmas jumpers and Christmas hats were a must. She smiled as she recalled how her parents had always dressed up as Santa and Mrs Claus for Christmas day when Lexi and her brothers were young.

She decided to meet Ben from work when she'd finished her shopping so they could go for a drink and have a catch up. They'd both been so busy lately they'd barely had time to mumble more than 'what shall we have for dinner?' or 'do you want a coffee?' Perhaps they could grab a bite to eat before they came home too, that would make the evening more relaxing. She knew that Ben was working a half day tomorrow, so she decided she'd put up the Christmas tree as a surprise for when he came home. Maybe she could get a small turkey crown and they could have their own Christmas dinner on Sunday – it would give them chance to celebrate as a couple. She could get a box of crackers too, and they could open one or two of their presents, have their own early Christmas Day. That would be so romantic.

The shops were packed with long queues everywhere. By the time Lexi had bought some new lights – she'd plumped for warm white ones that changed to multicoloured then back again – and a couple of stocking fillers for Ben, there was only half an hour before Ben finished work. *I'll get the rest of the shopping on Monday*, she decided, as she headed for the car park.

It was bitterly cold. Lexi shoved her hands in her pockets, wishing she hadn't left her gloves in the car, and glanced over at the entrance to the big office block where people were starting to trickle out. Ben should be out any minute now, he finished work at five thirty and it was twenty to six. Unless he was working late. He had worked late quite a bit lately. It was stupid of her to come and meet him on impulse like this, she should have messaged him first, she realised. She'd text him now, she could wait in the café around the corner if he was working late, or maybe he would be able to leave if he knew she was waiting for him.

She took out her phone then paused, a smile springing to her lips as the doors opened and Ben walked out, looking endearingly handsome as he buttoned up his long black overcoat, the grey-cashmere scarf she'd knitted for him wrapped around his neck. She always thought that there were two different Bens, the easy-going Ben that lounged around in jeans and T-shirts at home and the sales manager Ben who always dressed impeccably for work in a suit, shirt and tie. She loved both versions. She waved and stepped forward but Ben had turned back to the entrance. *Has he forgotten something?* A woman with short, dark hair, dressed in a long camel coat with knee-high, brown-leather boots, and a brown-leather handbag swinging on her shoulder, walked out and her face lit up in a smile. Lexi watched, stunned, as Ben stepped forward to meet her and the woman wound her arms around his neck and kissed him. Kissed Ben. *Her* boyfriend. And Ben was kissing her back. Then they were both walking off hand in hand and Lexi was watching them, too shocked to move. *Ben and another woman?*

Suddenly she found her voice and shouted 'Ben!' so loudly that other office workers leaving the building stopped and stared.

Ben turned around and she saw the surprise on his face as he registered her standing there, then quickly released the woman's hand. 'Lexi?'

He was walking back towards her now, swiftly composing himself and changing his expression to one of delight. 'Lexi, darling . . .'

Here it came, the big excuse for why he had kissed another woman and was walking off with her. Did he think she was so gullible that she would accept anything he said? The look on that woman's face when she spotted Ben waiting for her had said it all.

'Rosa and I were just . . .'

Lexi folded her arms and waited to see what explanation would trip out of his mouth.

'Just tell her the truth, Ben. She deserves that.' The woman – Rosa, apparently – had joined them. She linked her arm through Ben's, a smug expression on her face as she looked at Lexi. 'I'm sorry you had to find out this way. Ben was going to tell you after Christmas, weren't you, Ben?'

Ben opened his mouth but no sound came out.

'Tell me what exactly?' Lexi asked, fighting to keep the tears from her eyes and the wobble out of her voice. She would not break down in front of them. She damn well would not!

'Lexi . . .' Ben had found his voice now, his eyes were on hers, pleading for her to understand.

'We're in love. We've been seeing each other for a while.' Rosa was looking at her with pity in her eyes. Lexi jutted out her chin, holding her head higher. She didn't want this bloody woman's pity. Nor Ben's.

'Is that so? Well, in that case, you're welcome to each other.' She fixed her eyes on Ben's face, ignoring the woman. She held out her right hand, palm upwards. 'I'll have the keys to my flat, thank you.'

Ben looked shocked. 'You're throwing me out?'

Is he for real? 'You expect to keep living with me when you've just told me that you're seeing someone else?' She wriggled her hand. 'Give me my keys. I'll pack up your things and put them outside the door of my flat at eight o'clock tonight. You can pick them up then.'

The colour drained from Ben's face. 'You can't do that . . .'

'I think you'll find I can. The flat is in my name.' She'd been renting it for two years before Ben had moved in and, thankfully, hadn't got around to adding him to the tenancy.

'I'll give you the key when I've collected my things. I don't trust you. You might throw them away in revenge.'

Lexi summonsed up the most contemptuous look she could manage. 'Revenge for what? For you cheating on me? Don't flatter yourself that I'm upset about it because I'm not. I was getting bored with you anyway.' It was a lie but she was damned if she would let either he or bloody Rosa know how upset she was.

'Don't worry about it, darling, you can move in with me. Let's go and collect your things now and take them straight over to my house.' Rosa emphasised the word 'house' as opposed to 'flat', her eyes taking in Lexi's short, grey faux-fur coat, red-and-black checked miniskirt, thick black tights and black over-the-knee boots. She obviously considered Lexi inferior to her.

'Go ahead, but *she* isn't stepping foot in *my* flat,' Lexi told Ben firmly. '*She* can wait in the car.'

She turned on her heels and marched away, her head held high. It wasn't until she reached her car and was safely sitting in the front seat that a sob wracked her body. *Pull yourself together. You're not going to do this in front of them. You don't want Ben to arrive at the flat for his things and find you crying. Don't give him the satisfaction.* She took a few deep breaths, then started up the car. She would give Ben a quarter of an hour or so to pack his things and get out. Then she could give way to the devastation and shock his betrayal had caused her.

Chapter Two

Lexi had been home just long enough to pour herself a glass of Sauvignon Blanc for Dutch courage – and shock – when the door opened and Ben walked in. He paused in the doorway and looked at her as though assessing whether he needed to duck from flying missiles. 'I never meant this to happen . . .'

'I don't want to hear any excuses.' She held out her hand. 'Key.'

He shuffled his feet awkwardly. 'Lexi, can't we talk about this? Let's not be hasty.' He gave her his best puppy-dog look, the one that usually melted her heart. *Well, not this time.*

'Talk about what? That you've been cheating on me for goodness knows how long?' She glared at him. 'There's nothing to talk about. You want someone else. I'm not going to stand in your way.'

'I don't know whether I do. I still love you . . .'

'Tough. I no longer want you. Now if you would please pack and go.'

'I'm sorry, I never meant it to happen. It doesn't have to end like this . . .' He gazed at her imploringly.

'It certainly does. We're over.' What was he on? Did he think she would just forgive him, beg him to come back? Lexi was a tolerant person and believed in giving people a second chance, or even a third, depending on the circumstances, but loyalty was the one thing that was non-negotiable in a relationship as far as she was concerned. Much as she loved Ben, she couldn't – wouldn't – forgive him for cheating on her.

He scowled. 'Well, if that's the way you want it.' He dropped the key on the coffee table. 'I'll be out of your way in a few minutes.'

She took a long gulp of wine. How dare he act as if she was the one in the wrong? She wanted to scream and pummel him with her fists, throw his clothes out of the window, but she had no intention of doing either. She would remain calm and dignified if it killed her. She wasn't going to give him the satisfaction of any other reaction.

She sat on the sofa in the lounge area sipping her wine and pointedly ignoring Ben as he stamped about packing his things, then took them outside to where Rosa was waiting. Finally, he stood in front of Lexi. 'That's it then. Everything.' There was a tragic edge to his voice.

She forced herself to calmly meet his gaze. 'Goodbye, Ben.'

He shook his head in disbelief. 'I can't believe you're being so cold about this.'

She surveyed him over the rim of her glass. 'What do you want me to do? Cry? Beg you to stay with me?' She shook her head. 'Not my style. Now let yourself out.'

'You're not the person I thought you were, Lexi. I thought you were warm, loving . . .'

She eyed him contemptuously. 'Says the man who's been shagging another woman behind my back.'

He flinched as if she'd slapped him across the face. Then he turned and walked out, slamming the door behind him.

As soon as the front door closed, the tears that Lexi had been fighting back for the past hour spilled out of her eyes and poured down her cheeks. She put the now-empty wine glass down on the table, curled up into a ball, pulling her feet up underneath her and resting her head on her bent knees, and sobbed. She'd really thought that she and Ben were happy together, that he might be 'the one'. They'd rarely argued, had rubbed along together so well. How wrong she was. She couldn't believe that he had betrayed her so badly. How long had it been going on? While she'd been planning their first Christmas together, Ben had probably been plotting how to avoid spending Christmas Day with her, preferring to be with Rosa instead. No wonder he had suggested that she go down to Devon to spend time with her family by herself. She'd bet he'd been intending to say he was too tired to travel down to join them and would have Christmas dinner at his mum's instead, only he wouldn't have been at his mum's, would he? He'd have been at Rosa's. The two-timing rat.

She wiped away her tears with the back of her hand, poured herself another glass of wine and wandered into the bedroom. The wardrobe doors on Ben's side were open. She walked over and looked inside at the empty space where his clothes had hung. The very clothes that he would soon be hanging up in Rosa's wardrobe. Then she turned to the bed, her eyes resting sadly on the empty spot where Ben would no longer sleep. Tonight, she would sleep alone and Ben would be cuddled up to Rosa. A lump formed in her throat again and tears welled in her eyes. Her mother would tell her to cry it out. 'Crying is good for you,' she always said. 'It's nature's way of getting rid of the sadness in your heart. Once it's all out, you can start building your life again.'

Lexi kicked off her shoes, yanked back the duvet and lay down, then she pulled it around herself, buried her head in the pillow and cried out her sadness. It took a long time, but finally, she fell asleep.

Lexi awoke the next morning feeling exhausted but calmer. At least she had found out what a lying scumbag Ben was. Now she was going to pull herself together, go down to Devon and have a brilliant family Christmas. She certainly wasn't going to spend it crying over Ben. And she could go down today instead of waiting for Ben to finish work on Christmas Eve. There was nothing to keep her here, she could take her laptop and do her lesson planning in Devon. She'd tell her parents that Ben had insisted that she come down without him as he had to work over Christmas. They were so excited about the whole family being together again that she didn't want to put a dampener on it with the news that she and Ben had split up. Nothing was going to spoil this Christmas, she'd make sure of it. She'd wait until this afternoon before she set off, though, make sure the wine was out of her system. Lystone, the village where her parents lived, was only a couple of hours' drive so she would get there before it started to get dark.

She made some toast, to give herself some energy, even though eating was the last thing she felt like doing, and a strong cup of coffee. The flat looked so dull and un-Christmassy, with only a couple of cards on the wall unit. Several of her pupils had given her cards yesterday, and presents too. She'd planned on putting up the Christmas tree today, placing the presents around it, hanging the cards up along the wall, draping fairy lights around the window – making it look festive for when Ben came home. She blinked back the tears. Well, Ben was never coming home again and it was a waste of time decorating the flat when she was going away for Christmas. She'd take the lights for her dad, he could always find use for a string of Christmas lights, and she'd return Ben's presents after Christmas. She might as well take the Christmas jumper she'd knitted him with her, though, one of her brothers might want to wear it.

She took the shopping bags into her bedroom, and slipped the box of lights into her suitcase. Then she took the carrier bag containing Ben's Christmas jumper out of the wardrobe where she'd hidden it and spread the jumper out on the bed. It was white with rows of red reindeer and green Christmas trees running across it. She had designed and knitted it herself. She'd knitted herself a long, hooded Christmas cardigan in the same pattern and Ben had remarked how festive it was, which had really pleased her. She loved creating original knitwear to either wear herself or sell on her own website – LexiKnits – and Etsy. Although Ben had teased her when he'd first seen her knitting, saying it was an 'old lady's hobby' he'd been impressed with the grey-cashmere scarf she'd made him, saying it was classy, and she'd been so proud when he wore it to work. Ben had been so supportive of her, so kind and loving. She was sure he'd have been willing to wear this jumper when he saw everyone else wearing one – he might even have liked it!

She looked at the empty side of the bed, remembering her and Ben cuddling, making love, sitting up sipping tea and reading on Sunday mornings, the late breakfasts, the movie nights cuddled up in front of the TV, how Ben had made her a hot chocolate with marshmallows when she was crying at a sad romantic movie, or came back from work late with flowers or chocolates.

But they were 'guilt presents', weren't they? Ben hadn't been working late, he'd been with Rosa.

She thought of Rosa, so elegantly dressed, looking every inch the career woman, and imagined her and Ben discussing spreadsheets, sales charts, targets and contracts. Not like Lexi, who wore comfy clothes for her work at the school, spent her evenings marking or doing lesson plans or knitting while she watched the soaps. Ben had often teased her that she had no ambition.

'Ambition is for people who want their life to be different,' she'd told him. 'I'm happy with mine exactly how it is.'

And she was happy – at least, she had been until today. But obviously Ben wasn't. He wanted someone more ambitious, more glamorous, more exciting than Lexi. All those times he'd held her in his arms, told her he loved her, that she was perfect, he'd been lying. Did he say the same things to Rosa? she wondered, tears filling her eyes again. She blinked them back. She was done crying over Ben. She folded the jumper up, slipped it back in the bag, then put it in her suitcase. She grabbed her laptop and put that in too, then zipped the case shut. She did a final check of the flat to make sure all the taps and electric sockets were turned off and headed down to the car. In just a couple of hours' time she would be in Lystone, back in the warmth of her family home, and then she could shut Ben out of her mind. She'd deal with her heartbreak after Christmas, when she felt stronger.

The roads were busy with Saturday-afternoon traffic and it was dusk when Lexi pulled up in the driveway of her parents' home, which, as she'd expected, was ablaze with colourful fairy lights. Her father had strung lights on the tree in the front garden, and all up the drive, and around the guttering – just as he used to do when she, Ryan and Jay were all young. She was pleased she'd arrived a little later than she'd intended as she could now see the decorations in all their glory. She stepped out of the car and looked around at the sparkling Christmas tree in the porch, the colourful lights twinkling on and off around the windows, the huge Santa figure by the door, the reindeer and sleigh glowing on the roof – trying not to worry about her father climbing ladders at his age – and felt as if she'd been jolted back to her childhood, when life was simpler and she'd had no idea how falling in love with someone could crush your heart into tiny pieces.

There were no lights on in the house, though – her father had the Christmas lights on a timer so they came on automatically when it was dark. She guessed that her parents were still at work. They had run a small bakery and tearoom in the village for years, it was very popular, and it would be especially busy this time of year. She glanced at her watch: quarter to five. Her parents always used to close up at four on Saturdays, but maybe they had stayed open later as it was almost Christmas.

Perhaps Granny Mabe is in? she thought. You would think that her eighty-four-year-old granny would be safely tucked up at home at this time of day in the winter, but her mother frequently remarked during her phone calls to Lexi that Granny Mabe was always out and had a better social life than Paula and Craig, Lexi's parents.

14

Suddenly, a car pulled up behind her. Lexi turned, thinking it must be her parents returning home, but it was Granny Mabe who stepped out of the car. She was small – Lexi had inherited her genes – and dressed in a thick, green parka jacket, black trousers, ankle boots and gloves. She had round-rimmed glasses perched on her nose and wisps of her silver hair peeped out of the green-and-red snowman-patterned hat on her head that matched the scarf around her neck, which she had probably knitted herself. She looked like a little Christmas gnome. Her face was wreathed in smiles as she held out her arms.

'Lexi, darling, how good to see you. Come and give your gran a big hug.'

Lexi walked into her arms, just as she used to do when she was a child and had had a row with her brothers or her parents. As she nestled into the warmth of Granny Mabe's embrace, she felt herself relax. She was home. And despite the horrible break-up with Ben, she was going to have a fantastic Christmas, because there was *nothing* like a Forde family Christmas.

Chapter Three

Saturday, seven days before Christmas

'Well, this is a lovely surprise! Paula said you wouldn't be arriving until late on Christmas Eve.' Granny Mabe stepped back and looked over Lexi's shoulder to the car. 'And where's Ben?'.'

Lexi swallowed and forced a cheery tone to her voice. 'He can't come, he's working until late on Christmas Eve and has to write up a proposal for when he goes back on Monday so he told me to come down without him,' she replied, trotting out the excuse she'd planned on the drive down, not wanting her sadness to spoil the celebrations, or for her family to feel sorry for her, especially as her brothers were happily partnered-up. 'He's going to his mum's for Christmas Day.'

Her gran frowned. 'What a shame that you're spending your first Christmas apart.'

Lexi summoned a bright smile. 'Honestly, Gran, it's no big deal. We're going to have a lovely New Year together instead. I hope it isn't a problem that I've come a few days early? I didn't phone because I wanted to surprise you all. Do you think Mum and Dad will mind?'

'Of course not! They'll be made up that they've got you for a few extra days — and all to themselves as well. Although, of course, Ben was very welcome.' Granny Mabe reached into her pocket for her keys. 'Let's have a cuppa and chat. Craig and Paula won't be home for another hour or so.'

'Yes, please,' Lexi replied, linking her arm through her granny's and walking with her to the front door. Granny Mabe was right, it would be good to have time alone with her family without having to worry about whether Ben felt comfortable, or wanted to do anything different.

I'll never have to concern myself with what Ben wants again.

She pushed the thought from her mind. She wasn't going to think about Ben, she was going to enjoy Christmas with her family.

'Are you all right, love? You seem miles away.' Granny Mabe had unlocked the door now and was staring at Lexi, concern etched on her face.

'I'm fine,' Lexi said brightly, following her gran into the cosy hall. Her parents always left the heating on low when they were at work so that the house was warm to come home to.

Granny flicked a switch and a string of colourful fairy lights danced across the wall. Lexi grinned. She knew that it would look like a Christmas grotto inside. Just as Lexi's flat usually did every Christmas. Apart from this one. A wave of sadness surged through her and unwanted tears sprang to her eyes as she thought of the festive weekend she'd planned with Ben. Hoping her gran hadn't noticed, she turned her head quickly, pretending that she was looking at the changing lights.

'Let's go into the kitchen, it's cosier,' Granny suggested as she and Lexi shrugged off their coats. 'Is it tea, coffee or hot chocolate that you're wanting?'

'Hot chocolate, please.' Her emotions now under control, Lexi followed her gran into the kitchen. 'Do you have marshmallows?'

'We certainly do. You'll find them in that top cupboard,' Granny Mabe said as she filled the kettle and switched it on.

Lexi opened the cupboard, spotted the jar of small pink-and-white marshmallows amongst all the other jars, tins and packages, took it out and carried it over to the worktop where Granny Mabe was spooning chocolate powder into two mugs. 'It's already got milk in it but do add some more if you want,' she said.

'It'll be fine. I often buy that brand.' Lexi opened the jar of marshmallows as her gran poured the hot water from the now-boiling kettle into the mugs and stirred. They both scattered a tablespoonful of marshmallows over the top, then took the mugs over to the table, pulled out chairs and sat down.

As she sipped her drink, Lexi remembered the evenings when she was little and had stopped over at her grandparents' house, sitting by the fire drinking hot chocolate while Granny Mabe told her tales of her childhood in Jamaica as she knitted. Her granny's mum had been Jamaican and her father British, they had fallen in love and had two children, Granny Mabe and Great-Uncle Tobias. When her granny's father had been offered a job in England, they had returned to the UK and lived there ever since, and later, Granny Mabe had got married to Grandpa Huey and then had three children, one of them being Lexi's father, Craig. Craig had the same dark hair and golden skin as his mother but was tall and slim with the high cheekbones and Roman nose of his father, making him look – even now, with his full head of curly silver hair – very distinguished.

'So, how are you really?' Granny Mabe asked. 'I saw the tears spring to your eyes in the hall. If you don't want to talk about it, that's fine, but if you do, I'm a good listener. And it will go no further, if you don't want it to.'

Lexi thought of all the times she'd confided in her gran when she was younger, especially during her rebellious teenage years, and the good advice her gran had given her. She'd always felt that she could tell her anything.

'Me and Ben have split up. I found out yesterday that he was having an affair,' she admitted, her voice breaking into a sob.

'Oh, my darling.' Granny Mabe was out of her chair and beside Lexi in a moment, her arms around Lexi's shoulders, squeezing them tight, as Lexi burst into tears. 'There, there. You cry it out.'

Lexi dug her hand into her pocket for the tissue she'd put there before leaving today, and wiped her eyes. 'I don't want to cry over him. I want to forget all about him. He's not worth crying over,' she said, sniffling.

Granny Mabe sat back down, her brown eyes looking at her tenderly through the glasses that had slipped down to her nose. 'Men who treat us badly are never worth crying over, but we do it anyway. We cry for our lost dreams, for the man we thought we were with, for the love we thought we had.' She reached out and placed her hand on Lexi's. 'But when we've finished crying, what do we do?'

Lexi gave her a watery smile, remembering all the similar talks she'd had with her gran when some lad or other had broken her heart in her teens. 'We rise up, stick our lippy on, put a smile on our face and go out with our head held high and show them just what an amazing life we're going to have without them.'

Granny nodded. 'That's my girl.'

Lexi wiped her eyes, her gran's words making her feel much better, as she remembered the other times she'd thought her heart was broken. 'That's why I don't want to tell anyone, Granny. I don't want my break-up to spoil Christmas. Especially as this is our first family Christmas for years.'

'And it won't.' Granny Mabe raised her mug of hot chocolate and held it out to Lexi, who immediately picked up her own mug and clinked it with her gran's. 'To the best Christmas ever,' they both chorused.

Granny Mabe took a big sip of her hot chocolate then put her mug back down and leant across the table. 'Now, I've got a secret to share with you, but not a word to your mum and dad. Promise?'

Lexi's interest was immediately piqued. 'I promise.'

Granny Mabe leant forward conspiratorially. 'I belong to the local Yarn Warriors group. You know what yarn-bombing is, don't you?'

'Yes, it's a kind of street art – people cover trees, benches and other things in knitted squares and stuff,' Lexi replied, thinking it should be her asking her gran that question.

Her granny nodded. 'Yes, but we don't do it just for the sake of it. We do it to pretty something up, or to make a statement, or draw attention to something. Last year we yarn-bombed some rusty benches in the park, it drew lots of attention to them and finally the council sent someone to give them all a coat of paint. There's a lot of people who don't like yarn-bombing, though, they think it's a sort of graffiti, so we do it when no one is around and keep our identities a secret.'

Lexi stared at her. She hadn't expected her eighty-four-year-old gran to know what yarn-bombing was, never mind take part in it! And belong to a secret organisation! Before she could find the words to reply, Granny Mabe looked around as if to make sure no one was listening, although there was only the two of them in the house, and continued.

'We've been yarn-bombing in the village to make it more festive for Christmas. We've made postbox toppers, knitted baubles to string from railings and glittering wool "scarves" to wrap around the trees. You'll see them as you walk around.' Her eyes were wide with excitement. 'Not a word to your parents, mind. I doubt they will approve.'

'But don't they see you knitting? Or do you knit when they're at work?' she asked.

Her granny picked up another marshmallow and popped it into her mouth. 'They're used to me knitting. They think I'm knitting blankets for the old folks.'

Granny Mabe had knitted for as long as Lexi could remember: blankets for babies, hats and scarves for the homeless, cuddly toys for children in hospital, orphanages or overseas. It was Granny Mabe who had taught Lexi to knit as a young child. Later, whenever she had a problem in her teens, she would take her knitting to her gran's and they would knit away as Lexi confided her worries to her. Whenever Lexi turned up with her knitting, Grandpa Huey would disappear into the garden for a bit and leave them to talk. An hour or so later, he'd reappear bearing a tray laden with mugs of hot chocolate and marshmallows and

21

ask, 'all sorted?'. Lexi had always nodded and taken the hot chocolate gratefully. Although Granny Mabe couldn't always solve Lexi's problems, her sage advice had made Lexi feel like she could deal with them. She didn't know what she'd have done without Granny and Grandpa back then. She was so glad that her parents had had the garage converted for them, it meant that Granny Mabe wasn't alone now that Grandpa Huey had died. Poor Granny had been heartbroken to lose the love of her life, but her friends and Lexi's parents had rallied around her, and now she seemed to have a new lease of life. *And a secret one!*

'Isn't it a bit risky? Doesn't anyone see you doing it? There's a lot of people about in the village in the day.'

'We don't do it in the daytime. We're not that daft. We sneak out when it's dark. I tell your parents that I'm going to bingo.'

Lexi nearly choked on her marshmallows. She couldn't believe that her gran was secretly part of a guerrilla movement that sneaked out in the dark to cover objects with their 'knitted graffiti'. She'd bet Granny Mabe had been a right rebel in her youth.

'We're working on a top-secret project—' her granny started to say, but then the front door opened.

'Lexi, are you here?' Her mother had returned from work and had obviously spotted her car in the drive.

'We're in the kitchen!' Granny Mabe shouted. Then she put her finger to her lips and winked.

Chapter Four

'Sweetie! Come back!' Joel Dexter shouted, but the little Maltese terrier ignored him and bounded off down the street in the opposite way Joel had intended to walk, dragging her lead behind her. She'd taken advantage of him struggling with the latch of the gate to pull the lead out of his hand and had made her big escape.

Joel charged after her. 'Sweetie!'

Sweetie ignored him and scampered off far faster than he thought she was capable of.

'Sweetie! Come back!' he shouted again, quickening his pace and wishing his sister and her husband had given the Maltese a different name. He felt stupid running up the street shouting 'Sweetie'.

Honestly, who knew that the little dog would be so much trouble? He was beginning to wonder if he'd done the right thing moving to Lystone just before Christmas. Now the divorce from Toni was almost finalised, he'd wanted to make a fresh start and move right away. So when his sister, Hazel, and her husband, Al, were offered work in Dubai for six months, he'd taken up their offer of renting their house; the idea of living in a little rural village in Devon had appealed to him and he'd thought it would give him time to sort out his life, decide what he wanted to do. His love of the countryside was behind his decision to become a tree surgeon, rather than follow in the footsteps of his parents who were both doctors, and lived and worked in Glasgow, where his father had grown up. Joel had met Toni when he'd moved to Somerset where he'd got a job looking after the woodland belonging to one of the large estates where she was a PA. They'd got married a year later, and then split up two years after that. Toni was a go-getter, and now she had gone.

Lystone was a lovely village, and Hazel and Al's cottage very comfortable, but they had left their Maltese terrier, Sweetie, in Joel's care. Sweetie was eight now, and Hazel had assured Joel that she was very sweet-tempered, content to be left all day while she and Al went to work, and only required feeding, watering, cuddling and walking each day to keep her happy. Joel had soon discovered, however, that Sweetie was one spoilt pooch, and missed her pet parents – as Hazel called her and Al – terribly. She howled every night unless Joel let her sleep in his room, and then she insisted on getting into bed with him and snoring so loudly he barely got any sleep. He was exhausted. And whenever he had to leave her to go out, she barked consistently – at least, he thought she did, because he could hear her barking as soon as he got out of his van. He was worried that the neighbours – who he hadn't met yet – would complain. This week had been tiring and he was desperate for a Sunday-morning lie-in, so had decided to take Sweetie for a walk this evening in the hope that the exercise would wear her out and she'd sleep in late. Sweetie, however, had decided to run

24

not walk and was already disappearing down the street, her lead flying behind her. Joel legged it after the white bundle of fluff, shouting 'Sweetie!' at the top of his voice.

Sweetie had disappeared around the corner now, so Joel pushed himself for an extra spurt. Hazel would never forgive him if he lost her precious pooch or – Heaven forbid – she got run over. The thought brought him out in a sweat of panic. Sweetie might be a thorough nuisance, but he didn't want anything to happen to her.

'Sweetie!' he shouted, sprinting breathlessly around the corner and then skidding to a stop as he saw a young woman with long, honey-brown hair flowing from underneath a grey woolly hat with two fur bobbles on the top, crouching down, stroking the little Maltese. Sweetie was wagging her tail as if she was greeting a long-lost friend.

'Oh, there you are! Thank goodness!' he said between gasps. He'd thought he was fairly fit but that run had left him breathless.

The woman looked up, her dark brown eyes full of surprise as they rested on him – she was probably thinking that a tall, muscular guy like himself should have a Boxer with a name like Bruce instead of a little white Maltese called Sweetie. *Thanks, Hazel.*

'I'm so glad you caught her. She pulled her lead out of my hand while I was shutting the gate,' he said, his breathing more regulated now. 'Come on, Sweetie.'

Sweetie slunk away from him, wriggling closer to the woman. *No recognition. No tail wag. Great.*

The woman scooped Sweetie up in her arms, nestling her close to her chest, and then studied Joel thoughtfully, as if she

25

could tell that the dog wasn't really his. *Oh no! What if she thought he had stolen her?* Sweetie was certainly acting as if he was a complete stranger.

'Thanks for catching her but I'll take her now,' he said levelly as he walked closer and reached out to stroke Sweetie's head. 'Come on, Sweetie.'

The perishing dog snuggled her head into the woman's shoulder as if she had never seen Joel before and this woman was her owner.

'She doesn't seem to want to come with you,' the woman said hesitantly.

He sighed. 'She probably doesn't, but we're stuck with each other. She's my sister's dog,' he added, seeing the woman's look of concern. He filled her in about housesitting for his sister, then got his phone out of his pocket, swiped to his photo gallery and showed her a picture of Hazel, Al, himself and Sweetie, taken the day before they left for Dubai. 'Hazel and Al only left last week and Sweetie hasn't got used to me yet. I'm Joel, by the way, Joel Dexter,' he added, thinking he'd better introduce himself.

The woman nodded slowly. 'Lexi Forde. I've come down to spend Christmas with my parents, they own the bakery. Sorry for doubting you but she does seem hesitant to come to you.'

Lexi. He liked that. It suited her. 'I wish she'd be a bit more hesitant about sleeping in my bed all night and keeping me awake with her snoring! I don't think I had more than three hours sleep last night.'

Lexi giggled. 'You sound like a new dad.'

'I am. I've never had a dog before. Hazel assured me that Sweetie would be no trouble at all but she's a nightmare! And as for her name. Have you any idea how embarrassing it is for a tall guy like me to go running down the street shouting "Sweetie!"'

Lexi burst out laughing at that. 'Oh, I'm sorry – but it is funny! That's one of the reasons I wasn't sure she was your dog.' She stroked Sweetie's head. 'I think you'd better go back to your new master.'

Sweetie licked Lexi's face, then allowed herself to be passed over to Joel. She licked his face happily as soon as she was in his arms.

'Oh, you want to know me now, do you?' he said, tickling her under her chin. 'It's a good job that I've got a forgiving nature.'

Sweetie nuzzled into him. It was hard to believe that she'd refused to come to him only a few minutes ago. She really was a little terror!

'Well, I must get back,' Lexi said with a smile.

'Thanks again,' Joel said.

He turned to watch as Lexi walked past him, then headed around the corner he'd just sped around. She paused, as if sensing that he was watching her, looked back and waved. She seemed nice, he thought, shame she was only here for Christmas.

He put Sweetie down on the ground, keeping a tight hold on her lead. 'Right, menace, now let's go for that walk. And no more tricks!'

Lexi hurried on along the street, a smile still on her lips. What an adorable little dog, and Joel seemed nice too. He had such a deep, rich, pleasant voice, with a touch of a Scottish accent. She

27

felt some sympathy for him having to walk a little dog like that, and with such a girly name! His sister and partner must have glam jobs to jet off to work in Dubai for six months, and how lucky that Joel was available to house sit during their absence. She wondered if he lived close or had moved completely out of his area, fancying a change. She shrugged, what did it matter?

After giving her mother a hug and trotting out the excuse about Ben working, Lexi had decided to go for a short walk around the village, wanting to give herself time to pull herself together before facing the questions her mother would inevitably be asking over dinner. She knew her mother's quizzing came from a good place but even talking about Ben brought tears to her eyes. She couldn't believe how he had betrayed her, and at the worst possible time of year, too. Excusing herself by saying she wanted to take a look at the Christmas lights, and the decorations outside the houses – something she had always loved doing – she had grabbed her coat and set off, with her mother calling after her that dinner would be served in an hour.

As she headed along the street, Lexi remembered her parents taking her, Ryan and Jay on a tour of the village to see the lights when they were children. The villagers in Lystone always put on such a spectacular show, and many families from other villages often drove over to see them, and the dazzling light displays the council always put on.

Her favourite special Christmas tradition was the lighting of the big Christmas tree on the green, followed by a carol service, then everyone piling into the Olde Tavern for drinks and snacks. She'd been really looking forward to introducing Ben to the Forde family Christmas traditions, she was sure he would have loved the Christmas carol service. A lump formed in her throat and she swallowed it down. She couldn't believe they were finished; she'd adored Ben and thought that he'd loved her too.

She carried on up the street until she came to the green, separated by the road from the houses and shops that circled it. She looked over at the big fir tree that stood in the middle. To her surprise, there wasn't one single decoration on the tree and there was a cordon of red-and-white tape all around that section of the green. The council were leaving it late, it was only just over week until Christmas and although the lights were never switched on until Christmas Eve it was usually decorated a couple of weeks beforehand. Perhaps someone would come and decorate the tree on Monday, she thought. *That's probably why they've cordoned it off.*

She carried on with her walk, smiling as she spotted a cute, knitted snow-family decorating the top of a postbox. The woolly figures were gathered around a Christmas tree and a carol book on a stand. *This must be one of the postbox toppers Granny Mabe mentioned!* Maybe her gran had even helped make it.

'Ridiculous, isn't it?'

Lexi turned at the sharp voice to see a man, probably in his late fifties, standing behind her.

'Sorry?' she asked, puzzled.

'I saw you looking at that!' The man pointed to the postbox topper. 'They call it art! Well, I call it a mess. Look how dirty and discoloured it is. And there's plenty more scattered all over the village. It's a disgrace!' The man tutted and walked off.

Lexi stared after him. It seemed that not everyone approved of her gran and the other Yarn Warriors' attempts to add a festive touch to the village.

She shivered, it was a bit chilly now and dinner would be

ready soon. She decided to go back home and catch up with her parents. She could look around the village a bit more tomorrow.

Her mother was laying plates on the table when Lexi let herself in the back door. The delicious smell of steak and kidney pie wafted from the oven, and Lexi's tummy rumbled. She was hungry. 'Just in time! I was about to dish up. Did you enjoy your walk?' she asked, glancing up at Lexi.

'I did,' she said, taking off her coat and hanging it up in the utility room and slipping her boots off before joining her mum back in the kitchen again. 'I love how festive Lystone looks at Christmas.' She opened the cutlery drawer and grabbed some knives and forks.

Then her father came in. He beamed when he saw her and gave her a big hug. 'It's so good to see you, darling.'

Lexi lay her head on his shoulder for a moment, her father's hugs had always managed to make the world feel a better place.

Granny Mabe joined them and they chatted away as they sat down to eat. Lexi felt happy and relaxed, sitting in the cosy kitchen with her family, remembering the years they'd all crowded around this table, Jay and Ryan too, talking and eating. Sometimes the conversation would get a bit heated, sometimes one of them would storm out, but only to return a few minutes later when dessert was served. No one in the Forde family ever stayed angry for long.

'Your mum said you went for a walk to look at the lights. You always used to love doing that at Christmas time,' her dad said. 'The village looks beautiful all lit up, doesn't it?'

'Gorgeous! Although, I only went as far as the green.' Lexi swallowed a mouthful of the pie before continuing. 'I was surprised to see that the fir tree isn't decorated yet. I thought they always did it the second week of December. I notice that it's cordoned off, though, so I guess they're going to do it on Monday.'

'They're not decorating it at all. The council want to chop the tree down. They said that it's unsafe.' Granny Mabe told her. 'Load of rubbish if you ask me.'

'What? Surely not?' Lexi asked incredulously.

She saw her parents exchange looks. Then her father said, 'I'm afraid so, that's why that part off the green is cordoned off. They don't want anyone going on it in case one of the branches falls off the tree.'

Lexi was stunned. She couldn't imagine Christmas without the traditional Christmas Eve carol service around the huge fir tree on the green. 'When did they say this? Can't they do anything to save the tree?'

'Apparently not. We weren't told until this Thursday, which didn't give us much time to do anything. We kept expecting the tree to be decorated any day, and when we enquired, the council replied that they were dealing with it. Then on Thursday we were told that the tree was too dangerous and would probably have to come down. Some of the branches are dying back and they're worried that the pressure of the lights and decorations might cause the branches to break and injure someone.'

'Oh no! That's awful! Can't they simply chop off the affected branches?' Lexi asked in dismay. The huge fir tree was an important feature of the village. She couldn't bear to think of it being chopped down.

'I don't know, dear. There were a couple of men looking at it last week – I think they must have been tree surgeons; one of them was on one of those mobile platform things and checking out the branches at the top of the tree. He must have declared it unsafe,' her mother said. 'Everyone's really sad about it. There's talk of moving the carol service to the square, but it won't be the same.'

This was awful, Lexi thought. The carol service around the Lystone Christmas tree was such a big part of Christmas. People came from miles around to take part. And it was such a shame for it to happen this year, too, when Jay was coming over from Canada. It was their first family Christmas for years and it would have been lovely for them all to attend the traditional 'lighting the tree' carol service together, just like they used to do.

Surely there was something they could do to save the tree.

Chapter Five

Thankfully, the walk had tired Sweetie out and, to Joel's relief, after a meal she had gone straight into her basket and fallen asleep. Hopefully he might actually get to sleep the whole night alone in his bed without her fidgeting and snoring beside him. It was fine for Hazel to insist that he had to be kind but firm but that was easier said than done at two o'clock in the morning when Sweetie was whining outside his bedroom door and he had to be up for work at six.

As he sat on the sofa drinking a nightcap, his mind went back to Lexi. She said she'd come down to spend Christmas with her parents so he guessed she was only in the village for a week or so. He wondered if he would bump into her again. She was gorgeous with her soft brown eyes, the cute smattering of freckles over her nose, and long, wavy golden-brown hair. She seemed fun too, he thought, remembering the hat with the double fur ball on the top. The thought that it was a shame she didn't live in Lystone drifted across his mind and he batted it away. The last thing he needed was to be thinking about getting

33

involved with another woman. It had taken him two years and thousands of pounds to extract himself from his marriage with Toni. All he wanted to do now was concentrate on working and getting himself a new home. Living at Hazel and Al's for the next six months at a nominal rent would provide him with the chance to get his life back on track. And he had his first commission too – the council wanted him to give them a quote for felling a fir tree on the village green. He was going to take a quick look at it tomorrow but would return with Andy and a hoist on Monday. He'd met Andy at university, they'd worked at the Forestry in Scotland together and had kept in touch, sometimes working on bigger jobs together once Joel moved to Somerset. Andy was based in Exeter, which was pretty central, and they were hoping to form a business partnership together if they could get enough work. Joel had his van and some equipment, including a branch chipper stored in a nearby lock-up and Andy had a truck, other equipment and a platform to enable him to reach the top branches on taller trees. Between them, they could tackle most jobs.

Martin, an old colleague of Joel's, now worked on the local council and had promised him that if they offered the lowest quote and could do it before Christmas, they would get the job. Although Martin hadn't come right out and told Joel the other quotes he'd received, he had given him a hint of the price he was looking for, and Joel was confident that they would be able to beat it, providing it didn't take more than a couple of days to fell the tree. If they could get this job with the council it might lead to more work with them. And right now, Joel needed all the work he could get. He was currently without his own house, or a job. Although, thankfully, the divorce hadn't completely bankrupted him and he still had some money in the bank.

He had promised to meet Toni, his soon-to-be ex-wife, tomorrow too. He had tried to keep the divorce civil to save on solicitor's fees, and because he didn't want to turn the love they had both once had for each other into a cat fight. Toni no longer loved him and wanted out, to be free to live her own life with a new partner. Fair enough. Even though it had come as a shock and broken his heart, Joel had no desire to stay with someone who didn't love him. It had taken them two years to get to this stage: the house was sold, the Decree Absolute would be through any day now, and they were all set to go their separate ways, then out of the blue he'd had a request from Toni to meet him for lunch on Sunday. He'd wanted to say no, meeting Toni always drained him, but she'd sounded desperate, and he didn't want anything to hold up the final divorce proceedings, so he'd agreed.

He sighed and looked again at Sweetie snoring softly in her basket. She'd already been out and done her business. If he crept up to bed now, he might actually get a good night's sleep.

He'd washed, and brushed his teeth, and just pulled back the bedcovers when he heard Sweetie barking and bounding up the stairs. *Damn.* Maybe he should ignore her a bit and see if she settled down. He climbed into bed and pulled the duvet over his head.

Sweetie started to howl.

Joel threw the duvet back and padded across the floor to open the door. Sweetie wagged her tail happily, then bounded across the room and onto the bed.

Joel sighed. This was going to be a long six months.

*　　*　　*

'Well, it's lovely to have you here, it really is,' Lexi's father said when meal finished, they all sat down in the lounge to chat over hot drinks – coffee for Craig and Paula, hot chocolate for Lexi and Granny Mabe. 'And we're pleased that you managed to get away earlier than planned, but it means we haven't decorated your Christmas tree yet. We were going to decorate all the Christmas trees in the bedrooms tomorrow.'

Her parents had always put a Christmas tree in every bedroom when Lexi and her brothers were young, and still followed that tradition whenever any of them came home for Christmas.

'That's fine, I'll do it,' she said. 'And I'll help you with the other trees too.'

Her dad's face broke into a big grin. 'That'd be great. Just like old times.'

Her mum nodded. 'I can't wait to have all the Forde family back together again.'

There was an awkward silence, and Lexi knew that they were all thinking the same as her: if only Grandpa Huey was here too. It was Granny Mabe who spoke first. 'Huey would have loved to be here with us, but he's watching over us and will be happy that we're all together.'

Lexi knew she was right. Although, she couldn't help wondering what Grandpa Huey would think about Granny Mabe and her 'Yarn Warriors'. Had she been yarn-bombing when he was alive? she wondered, or had she only joined the group recently in an attempt to fill her days without Grandpa Huey. Her gran had been devastated when her husband had died, but looking at her now made Lexi feel stronger, more positive. Her granny and grandpa had been together forever, whereas Lexi had known Ben a little over a year. If Granny Mabe could carry on without the love of her life, then Lexi could make a new future for herself without Ben.

They all sat chatting for a couple of hours, sharing family anecdotes and news. Luckily, her parents didn't ask much about Ben, accepting Lexi's explanation as to why he wasn't here. Lexi was amused to see that, although her phone didn't ping once all evening, Granny Mabe had several texts.

'Who's sending you all those messages?' Craig asked as yet another message pinged in.

'It's just the knitting group,' Granny Mabe announced as she peered at the message and quickly replied.

Paula raised her eyebrows. 'She's never off that phone.'

Lexi had to supress a giggle. If only her parents knew what her gran and her knitting group were up to!

Finally, feeling exhausted after her restless sleep the previous night, and the long drive down here, Lexi excused herself and went up to bed just after ten.

'You'll have to make up the bed, that's another thing I was going to do tomorrow,' her mother suddenly remembered. 'The bedding is folded up on the bottom of the bed.'

'No problem. Night, everyone,' Lexi said.

'Night, love. No rush to get up in the morning,' her father told her.

Lexi went upstairs to her old childhood bedroom. She pushed open the door of her room and stepped inside, loving the familiarity of it. Nothing had been changed since she left home ten years ago, after qualifying to be a teacher and deciding to take the job she had been offered in Gloucester. The same red, rose-patterned wallpaper, white shelves laden with books, red fluffy carpet. She'd always loved red. Standing in the corner of the bedroom was a medium-sized white artificial Christmas tree. *Her* Christmas tree. Every year when she was living at home she had decorated it in a different colour scheme, and every time she had come home for Christmas her parents had put it in her room. She thought of the white Christmas tree back in her flat that she had been planning on decorating with gold baubles and white bows. *Today*, she remembered. Today was the day she'd been going to make the flat look all festive as a surprise for Ben when he came home. Only it was Ben who had given her the surprise, wasn't it? Tears sprung to her eyes again.

I am not going to let Ben spoil Christmas!

She glanced over at the windows where the fairy lights were twinkling and smiled at the Christmas-themed curtains hanging there – red with white Christmas trees and reindeers dotted over them. There was a matching duvet cover folded up on the bottom of the bed, and she knew that there would be Christmassy curtains in her brothers' bedrooms too. Her mum had made the duvet covers and curtains herself years ago, and got them out every December.

Lexi walked over to the window, and peered out into the darkness for a moment, watching the twinkling lights on the tree in the back garden. She wondered how her parents had time to put up a tree in every room, the porch, the front and back garden, and the shop, when they worked every weekday. She knew that they enjoyed doing it, though. They loved Christmas and had gone out of their way to make it as special as they could when Lexi and her brothers were growing up. Their excitement at having the family together for Christmas again, and having Toby – a young child in the house – was evident, and she wasn't about to spoil it for them by crying over Ben. She closed the curtains and then went over to the double bed. More fairy lights adorned the wall above the bed, as they had done when she was young. She bent down and flicked the switch, smiling as the warm white lights glowed comfortingly. Then she sat down on the bed and pulled her phone out of her bag to check if there were any messages, wondering if news of her and Ben's split had reached any of her friends yet.

No messages from any of them. Nothing about their split on social media but then she had blocked Ben from all her social media accounts the previous night, not wanting to see cosied-up pictures of him and Rosa. There were a couple of messages from her LexiKnits website and, she was glad to see, several orders from her Etsy shop. Her quirky knitwear was proving to be very popular. It was just a hobby, and she didn't churn them out, but it gave her a lift when someone ordered one of her own-design hats, scarves or jumpers.

Satisfied, she set about making her bed, then went to the bathroom to wash, and clean her teeth, suddenly feeling very weary. *Tomorrow, I'll decorate my tree and have a longer walk around the village*, she decided as she ran her toothbrush under the tap and squeezed on some toothpaste. *I'll see if I can spot any more of Granny Mabe's yarn-bombings*. It was good to be back home and have a family Christmas again, singing carols, playing party games, exchanging news. Wearily, she climbed into bed, her thoughts going back to Christmases when she was young, and the excitement of Christmas Eve, when they had all crowded around the fir tree on the green for the carol service, then piled into the Olde Tavern for mince pies and hot chocolate – or something stronger for the adults.

If only we could still have the carol service around the Christmas tree on the green, she thought. It wasn't a proper Lystone Christmas without that.

Chapter Six

Sunday, six days before Christmas

Lexi pulled back her curtains the next morning and gasped in delight at the beautiful scene that met her eyes. It was snowing! It had been so cold last night that she'd slept with the electric blanket on all night, but she hadn't expected to be greeted by the ground covered in snow when she woke up. She felt ridiculously excited, like she used to when she was a child. She and Ryan would go sledging, and build a family of snowmen in the backyard. Sometimes Jay would join in too, but he was two years older than Lexi and preferred to hang around with mates his own age, whereas Ryan, at eighteen months younger than her, would be happy to play with her sometimes. Although, as the two boys got older, they'd often hung out together whilst Lexi had her own crowd of friends.

She quickly pulled on her onesie and hurried downstairs. 'It's snowing!' she announced.

Her mother looked up from the toast she was buttering and

grinned. 'I had noticed. Don't tell me you're going out to build a snowman.'

Lexi grinned back. 'No, but I am going for another walk as soon as I've decorated my tree.'

'I thought that would be the first thing you'd want to do,' her mum told her. The bakery was always closed on Sundays so they had a well-earned day off. 'Your dad's left some baubles in the conservatory for you. There's an assortment of colours, tinsel and lights. Take whatever you want.'

'Thanks. Do you want me to do anything before I go for a walk? I could help out at the bakery this week, give you time to get things done here before Jay and Ryan arrive?' Jay, Sonia and Toby were arriving on Wednesday and Ryan and Nell on Friday.

'That's kind of you. We've got Claire and Brad so I think we can manage but do pop in for a cuppa and a cake whenever you're passing. It'd be good to see you, and if it's quiet, I'll join you.'

'I will,' Lexi promised. She was determined to keep busy so that she didn't have time to think about Ben. It was working – most of the time. And she had lesson planning to do, she reminded herself. She might make a start on that this evening.

'Do you want some toast and a cuppa?' her mother asked, passing the plate over to Lexi's dad who put it in the middle of the table.

'I'd love some, but you sit down and I'll make my own, and a drink. I don't want you waiting on me, you work hard enough.'

'If you're sure.' Her mum sat down at the table with her dad and picked up a slice of toast, while Lexi put two slices of bread in the toaster.

42

'The kettle's just boiled,' her dad told her.

Lexi flicked the switch to re-boil it, popped a teabag in a mug, then poured the now-boiling-again water onto it and added milk. She never took sugar in tea. The toast popped up and she quickly buttered it and joined her parents at the kitchen table.

'So, what are you two up to today?'

'We've got the Christmas trees in the bedrooms to decorate,' her dad said as he spread jam onto his toast. 'You choose your baubles first, though, then I'll do the other trees. There's plenty to go around.'

'Do you have any gold ones?'

'I do.' He grinned. 'And some shiny gold stars.'

'Perfect!'

As soon as breakfast was finished, Lexi went into the conservatory with her dad and rummaged through the boxes of Christmas baubles and decorations there, choosing some gorgeous large gold baubles, some smaller white ones and some gold stars.

'I thought I'd use all different colours for Jay's tree and hang some sparkly Santas on it too. Toby will love that,' her dad said.

'These blue and silver ones would be nice for Ryan and Nell.' Lexi pointed to the box of baubles. 'We could hang some silver bows on it too. Do you want me to do it later?'

'Thanks, love, but we've got it covered. Your mum is doing the tree in Ryan and Nell's room and I'll do the one in Jay, Sonia and Toby's.'

'Okay, well, I'll leave you to it.' Lexi carried the box up into her room, propped her iPhone up on the stand she'd brought with her, and told Siri to play some Christmas carols. As the

43

music filled the air she felt her mood lighten, and as she hummed away, she started decorating the Christmas tree.

She was really pleased with it when she'd finished. It looked so pretty and the star lights twinkled delicately. Feeling much happier now, she had a shower, pulled on a long, grey cable-knit jumper and skinny jeans, put a bit of make-up on her face, brushed her hair so that it was bouncing loosely around her shoulders, and she was ready to go.

Suddenly, her phone pinged in her pocket to announce an incoming text. She took it out and looked at the screen, surprised to see that it was Ben. Well, she wasn't even going to open the message. She wasn't the slightest bit interested in what he had to say. She put her phone back in her pocket and went downstairs, where Granny Mabe was putting a roast in the oven, her dad was peeling potatoes, and her mum was putting washing into the dryer.

'I'm off for a walk now. Do you need anything from the corner shop?' The shop sold all the basics and was always open on a Sunday morning.

'No thanks, love. Enjoy your walk. You look a bit peaky. I think you've been working too hard. A few days' rest down here will do you the world of good,' her mum said. 'Lunch will be about three.'

'I won't be late,' Lexi promised. She grabbed her coat from the hall and pulled on her boots and scarf, before opening the door and stepping outside.

The snow had stopped now and had formed a crispy layer over the ground, so Lexi was pleased her boots had soles with good grip, the last thing she wanted was to fall over. As she set off, she wondered if she would bump into Joel and his cute little dog again. Sweetie had been absolutely adorable, but Lexi could see that she was a handful for Joel.

The snow was soft and crunchy under her feet, and the air brisk. She felt the tension leave her as she walked down the street, admiring the snow-covered bushes and plants in the gardens she passed. It had only been a light fall of snow but it was enough to make everywhere look like a winter wonderland. It would be Christmas on Saturday, she hoped it would be snowing then. It would be wonderful to have a white Christmas.

Some children were already scooping up handfuls of the fallen snow and giggling as they threw snowballs at each other. She stopped to watch them, her spirits lifting. She was so glad she'd come to spend Christmas with her parents, already she felt a lot happier.

'Uuurgh!' Joel spluttered as something wet and slobbery licked his face. He opened his eyes, then quickly closed them again as the dog's tongue aimed for his eyelid. 'Sweetie!'

'Woof!' Sweetie barked happily. He felt the dog move and risked opening his eyes again. 'Woof! Woof!' She was standing up now, wagging her tail, obviously ready to go out and do her business. He glanced at the clock – almost eleven! He'd overslept – hardly surprising, as Sweetie had kept him awake half the night.

'Okay girl, I'm getting up,' he said, edging himself up on his elbow. Sweetie jumped off the bed, trotted over to the door, then turned to him, wagging her tail.

'Coming!' He got out of bed, grabbed his jeans and jumper off the chair and pulled them on, then went downstairs to let the little dog out. Snow still covered the ground and Sweetie didn't seem that fond of it. She quickly squatted down to do her business then came running back in through the back door he'd left ajar for her.

'A bit chilly for you, is it?' he said, stroking her head. 'Want something to eat?'

Sweetie wagged her tail and went over to her bowl. He wasn't sure if that was because she understood him or had learnt the routine. Hazel said she always gave Sweetie a small meal in the morning, and her main meal in the evening.

Leaving Sweetie to eat, Joel made a black coffee and scrambled eggs on toast. He was feeling hungry this morning, and also more than a bit apprehensive. What did Toni want to talk to him about?

After breakfast was finished, he took Sweetie for another trip outside then she curled up in her basket to sleep. Joel went up to have a shower and get changed. When he came back down, Sweetie was still fast asleep. He looked at her, wondering if it would be best to try and sneak out while she was still asleep, or to say goodbye to her. He was hopeless at looking after a dog, he realised. As though she knew he was staring at her, Sweetie suddenly opened her eyes. She looked at him for a moment, then slowly got out of her basket and came over to him. He knelt down and fussed her. 'I've got to go out, girl, and I'm sorry but you can't come. I'll be back soon, though, and then I'll take you for a walk,' he promised, although he wasn't sure that Sweetie would actually like walking in the cold, wet snow. He'd probably end up carrying her.

Giving her a last fuss, he went out the front door, with Sweetie trying to squeeze past his legs and yapping furiously when she didn't manage it. He shut the door behind him feeling guilty and worried. He hoped that she didn't yap for long, it was distressing for her and disturbing for the neighbours. This arrangement wasn't working out as well as he'd hoped – Sweetie was so demanding and unsettled. Hazel had promised that Sweetie was happy to be left for a few hours, and she must be, as both Hazel and Al worked, although Hazel was based from home a lot, she still had meetings to attend. Hopefully, the Maltese terrier would get used to him and settle down soon.

He zipped up his jacket as he strode up the garden path, glancing left towards his van which was parked a little way up the road – he really should put it in the garage around the back – as he opened the gate and stepped out. An elderly man was walking towards him, carrying a bag of shopping, when suddenly, he lost his footing and slipped. Joel immediately dashed forwards, reaching for the man's arm to prevent his fall.

Ouch! Someone else had noticed the old man's predicament and raced to save him too, coming from the right, and they'd both collided with a bang. Joel's elbow hit the other person hard, and the impact of hitting his funny bone sent Joel reeling. He grabbed the fence nearby for support, while still holding onto the old man's arm to stop him from falling.

'Sorry,' he apologised, steadying himself and looking around to see who he'd bumped into. Horrified, he saw the woman he'd met last night – Lexi – on the floor, her jean-clad legs sprawled out in front of her. He had obviously knocked her flying off her feet. *Damn.* Why hadn't he looked before he leapt? Because the old man would have fallen over, that's why, and at his age that could be fatal.

'I'm so sorry! I didn't see you,' he apologised, checking that the man was holding onto the fence securely before going over to help Lexi. 'I think I caught you with my elbow. I guess we were both too busy trying to stop this man's fall to notice each other. Are you hurt?'

'Hello, again.' She smiled and glanced up at him. She looked even more gorgeous than last night, he thought, trying not to stare at her cute button nose and rosebud lips. Then his eyes rested on the lump peeping out from below the rim of her hat, which had been pushed back when she fell. 'Oh God, I'm so sorry! You've got a huge bump coming up on your forehead. I feel dreadful.'

'It's fine, don't worry.' She grabbed the hand he held out to her and scrambled to her feet. Then she brushed herself down and rubbed her head where his elbow had obviously hit her.

'I really am sorry.'

'Seriously, it's okay. How's your elbow?'

'Sore. I suspect that there might be a bruise there too.'

'We're a right pair, aren't we?' She turned to the elderly man, who was clutching the fence, his shopping bag still in his hand. 'Are you all right? You did slip a bit before we could catch you. Have you hurt yourself?'

Good-natured as well as pretty, Joel thought as the old man shook his head.

'I managed to grab the fence in time. I always try to walk near a fence when the ground is a bit slippy, in case I lose my footing. The snow is beautiful but treacherous.' He looked from Joel to Lexi. 'Thank you both for coming to my rescue' His eyes rested anxiously on Lexi's forehead. 'I'm so sorry that you clashed in the process. I think you're going to have a nasty bump there. Would you like to come in and put some ice on it? Have a cup of tea while you're there.' He turned to Joel. 'You too.'

'That's very kind of you. Do you live far?' Lexi asked him.

He shook his head. 'The next house is mine. It's so annoying that I almost got home before I slipped. I'm Lloyd, by the way, Lloyd Winston.'

Two doors away. Joel hoped Sweetie wasn't being a nuisance to him. 'I'm Joel Dexter, I'm temporarily living next door but one.'

'Ah, you must be Hazel's brother. She said that you were going to look after the house, and Sweetie, while she and Al were away.'

'And I'm Lexi and I'd love a cup of tea – and to put some ice on this bump before it swells into a golf ball.'

'I'm sorry but I have to dash,' Joel admitted reluctantly. 'If you're sure you're both okay? Shall I at least see you to your front door, Lloyd?'

'You carry on, we're both fine and I can walk Lloyd to the door.' Lexi reached over and opened the latch on his gate, then linked arms with Lloyd, who was still clutching his shopping bag. 'We can lean on each other,' she said.

Lloyd grinned at her. 'I'm not going to deny that it's good to have a beautiful woman hanging onto my arm.'

Lexi grinned back.

Honestly, he was a charmer, Joel thought. And Lexi was beautiful. Kind, too. He wished he had time to stop and have a cup of tea with them both.

Joel stood at the gate, watching as they walked down the path. When they reached the front door, Lloyd fumbled in his coat pocket, took out a bunch of keys and inserted one in the lock, his hand trembling. That stumble had shaken him up.

'Let me.' Lexi took the key out of his hand and then turned

49

it and pushed the door open for Lloyd to go through first. They both turned to wave to Joel.

'Right, I must go. Remember to put some ice on that bump, Lexi – and I apologise again. I'll pop in and see you later, Lloyd.' He gave them another wave and headed for his van, glancing at his watch. He was going to be late and Toni hated to be kept waiting.

You're not married to her anymore, he reminded himself.

Chapter Seven

Lexi wondered if Joel really did have to dash off, or whether it was an excuse not to come in for a cup of tea? Some people didn't have time for old folks. He seemed kind, though, and had been very concerned about her head. And had stopped to make sure that she and Lloyd both got safely inside.

He was a looker too, not in a 'film star' kind of way, but in an interesting way. Tall, with short, thick, light-auburn hair, vivid green eyes, a wide mouth that looked like it laughed a lot, and a sexy smattering of designer stubble. He looked strong and muscular, like he worked out. Maybe he was a fitness instructor.

'Are you coming in, lass?' Lloyd asked, and she suddenly realised that she was still staring after Joel, and that Lloyd was standing inside the hallway.

'Err, yes,' she stammered, stepping in and closing the door behind her.

'Take your coat off, dear, and go into the living room – first door on the right – and make yourself at home. I'll go and put the kettle on,' Lloyd said.

Her head was throbbing, she had to admit. She glanced at

her reflection in the hall mirror and looked at the big bump peeping out from under her hat. That would turn into a bruise soon. Had Joel got a bump on his elbow? she wondered.

'I'll come through to the kitchen and get some ice, then I can chat to you while you make the tea,' she said, wishing that Lloyd would let her make it, slipping like that must have been a nasty shock to him. If she and Joel hadn't been around to prevent his fall, he could have ended up breaking his hip – and she knew how serious that could be for someone of Lloyd's advanced years.

'That would be very pleasant.' Lloyd took off his coat and hung it on one of the pegs on the wall, then replaced his shoes with slippers. Lexi did the same with her fake-fur coat, then looked down at her boots, wondering whether to take them off.

'Leave them on, dear, they're fine,' Lloyd told her as he set off up the hall. 'This way.'

Lexi gave her feet an extra wipe on the mat, just to make sure that the soles of her boots were clean, and followed him. The house felt warm and cosy, she noticed; she knew that a lot of elderly people worried about heating bills and lived in one room in the winter. She wondered if Lloyd lived on his own. There was no sign of anyone else living here, but they could have popped out for a bit. There were no Christmas decorations about either, she observed, but then not everyone was as Christmas-mad as her family! Lots of people just decorated one room or put up a small tree.

The kitchen was clean and tidy, if a little dated. In the corner was a small wooden table with two chairs. Did that mean someone else lived here?

'At least let me put the kettle on while you put your shopping away,' Lexi said as Lloyd took a carton of milk and some butter out of his bag and put them in the top part of the fridge-freezer that stood in the corner of the kitchen. Then he opened the freezer, took out a bag of frozen peas and wrapped it in a tea towel before handing it to Lexi.

'Sit yourself down and put this on your forehead. I'll make the tea,' he insisted.

She obviously wasn't going to get anywhere with him, Lexi thought, and he did seem to have pulled himself together now, so she gave in. 'Thank you.' She sat down at the kitchen table, took off her hat and placed the bag of frozen peas on her forehead. She could feel the relief already.

'So, you know Joel, then? Do you live nearby too?' Lloyd asked as he filled the kettle up. 'I can't recall seeing you before, but then I don't get out much in the winter.'

'No, I live in Gloucester but I bumped into him last night. Sweetie had escaped when he was taking her for a walk. Luckily I caught hold of her. I've come down to spend Christmas with my parents. They own the village bakery,' she added.

'Ah, Paula and Craig. Lovely couple.' Lloyd put a small loaf in the bread bin on the worktop then glanced over his shoulder at her. 'Your gran lives with them too, doesn't she? She's quite a character.'

'You could say that,' Lexi agreed, wondering how well Lloyd knew Granny Mabe and if he was aware that she was part of the Yarn Warriors.

'We'll take this into the lounge, it's cosier in there,' Lloyd said putting the two mugs of tea and a tin of biscuits on a tray.

'Let me carry that,' said Lexi. She took the bag of frozen peas off her forehead. 'Has my bump gone down a bit?' she asked. 'It doesn't hurt as much.'

Lloyd's gaze rested on her forehead and he shook his head. 'Not yet. I think you're going to have a nasty bruise. I feel so guilty about that. You and Joel were trying to help me.'

'Accidents happen, and I'm glad we managed to break your fall,' she said. 'Now, please let me carry that tray.'

'I can manage. You put those frozen peas back on that bump.' Lloyd was already on his way out of the kitchen. He really was stubborn, she thought, holding the frozen peas onto her forehead with one hand, and picking up her bag and hat with the other. She followed him into the living room, where he was now putting the tray down on the coffee table.

'Sit yourself down, lass,' Lloyd said, indicating the sofa. He sat down in the big armchair opposite and reached for his mug.

Still holding the frozen peas on her forehead, Lexi eased herself down onto the sofa, her backside felt a bit tender from where she had fallen, and quickly glanced around. The room looked cosy and tidy, although the carpet and three-piece suite were a bit worn. There were a couple of Christmas cards on the sideboard, and some tinsel draped around a photo frame with a picture of what she could see was a younger Lloyd with his arm around the shoulder of a woman, probably his wife. There was no Christmas tree or any other decorations, though. She wondered if that was because putting up the tree was too difficult for him. She'd try to steer the conversation around to it, then offer to help him if he did want to put up a tree or any decorations, she decided.

'This is a lovely cosy room,' she remarked. 'Have you lived here long?' she asked.

'Me and my Ruby moved here over thirty years ago,' he said. 'Ruby died fifteen years ago. I've been on my own ever since.'

'I'm sorry to hear that.' She picked up her mug of tea and took a sip. That was so sad. She felt really sorry for Lloyd, on his own in his twilight years. She wanted to ask if he had any family but didn't want to overstep the mark. Old folk could be proud and hated anyone interfering.

'We had a good marriage, she was the love of my life and her death broke my heart, but it was a long time ago now. Time heals.'

'It was the same with Granny Mabe. We thought she would never get over Grandpa Huey's death but thankfully she did.' She took another sip of her tea. Granny Mabe had Lexi's parents, though, and a group of friends. Lexi had the feeling that Lloyd was alone. That was such a shame.

'You're late,' Toni said with a pout as Joel strode over to the table where she was sitting. 'I've been waiting ages. This is my second skinny latte.'

Joel looked at the half-full glass cup in front of his soon-to-be ex. 'Sorry. I got a bit caught up.' He sat down in the chair opposite her. 'What's the problem?'

Toni had sounded distressed when she'd called him and had insisted that she couldn't discuss the matter over the phone but had to talk to him personally. He studied her face. She didn't look distressed now. Her shoulder-length blond hair was perfectly styled, her make-up carefully applied to achieve the natural look she loved – and he knew took at least half an hour to achieve. She was wearing a red coat with a black faux-fur collar and black trousers. She looked dressed to impress.

She bit her lip, tears welling in her eyes.

Okay, so she is distressed. He softened his tone. 'Has something happened?' he asked gently.

She nodded, her eyes holding his, but before she could speak, a waiter came over to take his order. 'Black coffee, please, no sugar,' Joel said, waiting for the waiter to leave before asking again. 'What's happened, Toni?'

Her bottom lip quivered. 'I've made a mistake, Joel. A terrible mistake . . .'

What the hell has she done? How serious is it? Her distress was making him panic now, Toni always had been impetuous, jumping into things before weighing up all the consequences. *She's not your problem now*, he reminded himself.

She leant forwards and placed her hand on his. 'I made a mistake, I realise that now. I don't want to divorce you. I love you.'

What? Joel pulled his hand away and leant back in his chair, staring at her. Was she serious?

'I know I hurt you and I'm so sorry, but Drake, he was a mistake. It's you I love. You I've always loved.' Her green eyes held his, tears brimming in them, her expression pleading. 'Please say you'll give me another chance. The Decree Absolute isn't through yet, we can still stop the divorce.'

Joel could hardly believe he was hearing this. When Toni had told him she wanted a divorce after only two years of marriage, he'd been devastated. She'd been upset, saying that she didn't want to hurt him, but that they were two different people on two different paths. He'd wanted to plead with her, to tell her to reconsider, but his pride wouldn't let him. If she didn't love him, then he didn't want to talk her into pretending to love him. And she was right, they were two different people who wanted different things, but he'd hoped that their love was

56

strong enough to see them through their differences. Apparently it wasn't. It was six months later before he learnt that Toni was involved with someone else. Drake Phillips, a hotshot with a company they liaised with. A good-looking go-getter like Toni. Even Joel could see that Drake was much more her type than himself; in her eyes he was a boring tree surgeon who loved walks in the country and the quiet life. Toni finally admitted that she'd been seeing Drake for the past year, and that he was the reason she'd wanted a divorce, so Joel had filed for it on the grounds of adultery. Toni had moved in with Drake, Joel had stayed in their house until it was sold and then split the proceeds in half. He'd kept communications as pleasant as he could in the circumstances and was now about to build a new life for himself. Then along comes Toni telling him it was all a mistake. Up until a few months ago, he might have been tempted to give her another chance, but now? Well, time was a great healer, and an eye-opener, and he realised that he hadn't been happy when he was married to Toni, but had simply plodded on, hoping things would get better.

'Please, Joel. I know that I hurt you and I'm sorry, truly I am.' Her bottom lip wobbled. 'I really love you and I think you still love me too. Please will you give me another chance?'

Joel finally found his voice. 'What about Drake?'

Toni licked her lips. 'He isn't the man I thought he was. He can be so cold and distant. And ruthless. Not like you. You were always so kind to me.'

Yes and where did that get me? He felt sorry for her, and she did look genuinely upset, but no, he couldn't go back to that life. He didn't love Toni any longer, hadn't for a while, and he suspected that despite her protestations, she didn't love him.

She'd probably split up with Drake and was using him as a fallback.

She reached out for his hand again. 'Remember how happy we were in the early days? We could get that back again. We can be happy together, I know we can. Can we at least try? Please.'

He shook his head. 'I'm sorry, Toni, but it's been over between us for a long time. When you said that you wanted to speak to me urgently, I had no idea it was about this. You said that something had come up.'

'It has. I realised that I didn't want a divorce. That I still loved you. I had to tell you before the Absolute went through.'

The waiter returned with his coffee and Joel drank it slowly, all the while his mind racing. He hated to see Toni so upset and suspected that Drake had probably taken up with someone else. He knew how that felt. But there was no way he was getting back together with his ex. 'I don't think you do love me,' he said gently. 'I think you've just come to me because you and Drake have split up. You'll find someone else, Toni. And you've got your money from the house sale so can get yourself somewhere to live. You'll work it out.'

'That money won't buy me anywhere decent! Drake's moved someone else in and I'm in a hotel at the moment. Have you any idea how much that is costing me?' She wiped a tear away from her eye. 'I was hoping that, well, if you don't want to get back with me, could you at least give me a bigger portion of the house money? It's okay for you, you're living at your sister's for a while and you'd be happy with a little terraced house anyway.'

'Whereas you want a big house like you had with Drake?' Joel pushed his coffee cup aside. 'I should have known what this was all about. Money. It was always about money with you. No, I don't want to get back with you and no, I won't give you a bigger share of the house money just because Drake has cheated on you, like you cheated on me.' He stood up. 'I hope things work out for you, Toni, but you and me are over.'

Chapter Eight

She'd better go after this, Lexi thought, as she drank her second cup of tea. She'd been here a couple of hours, and thanks to the frozen peas – which were now back in the freezer – the bump had gone down on her forehead, and Lloyd had perked up a lot, too.

'It's been lovely to have a chat,' she said. 'And thank you for the tea but I'll have to get going in a minute. I'll pop by again, if that's okay? And if you need any shopping, I could get it for you while the snow's on the ground. I don't mind, my parents only live a couple of streets back so it's not out of my way.'

'It's very kind of you, love, but I like to get out a bit. It breaks up the day, although I do worry about falling. If I break my hip, it takes a while to recover at my age, so I take it nice and steady.'

'Well, I promise it's no bother at all to me. I'll be here for a week or so and like I said, I'd be happy to get any shopping for you.' She picked up her bag and took out her phone. 'Let me give you my number, just in case,' she suggested knowing that a lot of people, especially older ones, didn't like to give their phone number out and wanted to be in control of any contacting.

Lloyd reached into his cardigan pocket and pulled out an old black mobile which he'd obviously had for years. 'Can you put it in for me, dear? I get a bit confused doing it.' He handed her his phone.

'Of course.' Lexi keyed in her details. 'Now let me know if you need anything. Anything at all,' she said as she handed the phone back.

'That's very kind of you, dear. I appreciate your help today. It did shake me up a bit but I feel much better now. There's nothing like a hot cup of tea and a chat to put the world to rights.'

'My gran says the same,' Lexi said with a smile. 'I'm going to the green to take a look at the fir tree. Gran said that the council are worried it's diseased and it will have to come down, so the villagers can't decorate it this year.'

'Really? I hadn't heard about that. What a shame, that tree has been there decades and when it's decorated it brightens up the village. I always have a wander over there Christmas Eve and join in the carol singing. I don't bother with a Christmas tree now, mine got broken years ago and it hardly seems worth buying one for just me, so it's lovely to look at the big one on the green.' He took a custard cream out of the tin and bit into it. 'It's always such a happy atmosphere, everyone wishing each other Merry Christmas. Cheers me up no end.'

Lexi was sure that there were lots of other people in the village who looked forward to the lighting-up ceremony and carol service on Christmas Eve and were going to be disappointed this year.

'It's a shame they've only just told us about the tree, it's a bit late to organise a carol service anywhere else,' she said.

'I know. It just won't be the same without the Lystone carol service around the tree.' Lloyd looked quite sad.

Lexi finished the last of her drink. 'Now, I'd better be going. Thank you for the tea and biscuits.' She put her cup down and stood up.

'A pleasure. It's been grand to have your company today. I don't see many people. Thank you for taking the time to chat to an old man. It's brightened up my day.' Lloyd got up out of his chair. 'Let me see you to the door. And do pop in again if you're passing this way.

'I will,' she promised as they walked out into the hall and she lifted her coat off the hook. 'See you soon'

'Make sure you do,' Lloyd told her.

Lloyd seemed lonely, Lexi thought as she waved again and set off down the path. She'd ask Granny Mabe if there were any groups he could join. She had a feeling Lloyd had shut himself away after his wife had died, some people did that. Her gran was always out and about so she was sure she could help Lloyd join in village life. She'd pop back and visit him tomorrow and bring a Christmas tree with her, Lexi decided. Her parents were bound to have a spare one, and some baubles, up in the attic. She could help Lloyd decorate it, that would cheer him up. She had an idea that if she mentioned it to him he would tell her not to bother but if she simply turned up with a tree he would be delighted.

As Lexi continued her walk around the village, she noticed lots of signs that her granny and her friends had been spreading the festive spirit. There were knitted Christmassy baubles dangling from railings, festive scarves wrapped around tree trunks and lamp posts and hanging from shop signs. A little girl walking with her parents was pointing at them, her face aglow with excitement. Lexi thought it all looked very merry. She stopped to look at one lamp post wrapped in a red knitted rectangle with a white snowman in the middle of it. Had her gran done that?

'It's a disgrace, isn't it? Nothing more than graffiti.'

Lexi spun around in surprise at the angry words. A woman was standing beside her, her face partly hidden by the hood of her black duffle coat.

'I think they look pretty,' Lexi said, stung on behalf of her gran and her friends.

'Nonsense. They look cheap and childish. And they soon become dirty and bedraggled. They make the village look tatty. It's irresponsible, if you ask me.'

'Perhaps people are just trying to make the village look festive. I'm sure they don't mean any harm.'

'Well, whoever it is had better watch out because the council are going to fine them when they catch them. And not before time, too. There was a number in this week's local paper for people to call if they see anyone doing this ridiculous "yarn-bombing".'

Lexi watched worriedly as the woman strode off. She had better warn her gran. She didn't want her, or her friends, getting a fine. And that was the second person who had complained about the yarn-bombings, so she wouldn't put it past someone to report them.

The huge village green was right in front of her now, the branches of the big fir tree sprinkled with snow. She remembered what an important part of her life that green had been, how she'd played there for hours with her friends as a child. There was plenty of room for family picnics and games of cricket, they'd even held summer fayres there, with various stalls selling produce, homemade gifts and treats. And the Christmas Eve carol service was always spectacular. She couldn't believe that the tree had to come down. It looked so majestic – and festive – with its snow-covered branches. She felt so sad to think that they wouldn't be able to gather around it and sing carols on Friday, like they always did on Christmas Eve. It was as if Christmas had lost part of its magic.

Then she spotted a man pacing around the tree. He was walking slowly, stopping now and again to look up at the branches, as if he was studying it. She could only see the back of him but he was tall and the hood of his parka covered his head. Was he from the council? But it was Sunday, she reminded herself.

Unless they are trying to see if they can save it in time!

Her hopes rising now, she crossed over the green and stood outside the cordon tape. 'Hi! Have you come to check out the tree?'

The man turned around, a hint of light reddish-brown hair falling onto his forehead. *Joel.* What was he doing here? Didn't he know that no one was supposed to go on the green? What did he think the cordon tape was for?

'Oh, hello, again.' He smiled at her warmly. His eyes scanned her face in concern. 'How's the bump? I hope that hat of yours isn't concealing a big bruise.'

'It's gone down a lot. Lloyd gave me a bag of frozen peas to put on it. I think there will be a bruise but I'll dab some of my mum's witch hazel on when I get home. That should help take down the swelling,' she said. 'How about you?'

'My elbow has a big bruise on it,' he admitted. 'Maybe I'll try witch hazel, too. I'm sure my sister will have some in her well-stocked medicine cupboard.' He pushed his hood back so he could see her more clearly. 'I hope you don't have any bruises elsewhere, you did hit the pavement with quite a thud.'

She flushed a little, remembering how she had landed on her backside, which was still tender. 'I haven't had chance to look yet, but I think I might have another bruise or two.'

'I do apologise ...'

'Think nothing of it, it was both of us ...' Wanting to change the conversation, she glanced back at the tree. 'You're not supposed to be that side of the cordon you know. The tree is dangerous. That's why they've taped off the whole area around it. It's such a shame that the lights can't be put on the tree and the carol service has had to be cancelled. It's an important Lystone tradition.'

Joel's eyes met hers. They were soft and green and framed by long eyelashes that she would die for. 'I know, I'm a tree surgeon, and my business partner Andy and I have been asked to submit a quote for cutting the tree down. I've just come for a quick look at it but will be back tomorrow with equipment to check it out properly.'

'Cut it down?' The rumour was true, then. Lexi rubbed her hands together, the cold going through her despite the gloves she was wearing. 'Is that really necessary? It's such a lovely tree and a big part of our village life. Can't you save it? Or at least make it safe enough for us to have one last carol service around it.'

'Ivy has wrapped itself around the tree and destroyed some of the branches. I don't know how much damage has been done until I examine it further, but I do know that it could be extremely dangerous for anyone to hang baubles or lights on it as this could cause the branches to fall off and injure someone. It's not safe for anyone to stand near it. That's why the council want it cut down as soon as possible.'

That was worrying. 'How soon?'

'Within the next couple of days.'

'You mean before Christmas?'

He nodded. 'Yes, it's a high-priority job.'

His words stunned her. The tree would be gone before Christmas.

'They can't do that! This tree has been standing here for decades! They can't cut it down!' She could feel the outrage rising in her and was aware of the slight shrillness to her voice. *Calm down, Lexi, you don't want him to think that you're hysterical, do you?*

'It's a shame, yes, but the council has to put safety first.'

'Cutting it down sounds so drastic. It's a beautiful tree, it's been standing on this green since my gran was a young girl, and years before that.' She remembered her gran telling her how she and Grandpa Huey used to come to the carol services on the green, and actually met at one when they were teenagers. 'If you're a tree surgeon, you should be able to do something.'

Joel frowned. 'Apparently another company have looked at it and declared it unsafe, which is why the council have cordoned it off. All I've been asked to do is provide a quote for cutting it down. It's normal practice for the council to have a few quotes, then choose the cheapest one.'

'Well, can't you at least tell them that you can't cut down the tree this side of Christmas? Then we can still have the carol service.'

He stuck his hands in his pockets and looked at her, a bit bemused. 'They'll just get someone else to do it, and I need the work. I've just moved down here, Lexi. I need to build up my business. Work from the council could keep me busy for months.'

This was awful. She couldn't believe it was happening. She shook her head in dismay.

His gaze rested on her, sympathetic yet detached. 'Look, surely you can have the carol service somewhere else? I do think people get too worked up over Christmas sometimes. It's just one day.'

Just one day! Lexi gasped, feeling her eyes widen at his words. 'Well you sound a right grinch!' she exclaimed. 'It's a very important day. Christmas brings people together, brings out the best in them. It's wonderful when the villagers gather around the tree to sing carols. Can't you see how important this is to everyone? It's part of Lystone's Christmas tradition.'

He nodded. 'I appreciate that, but saving lives is more important than traditions.'

'And making money is more important, too, isn't it? I've heard the rumours that the council plans to chop down the tree and build houses on the green. It's all about profit now, isn't it? The same with you, all you care about is the money you'll be earning from this job. People's feelings don't come into it!'

She turned around and stomped off. To think she had thought Joel was nice! Well, he had shown his true colours: it was clear that there was no way he was going to help save the Christmas Eve celebrations.

Joel watched in exasperation as Lexi stormed off. What was the matter with people? Why did common sense go out of the window at Christmas time? Couldn't Lexi and the other villagers see the danger they could be in if one of the branches fell off the tree and hit them on the head? It could be fatal. They were so obsessed with continuing with the traditional carol service that they didn't seem to care about safety. It was always the same. Lexi spoke about Christmas as if it was a magical time of peace and goodwill to all men instead of the most stressful time of year, when people got into debt to buy presents they couldn't afford, had accidents climbing onto roofs to put up ridiculously large Christmas displays, had too much to drink at Christmas parties. The whole world went mad for one single day of the year. It was crazy.

Chapter Nine

'Hello, Lexi. You've been ages! I think you must have walked around the entire village,' her mother said as Lexi walked into the lounge. She narrowed her eyes and frowned. 'What's that nasty bump on your head?'

Granny Mabe peered through her glasses. 'Goodness, what did you walk into?' she asked, her needles clinking as she knitted away at a sparkly gold square.

Is that for the yarn-bombing? Lexi thought. She had to find a chance to speak to Granny Mabe on her own and tell her about the council's plans to find and fine the yarn-bombers.

'It's nothing. An old man tripped up and I rushed to help him at the same time as Joel, his neighbour, did and we bumped into each other,' Lexi explained.

'Is the old man hurt?' her mum asked.

'No, he's fine, we managed to stop his fall.'

'That's good.' Her mother stepped closer and peered at the bruise. 'I'll get you something to put something on that,' she said, dashing out of the room.

'What about the man you bumped into?' Granny Mabe asked as she started a new row.

'He bumped into *me* actually, sent me reeling with his elbow.' Lexi swallowed. 'And guess what I've found out? He's a tree surgeon and the council have asked him to cut down the fir tree on the green – this week.'

Granny Mabe stopped knitting and stared at her. 'What? Before Christmas?'

'Here we are.' Paula returned with a bottle of witch hazel and some cotton wool. 'This will bring out the bruise quicker and it will heal faster.' She put some witch hazel on the cotton wool and dabbed the bump on Lexi's forehead.

Lexi bit her lip, it was painful when touched.

'Put it on a couple of times a day,' her mum told her.

Lexi's dad came in, a big plastic reindeer under his arm. 'I thought I still had this. I hope the lights still work, Toby will love it.' he said, holding a screwdriver in his other hand. Then he paused when he saw Lexi holding the cotton wool onto her forehead. 'What's happened?'

Lexi recounted it all to him, including her conversation with Joel on the green. Both her parents looked horrified.

'That's outrageous! They can't do that at such short notice. They're not even giving anyone time to try and save it,' her mum protested.

'Joel said that they've already had a tree specialist look at it who deemed it unsafe and they're now asking companies to submit quotes with a view of cutting it down in the next couple of days.'

'Well, that's a load of rubbish, there is nothing wrong with that tree that trimming a few branches won't put right,' Granny

Mabe said defiantly, clicking her needles even faster in her annoyance.

'Now, Ma, it must be unsafe if a specialist company has looked at it, and there's cordon tape around it,' Craig said, unscrewing the plug on the reindeer lights. 'We just have to accept it. It would have been nice if we could have had a final carol service there but it can't be helped . . .'

'We can all gather in the square and have a bit of a carol service there but it won't be the same,' Paula said with a sigh.

'We can't give up that easily!' Lexi retorted. 'We should start a petition, if we get enough support the council might think about saving the tree.'

Her mum shook her head. 'Martin Groves, the man on the council who's dealing with this, is a moderniser. He's not one for traditions. He's already up in arms about all this yarn-bombing that's going on in the village. He said it's nothing more than glorified littering. There's a hefty fine if he catches anyone doing it, but the stuff seems to appear overnight and no one has spotted the culprits yet despite there being CCTV everywhere. They wear hoods and black clothing, apparently.'

Granny Mabe's needles clicked more furiously.

'I bet it's because of those yarn-bombers that they're cutting down the tree before Christmas,' Lexi's dad said, carrying the reindeer over to the plug socket on the far wall and setting it down on the floor before plugging it in. No lights came on.

'What do you mean?' her mum asked.

Lexi looked over at Granny Mabe, who had stopped knitting and was listening avidly.

'Well, they've been putting all those festive yarn-bombs

everywhere,' her dad continued. 'Maybe the council think they'll start on the fir tree next, try to pretty it up as there's no lights and they don't want to risk that in case one of the branches falls off and someone gets badly hurt. The council could have an expensive compensation claim to settle.' He pulled out the plug and picked up his screwdriver.

That sounded plausible, Lexi had to acknowledge.

'That tree is as safe as houses. We can't let them cut it down,' Granny said, her eyes fixed firmly on her knitting. 'I think Lexi's right and we should get a petition up to protest. They could at least postpone cutting it down until after Christmas.

Lexi glanced over at her gran, were the Yarn Bombers planning something for Christmas Eve? She remembered her gran saying that she had something to tell her when she'd first arrived, but then her mum had come home. She had to get Granny Mabe on her own and find out what it was. She could imagine her gran and her friends tying themselves to the tree and singing 'this tree will not be removed!'

'Well, there's only a few days to go, let's hope they can't get it all organised in time,' Paula said. 'You know what the council are like, forms for this, forms for that. We'll get a petition going at the bakery and see if we can drum up enough support to make the council reconsider.' She got up. 'I'd better go and dish out dinner before the meat dries up.'

Lexi followed her mother into the kitchen. 'Can I do anything to help?' Both her parents worked hard and she didn't want them waiting on her.

'That's kind of you, dear. Perhaps you could lay the table?' her mum said as she opened the oven and took out a big piece of roast beef.

Lexi's tummy rumbled. Roast beef, roast potatoes and Yorkshire pudding had to be her favourite meal ever.

When they were all sitting around the table, tucking in to their meal, she remembered about the Christmas tree for Lloyd.

'Do you have a spare Christmas tree in the loft, Dad?' she asked.

'I think there's a couple up there. Did you want another one for your bedroom? We still have the small one you used to put on your bedside table,' he replied.

'Do you? I might put it up.' Lexi felt a bit nostalgic remembering the little tree. 'I was thinking of one a bit bigger, though. Lloyd, the old man who slipped, well, I helped him into his house with his shopping and noticed that he hadn't got a Christmas tree so I wondered if you had a spare one I could take to him.'

'I'm sure we have,' said her mum. 'Why don't you take a look up in the loft and see? You're welcome to take anything you want from there. You'd be doing me a favour, actually, I've been trying to persuade your father to sort out the Christmas stuff for years but you know what he's like. He won't throw anything away, but would give you the shirt off his back.' Her mum pushed a stray lock of hair behind her ear. 'Honestly, the shed and the loft are chock-a-block with stuff. He'll be taking over the spare bedrooms next!'

'Always been the same has Craig. He'd be upset if I threw anything away when he was a child,' Granny Mabe announced as she cut up her Yorkshire pudding. 'He'd put everything he didn't use any longer on top of the wardrobe. Had it piled that high that the top of the wardrobe fell through.'

'I am here, you know!' her dad said, mock-indignantly. He

speared some broccoli on his fork before saying to Lexi, 'You can take anything you like, love. I don't mind as long as someone can make use of it.'

Her dad hated anything being thrown away. Lexi remembered how he had been the same when they were young, whenever they had stopped using anything it went into the shed 'just in case they needed it again'. He'd put floorboards in the loft, and ladders leading up to it, so that he could use it to store stuff. She hadn't been up there for years, but it had been pretty full with things then, and she was sure there was even more stuff up there now. Her dad had not only kept things from when they were all small, but things from when he was a child, and he had also put some things of Grandpa Huey's up there too, when he and Granny Mabe had moved in. Her mum had wanted to move to a bungalow when Lexi and her brothers had moved out, but her dad had pointed out that there would be nowhere to put all his stuff. 'That's the point!' her mum had told him. But before she could persuade her dad to move, Grandpa Huey had taken ill and they'd started making plans for the garage conversion. Now, Lexi thought that her parents and Granny Mabe wouldn't want the upheaval of moving. Anyway, the spare bedrooms came in handy when Lexi or her brothers came to stay. Although, she thought her mother was right and her dad would soon start filling them up too.

'Thanks, Dad,' she said. 'Lloyd looked pleased when I mentioned it to him. He lives on his own.'

'Lloyd and Ruby ... that rings a bell. You must mean Mr Winston. He often pops into the bakery for a loaf of bread. I'm sure his wife was named Ruby,' her mum said.

'He had a son too, didn't he? I can't remember his name,' Granny Mabe added. 'He moved away years ago, as the young do.'

'I wonder if he's going to his son's for Christmas,' Lexi said. She hoped he was, she hated to think of the kind old man being on his own on Christmas Day. 'I'll ask him when I take the tree round, and if he isn't can I please invite him here?'

'We could squeeze him in couldn't we, Paula?' Granny Mabe asked. 'I remember Ruby, she was lovely. I met Lloyd a couple of times too, he seems a pleasant man'

Her mum nodded. 'It's no problem to me. We have plenty of food and one more at the table won't make any difference. What do you think, Craig?'

'Fine by me. The more the merrier.'

'Thank you so much. I'll help you, I promise,' Lexi said. She didn't want to make even more work for her parents.

Chapter Ten

After dinner, Lexi insisted her mother sat down and had a rest while she cleared the dinner things away and loaded the dishwasher. 'I'll go and find that Christmas tree now,' she said when the kitchen was tidy again

Her dad had returned to the reindeer-that-wouldn't-light-up. He wasn't one to let anything defeat him. 'I can't figure out why this thing isn't working. None of the wires are broken, I've checked them all thoroughly.'

'Where are you going to put it?' Lexi asked him, looking around. Every shelf and surface was covered with Christmas decorations: candles, snowmen, Santas, wind-up carol singers and other festive ornaments. Her parents always cleared the shelves and sideboard every December, putting the standard ornaments and photos away in a box, to make room for the Christmas decorations. Then in January, when the Christmas decorations had been put away, they all came out again.

'On top of the wardrobe in Jay and Sonia's room. I reckon Toby will love it and it will provide a night light for him.'

Lexi smiled. Having a child in the house again would give

her dad a good reason to go even more overboard with lights and decorations this Christmas. 'Are you and Mum dressing up as Father Christmas and Mrs Claus again?' she asked.

'We're planning on it, if I can find our outfits. If you spot them up in the loft when you're looking for the Christmas tree, bring them down with you, will you, love?' her dad asked.

'Sure,' Lexi agreed. She went upstairs and took the stick with the hook on the end out of the airing cupboard and used it to tug open the loft hatch and pull down the ladders. Making sure she'd secured them, she climbed up and reached inside for the light switch on the left wall and flicked it on. Immediately, the loft was flooded with light. She stepped inside and peered around. It was full of bags and boxes. She recognised the old rocking horse that she, Ryan and Jay had played on when they were small, and her doll's house. There were big trunks, too. She opened one and saw that it was full of clothes. She'd bet some of them were vintage. She knew that Granny Mabe had brought some of the boxes with her. It was like a treasure trove. She wished she had time to sort through it all – who knew what she'd find there – but she had to focus on finding the Christmas tree and decorations.

Although it looked like everything had just been dumped there, she knew her father did have some sort of order. The Christmas stuff would all be piled together, and probably still in its original boxes. Her dad always put things back in their wrappings, even the tools in his shed and some of the kitchen appliances, like the steamer. It drove her mum mad sometimes. When she needed something, she wanted to put her hand on it, not have to take it out of a box. Somewhere, amongst all this, would be a pile of Christmas stuff. All she had to do was find it.

Finally, she tracked down a big box over in the corner by the window, and a thin, long box standing upright behind it. That could be it. She walked over for a better look and saw the faded picture of a Christmas tree on the front. *Brilliant.* And she'd bet the other box was full of Christmas decorations.

It was.

Next, she searched through the other boxes of Christmas things to find the Santa costumes. Ah, there they were, neatly put away in a black bag with a label saying 'Santa outfits' on the front. She decided to take them down first.

'I've got the Santa outfits,' she said, walking into the lounge, just as the reindeer lights sprang on. Her dad looked chuffed.

'I knew I'd do it! I'll go up and put this in Jay's room now.' He stood up and brushed down his trousers. 'Do you want me to help you carry the tree and baubles down?'

'Thanks, Dad, that would be great . . .'

They stopped off at the big bedroom at the back that Jay, Sonia and Toby were sleeping in, first. Lexi gasped as she stepped inside. It was like a magical grotto with lights twinkling everywhere. A Christmas tree stood on the top of a low cupboard, with a Christmas scene around it, and festive duvet covers adorned both the double bed and the camp bed beside it. On the bottom of the camp bed were three soft toys: a Santa, a snowman and a penguin.

'I think you and Mum are going to enjoy having a child in the house again this Christmas,' she said.

'You bet we are.' Her dad carried the reindeer over to the wardrobe in the corner, placed it on the top and plugged it in, smiling triumphantly as the lights twinkled. 'There! It gives a lovely glow to the room and it's too high up for Toby to mess with,' he said.

'Toby will love it,' Lexi told him. She was looking forward to seeing Jay again, and meeting his wife and little Toby. Her first nephew, and her parents' first grandchild. No wonder they were both so excited.

They didn't go into Ryan and Nell's room but Lexi knew that it would be decorated just as festively.

Then they went up to the attic and her father picked up the box with the Christmas tree in it while Lexi brought down the box of baubles. They put the ladders back up and slid the loft door shut. Lexi had chosen a box of red and silver baubles for Lloyd, thinking they would look very Christmassy and traditional, and also some white lights. She checked the transformer to make sure they were working. She'd also picked up some red and silver tinsel and another string of lights for around Lloyd's bay window.

'I'll put them straight into the car and take them to Lloyd first thing in the morning,' she said. It was dark now and she guessed that Lloyd would be tucked up for the evening and wouldn't want anyone calling on him so late.

They all spent the evening sitting around the log fire, drinking mulled wine, eating mince pies and sharing past memories. When her parents went into the kitchen to get more wine and pies, Lexi reminded Granny Mabe about the fines being threatened for yarn-bombers. 'I don't think you should do any more for a while, Granny. Let the dust settle a bit.'

'Rubbish. I'm not letting mean-spirited people stop me from bringing a bit of happiness into people's lives,' Granny Mabe said.

Lexi remembered the wonder on the little girl's face when she saw the yarn-bombings on the railings. Some people did love them, she did too. But others didn't, and might report Granny Mabe and her friends. *There's always someone who's got to put the dampener on Christmas*, she thought, her mind going to Joel. He'd seemed such a nice man, one that you might think would be full of Christmas cheer and bonhomie. How wrong could you be?

'It's been so lovely to have a catch up with you, love,' her mother said, patting Lexi's hand. 'I know you must miss Ben, though. Is there no way he can join us, not even on Christmas evening or for Boxing Day? It's not that long a drive.'

Lexi felt a little guilty that she'd lied to them about why Ben wasn't with her. *It's only a little lie and it's better this way*, she told herself. It meant she could put him right out of her mind and not have everyone being all sympathetic around her.

'No chance, but it's fine, Mum. We can spend New Year together.'

I'm so glad that I came home for Christmas, she thought. It was good to have something else to think about rather than Ben's betrayal.

Well, she'd park her upset over that until she got home. Right now she was determined that they were all going to have a lovely family Christmas. And to try and talk Joel into saving the Christmas tree. He'd said he'd be there tomorrow with equipment to assess the damage, so she'd go and see him when she'd taken the tree to Lloyd. He might think that Christmas wasn't important, but she certainly didn't.

It had been an eventful day, Joel thought, as he sat drinking a brandy and watching the logs crackle on the fire. Sweetie was fast asleep, sprawled out on the rug. She looked so peaceful and cute.

He'd heard Sweetie barking as he got out of the van last night and hoped that she was just making a noise because she'd heard the van. He was at a loss as to what to do with her.. *She's probably missing Hazel and Al, and wondering what I'm doing in her house*, he reminded himself. He had to be patient with her. He'd only got a bit of work until New Year, so he could spend plenty of time bonding with Sweetie, then hopefully she would feel more secure and happier to be left.

He had meant to check on the old man – Lloyd – when he came back. But what with Toni dropping the bombshell that she wanted to get back with him, then checking out the tree and the subsequent fall out with Lexi, which had disturbed him far more that it should have, and coming home to find Sweetie so stressed, he had forgotten all about it. And now it was too late to knock on Lloyd's door and disturb him. He'd have to go tomorrow. Lloyd looked shaken up earlier, and that had bothered Joel, although he knew that Lexi had seen him home. He'd only met the woman twice, but had certainly picked up that she was a 'carer'. She cared about things, and about people. She seemed nice, actually. Shame they were at loggerheads about the perishing tree. It wasn't his fault if the council wanted him to cut it down, and if he didn't do it, another company would. Surely she didn't expect him to turn work down.

He sighed. He'd thought that life would be more peaceful when he moved to Lystone, but it was already turning out to be stressful.

Chapter Eleven

Monday, five days before Christmas

Joel opened one eye sleepily, glanced at the clock, then shot out of bed. He was late! Again! Thanks to Sweetie keeping him awake, alternating between snoring, hogging the covers and pacing around the bedroom all night, again. It was typical that she was fast asleep now, when he should have been up at least half an hour ago. He and Andy were checking out the tree properly today, and had arranged to meet at ten. It was already nine thirty.

As if sensing that he was up, Sweetie stirred, and sat up on the pillow, looking sleepily at him as if wondering what he was doing.

'Come on, girl, I need to let you out quickly or I'll be late for work,' he said, reaching for his dressing gown. Andy would be there with the van soon, and he'd promised Martin a report later that evening, as he knew he was determined to get the tree cut down this week.

'Woof! Woof!' Sweetie jumped off the bed and ran over to the door her tail wagging furiously.

'Give me a sec,' he told her as he pulled on a slipper and reached for the other one, thinking how his life was a bit out of kilter at the moment. Here he was, divorced – well, almost – and living in a rural village instead of a big city, which he'd assumed would be quiet and relaxing but was already turning out to be eventful. And if the council ordered him to cut down that blessed tree, he could well become public enemy number one if the other villagers reacted how Lexi had done last night. Not exactly a great start to village life, was it?

He went downstairs, Sweetie way ahead of him, and opened the back door for the Maltese to have an amble in the secure back garden, then topped up the water in the coffee machine, switched it on, put a pod of black coffee in and placed a mug underneath.

He must definitely check on Lloyd today and see how he was doing after his near fall. He secretly hoped he might bump into Lexi again, too – she seemed like the kind of person who would go the extra mile to make sure Lloyd was all right. He was surprised – and a little hurt – by her parting shot on the green yesterday. Anyone would think that he had cancelled Christmas. 'A grinch' she'd called him, referring to the Dr Seuss book about the grump who hated Christmas, which he presumed she'd read as a child, too. He thought that was a bit off. He didn't hate Christmas. He just didn't make a song and dance about it.

He sighed as he picked up the cup of coffee and took it over to the table. What was it with people and Christmas? As soon as December rolled in, all common sense seemed to go out of the window. Lexi had sounded almost fanatical about it. Honestly, the lengths people went to in order to have the mythical 'perfect Christmas'. It was as if nothing else mattered. What was the council supposed to do about the tree if it was dying? Someone could be killed. Christmas came second to saving lives. His parents, both doctors, had repeatedly said that when he and Hazel had begged them to spend just one Christmas Day with them instead of sending them off to their grandparents every holiday. He'd realised as he got older, that what they had been doing was vital, and unselfish. They'd put saving lives before their family and their own needs. He admired them a great deal now, still in Glasgow, working in A&E over the Christmas period. Neither he nor Hazel had wanted to follow in their footsteps, though, they'd seen first-hand the hard work involved in being a doctor. Especially at Christmas. Sweetie happily wandered back in, headed for her basket and was soon snoring away. Joel glanced over at her as he sat down to drink his coffee, he wished he could climb back into bed and sleep for a few hours longer, but there was work to do – and he needed this job. He just hoped it didn't make enemies for him in the village.

When he finished his coffee the little dog was still spark out, great he could have a quick shower then go and meet Andy, he'd take Sweetie out for a walk later and call in on Lloyd on the way home. He got up and crept out of the room so as not to wake her. He was halfway up the stairs when he heard loud barking and the scuffle of paws as Sweetie dashed out of the kitchen and up the stairs after him. Damn. It looked like he'd have to let her in the bathroom again while he showered. This was getting ridiculous. He could barely go to the loo on his own. He must try and get hold of Hazel today, and see if she had any suggestions as to how to settle the little dog.

*   *   *

After breakfast, Lexi decided to take the Christmas tree around to Lloyd. She pulled on her jeans and red polo-neck sweater, then her long Christmas cardigan – the one with the white background with rows of green Christmas trees and red reindeer that matched Ben's. It was long enough to reach her knees, and had pockets and a hood, she was driving there so wouldn't need a coat. She left her long hair hanging loose, and put in her flashing Santa earrings. She was determined to cheer Lloyd up.

'I'm going to pop the Christmas tree around to Lloyd's now, Gran,' she said. Her parents were both working in the bakery that morning. 'I'll invite him to Christmas dinner too. I hope he agrees to come.'

'Well, you look very festive!' Granny Mabe said with a smile. 'Now, don't be rushing back on my behalf. Some of my friends are popping round. We're having a meeting about the yarn-bombing.'

'Do you think you should carry on doing this, Gran? You could get a big fine,' Lexi pointed out.

'They've got to catch us first!' Granny Mabe replied.

Honestly, her gran was like a rebellious teenager, Lexi thought as she pulled on her long black boots.

As she pulled up outside Lloyd's house, she started to wonder if this was a good idea. Old people could be very proud. What if he looked on this as charity? Or if he didn't want a Christmas tree? She hadn't actually asked him, had she? She was always so impulsive – spontaneous she preferred to call it – but she knew not everyone appreciate surprises ... Maybe she should check before she took everything out of the car. And if he said he didn't want the tree she had to respect his wishes and not try to talk him into it. She knew she could be a bit over the top about

Christmas sometimes, what did everyone expect with a family like hers who all turned their houses into grottos and a mum and dad who insisted on dressing up as Santa and Mrs Claus, not only for the family Christmas dinner but also in the bakery every Christmas Eve!

She glanced at the house next door but one, the van had gone so it looked like Joel was out, which was good. She felt a bit bad about shouting at him yesterday. He was only doing his job, after all, and had been told that the tree was unsafe. Maybe when he checked it over today, he would decide that he could save it. She hoped so. She walked up the path to Lloyd's house and rang the bell.

'Who is it?' he called.

She opened the letterbox and shouted through. 'It's me, Lexi. Is this a good time to call? I can come back later if you're busy.'

The door was opened in a couple of minutes. 'How wonderful! I didn't expect to see you so soon, but do come in. It's a pleasant surprise. And I love the earrings. Very cheerful.'

She thrust her hands in her cardigan pockets and looked at him earnestly. 'I've brought something with me but please say if you don't want it all. I'm a bit worried that I might be imposing.'

Lloyd peered down at the ground by her feet then looked back at her, puzzled.

'It's in the car,' she explained. 'It's a Christmas tree. We had a spare one and I thought you might like it. I've brought some baubles and lights too. I could help you put it up. But if you prefer not to bother with it, I don't mind honestly. It was probably a bit presumptuous of me.'

His face creased into a warm smile. 'A Christmas tree? How

delightful! I haven't had one for years! What a lovely idea. Thank you. It's about time I brightened up the place and celebrated Christmas properly again.'

She grinned in relief. 'I'll go and get it out of the boot of my car.'

Two journeys later – Lloyd insisted on coming out to help her, and thankfully, the snow had almost cleared so she didn't have to worry about him slipping over again – and the tree and baubles were in the house.

'I've brought something else, too.' She took a small CD player out of her bag and two CDs of Christmas carols which she had also found in the loft. 'I love to have Christmas songs playing in the background while I put up the tree.'

Lloyd's eyes were sparkling. 'I'll plug it in right away,' he said.

'Right, now where would you like the tree?' Lexi asked as the words of 'We Wish You a Merry Christmas' rang out from the CD that was already in the player.

The old man looked around the room. 'I think over by the bay window,' he decided. 'Now, I'll fix us a hot drink, then we can get cracking.'

Lexi took off her long cardigan and put it over the arm of a chair, then carefully eased the Christmas tree out of the box, opened up the stand and fixed it on the bottom then started spreading out the branches. The tree was standing by the window, branches all outstretched, when Lloyd came in carrying a tray loaded with two mugs of tea and a plate of assorted biscuits.

'That's a grand tree. Are you sure you don't want anything for it?' he said.

'Positive. It was up in my parents' loft, they haven't used it for years. My dad won't throw anything away, but he's happy to give it away.'

'He sounds a kind man.' Lloyd placed the tray down on the table, then rubbed his hands. 'Right, let's get cracking!'

So, with the Christmas carols playing, they spent an hour or so decorating the tree, both singing along to the songs.

Chapter Twelve

'What do you think?' Andy asked when Joel was back down on the ground again.

'As I thought, the ivy growing around it has caused some of the branches to die back, but the general health of the fir tree is absolutely fine. There's no need to cut it down. It's a Douglas Fir, and in good health otherwise.'

Andy looked uneasy. 'I thought you said the council wanted it cut down?'

'They do. Martin is putting pressure on me to say that the tree is unsafe and needs to be destroyed.' Joel stuck his head on one side as he surveyed Andy thoughtfully. 'You know about the Christmas Eve carol service the locals usually hold here. Theoretically, there's no reason why it couldn't have gone ahead this year. It would only take a day, two at the most, to make the tree safe.'

'Maybe, but it's too late for that now. Even if Martin agreed, they'd never get the paperwork through in time. Or get the lights on.' Andy shuffled his feet. 'I don't see what we can do. If the council want the tree cut down then that's up to them. If we don't do it, someone else will and we'll lose a job, and probably future work, too.'

Joel rubbed his chin. 'I know, but I think we should at least say that it can be saved, and perhaps give them a quote for that? It's not ethical to put in a report saying that the tree is unsafe when it isn't. Reputation is everything in this business. If the council still want to cut the tree down, that's up to them. It's their decision at the end of the day, but it's our responsibility to be truthful about the state of the tree.'

'True.' Andy rubbed his hands together as a cold wind blew by. 'I need to get going. I've got another job this afternoon. You have to get your report over to Martin today, don't you?'

Joel nodded. 'I'll let you know what Martin says.' He didn't think that there was much doubt as to what Martin would say, the man was adamant that he wanted the tree cutting down, but Joel had to at least try. It was a beautiful specimen. It would be a shame to destroy it.

And it meant a lot to Lexi.

When Andy had gone, Joel stood back and gazed up at the tree, remembering how passionate Lexi had been about the annual carol service, saying how much it meant to the village. If the council agreed to save the tree, he could do it in time, and Andy had said he was free to help. It wasn't their decision, though, but would Lexi see it that way if the council insisted the tree had to come down? It was evident that Christmas, and all the surrounding traditions, were important to her.

Christmas. He'd enjoyed it as a child, but as he'd grown older it had little importance to him. In the period between Christmas and New Year, he'd seen his parents come home exhausted and often upset after spending a day in A&E, dealing with emergencies such as car crashes, drunken fights, and accidents, and had, from an early age, realised that the Christmas season often brought out the worst in people. As an adult, he had never bothered to celebrate it much, but Toni loved a party and Christmas to her was an excuse to do just that, and to buy expensive presents that they couldn't afford. In January, their bank balance was always in the red and whenever he complained she told him not to be a grinch, it was Christmas. It was as if Christmas was an excuse for over-indulging in anything. Last year, he – like most of the nation – had spent a quiet Christmas at home because of the lockdown restrictions, and he was happy to do the same this year. Hazel had left him a turkey crown in the freezer, a small Christmas pudding, a box of mince pies and a good brandy, and there were a couple of films on Netflix he wanted to see, so that was Christmas sorted for him. Right now, though, he'd go and check on Sweetie, pop in to see how Lloyd was, then send over the quote to Martin. After that, for the rest of the day, he could put his feet up. He was looking forward to that. He was exhausted.

Lloyd looked up as the doorbell rang. 'I wonder who that can be?'

'Maybe it's a parcel,' Lexi suggested. 'Are you expecting a delivery?'

'No.' Lloyd walked over to look through the window, then turned back, a smile on his face. 'It's Joel.'

Joel. Lexi felt her cheeks flush. *Keep calm*, she told herself, *don't sound off again.* She braced herself as Lloyd went to open the front door. She was in Lloyd's house; she would be polite but firm if Joel carried on dissing Christmas.

'Hello, Lloyd. How are you feeling? I'm sorry that I didn't get chance to pop by yesterday.'

'I'm fine, thank you. And you've got Sweetie with you. Hello, girl.'

'Yap! Yap!'

'Do come in. You too, Sweetie.'

Lexi turned towards the lounge door as she heard Joel ask, 'You know Sweetie?'

'Yes, I used to see Hazel and Al walking her. How are you getting on with her? She's a cute little thing, isn't see?'

'She is, but she's exhausting me. I know I've only been with her a few days but she just won't settle,' Joel said.

'She'll be missing Hazel and Al. They always make such a fuss of her. They're going to be away six months, aren't they?' Lloyd asked.

'Yes, they're helping set up a couple of new hotels over in Dubai.'

Sweetie bounded through the door and over to Lexi, wagging her tail excitedly. 'Oh you are such a cute darling!' Lexi said, making a fuss of the little dog.

Sweetie was followed by Lloyd and Joel, but Lexi studiously focused her attention on fussing the little dog.

'You wouldn't think that if you were woken up to her barking half a dozen times a night and came back from work to find she'd chewed up one of your sister's favourite cushions,' Joel said, smiling warily at her.

'Are you being a naughty girl?' Lexi asked Sweetie, trying to steel herself to apologise to Joel, who was now staring at her flashing Santa earrings. He probably thought she was stupid to wear them.

His eyes then flitted over to the half-decorated Christmas tree. 'This all looks very festive.'

'Lexi found out I hadn't got a Christmas tree, so she brought me one round and is helping me decorate it. Isn't that kind of her?' Lloyd told him. 'Come and join us. Sweetie is welcome, too.'

'Oh, I don't think Joel will want to do that, he doesn't approve of Christmas, especially not Christmas trees. He's about to cut down the big fir tree on the green,' Lexi retorted.

'Really?' Lloyd looked shocked and Lexi felt herself flush. She shouldn't have said that. She didn't even know if he was going to cut down the tree yet.

'That's a bit unfair.' Joel looked annoyed.

Lloyd looked from one to the other. 'Why don't you sit down and tell us all about it?

Lexi felt ashamed. Why did she let her tongue get carried away? 'Sorry, I know that you're only doing your job, but that Christmas tree means a lot to the villagers of Lystone.'

He met her gaze. 'I do understand, and I apologise if I sounded uncaring yesterday but it really isn't my decision to make. All I've been asked to do is submit a quote for the work the council want done.'

'It's a shame if the tree has to come down. Are you a tree surgeon, Joel?' asked Lloyd.

'Yes. I've been examining the tree today with my colleague. Ivy has wound itself around the trunk and some of the branches which is why several of them have died back.'

'And is it dangerous? Is any chance to save it?' Lexi asked, forcing herself to keep her tone calm and polite.

She saw the hesitation on Joel's face. 'I think it could be saved, couldn't it?' She held his gaze. She was sure that if the tree was so dangerous that there was no option but to take it down, he would say so instead of hedging as he was.

Joel sighed. 'Yes, it could be, but it isn't my decision. If the council ask me to cut it down, then that's what I have to do.'

'Surely you could cut off the branches that the ivy has wrapped around, then the tree would be safe?'

'Not without the council's permission, I can't.'

'And do you intend to tell them that you think it can be saved, and to offer to save it?' Lexi asked.

'I do, but I doubt if it will make any difference.'

Well, that's good that he's prepared to do that. 'And could you make it safe in time for Christmas?' She knew that she was putting him on the spot, but if there was any way of saving the Christmas carol service, she wanted to know.

'Theoretically, yes,' he admitted. 'But there would probably have to be another meeting about it, as a decision has already been made to cut the tree down. Which means that there wouldn't be time to prune the tree before Christmas. So we won't be able to put the lights on it and your carol service still won't be able to go ahead.'

'Can you please try to persuade them, at least?' Lexi asked.

He rubbed the stubble on his chin. 'I doubt that anything I say will have any clout.'

'You could try, though. Tell them how much this carol service means to everyone. It brings the village together. People exchange presents, meet old friends, go on to the pub and have mulled wine and mince pies.' She could feel her voice rising and took a breath to steady it, not wanting him to think she was getting emotional. 'My eighty-four-year-old gran looks forward to that carol service.'

'So do I, it's the only time I get to see people over Christmas,' Lloyd said.

Joel looked from one to the other. 'I will stress that the tree can be saved, and how much it means to the village. I can't make any promises, though. As I said, it's really not my decision.'

'Thank you for trying,' Lexi said, pleased that Joel wasn't as anti-Christmas as she'd thought. 'And I'm sorry if I was a bit over the top about it, but it means a lot to me.'

'I can see that.' Joel smiled at her. 'Apology accepted.'

'Good, now I'll go and put the kettle on and make us all a hot drink,' Lloyd said. 'I'm going to have to move this little doggy first, though.' He smiled down at Sweetie who was now curled up on his lap.

'She looks very comfortable with you,' Joel told him.

'Oh, she's used to me. I often stopped to make a fuss of her when Hazel or Al were taking her for a walk. Didn't I, girl?' Lloyd tickled Sweetie under her chin and she nuzzled into him.

'I have to admit that I'm at my wits' end with her. She insists on coming into my bed every night and spends most of the time fidgeting, snoring or barking.'

He sounded like a parent talking about a toddler, thought Lexi, and she couldn't help bursting out laughing.

'It's not funny, I can assure you. Sweetie might be adorable, but she is also a handful and definitely rules the roost. If I leave the house, even for a few minutes, she barks and whines, and has also started chewing up things.'

'Well, why don't you leave her with me when you're out at work, just until she gets used to you? It's a shame for her to be alone,' offered Lloyd.

Joel looked a bit taken aback. 'Are you serious?'

Lloyd nodded. 'It's no trouble and she'll be company for me. And speaking of company, thank you, both of you, for today.' He looked around the room, beaming. 'I can't tell you what it means to me to have you popping in, and bringing a Christmas tree over,' he said to Lexi. 'And for you to come and check on me, Joel.'

'Then, thank you, but only if you're sure it's no trouble. That would certainly be a weight off my mind,' said Joel. 'And I was wondering if you'd like a basket of logs? I had to chop a tree down last week – a diseased one,' he added hastily. 'The owner offered me some of the logs from it and now my wood store is overflowing. Could you make use of some? Call it payment for looking after Sweetie,' he added quickly.

Lexi guessed he was thinking that Lloyd might be too proud to accept his charity.

'In that case, yes please.'

'I'll go and get them. Do you mind if I leave Sweetie here for a few minutes while I do?'

'Of course. I'll put the kettle on and make us a pot of tea while you're gone.'

Chapter Thirteen

Joel's mind was full of thoughts of the fir tree as he went back home to get a basket of logs for Lloyd. He would obviously tell Martin that he thought the tree could be saved but, as he'd told Lexi, he didn't think Martin would take any notice of that. But it really was a magnificent tree and he would like to save it, if he could. Perhaps if he kept his price low and told Martin that he'd given a reduced quote on the condition he could save the tree in time for Christmas, Martin might agree. If not, maybe he could charge a low price for cutting down the tree but only on the condition that it was done *after* Christmas. The villagers might feel better if the tree was still standing for Christmas, even if there were no lights on it and the carol service couldn't go ahead.

Why was he trying to save the tree for Lexi? It was more important that people were safe. And Lexi would be gone back home in a week or so.

It's not just Lexi, it means a lot to the village, he told himself as he let himself in. And this was his new home, for now, anyway.

He filled the log basket with dry logs from the wood store in the backyard and took it back around to Lloyd, who had left the door on the catch for him. Lexi was standing on tiptoe, putting a gold, sparkly fairy on the Christmas tree, Lloyd was wrapping red and silver tinsel around the tree branches, and Sweetie was fast asleep on the sofa – she didn't even bother to look up when he came in. *Charming, after you've kept me awake half the night,* Joel thought.

'Shall I take them out to your wood store for you?' he asked.

'That would be grand,' Lloyd told him.

Joel returned a few minutes later, having filled the basket with dry logs from the shed so Joel had a fresh supply. 'I thought I'd save you the bother of having to bring some more logs in,' he said, putting the logs into the almost empty basket by the fire.

'That's very kind of you.' Lloyd pointed to a mug of tea, a sugar bowl and a milk jug on a tray on the coffee table. Both he and Lexi were holding their mugs. 'Sit yourself down and have a cuppa now. Help yourself to milk and sugar.'

'Thank you.' Joel added a drop of milk in his tea and then stirred it around before taking a sip. *Perfect. Not too strong, not too weak.*

'Fancy helping us put up the Christmas lights around the bay window?' Lexi asked, holding up a string of lights. 'They do work. I've tested them out.'

He saw the challenge in her eyes. She was determined to entice him into enjoying some festive cheer.

'Many hands make light work,' Lloyd said cheerily.

Why not? Decorating the room had obviously made Lloyd happy, and it would only take him a few minutes to fix the lights around the window. 'Sure.' Joel took a long sip of his tea then put the mug back on the tray. 'Anything to help.'

'Watch it, Lexi will be getting you wearing a Christmas jumper next,' Lloyd said.

Joel shook his head in mock-indignation. 'Never.'

'Never say never,' Lexi told him with a smile as she handed him the lights.

The atmosphere had lightened between them since he'd agreed to try and save the tree, Joel realised. He was glad, he hated being at loggerheads with anyone. He went over to the window and studied it. He could see some cable clips already dotted along the frame. 'You want the lights draped around the frame using the cable clips that are already here?' he asked.

'I'd forgotten about those. Ruby always liked lights around the window, so I put the cable clips up to hold them in place.' Lloyd looked sad at the memory, so Lexi reached out and squeezed his arm reassuringly.

She was warm and kind as well as hot-headed and obsessed with Christmas, Joel thought. And beautiful too, especially with that bit of red tinsel stuck in her hair and the slight flush to her cheeks. And those sparkling Santa earrings.

As Joel fixed the lights around the window, he could feel his mood brighten, he even caught himself humming to 'Santa Claus is Comin' to Town' which was blasting out from the CD player. He'd bet Lexi had brought the songs with her, too.

Sweetie had woken up now and was running around with a piece of red tinsel wrapped around her. They all chuckled at her antics And Joel took a photo of her. 'I'll send it to Hazel,' he said.

'It all looks wonderful, thank you both,' Lloyd said, when the tree was finally decorated and the lights were twinkling around the window. 'It looks so festive in here. It reminds me of Christmases when Ruby was here and Rocco was little.'

'Is Rocco your son?' Lexi asked.

'Yes. He's in his forties now, mind. Probably married with a child or two.'

'Probably? Don't you know? Don't you see him?' Lexi asked, astonished.

'We had a falling out a few years ago, not long after Ruby died. Rocco left and I haven't seen him since. He was always more his mother's son than mine.' Lloyd sighed. 'We had a difficult relationship.'

'Lots of families do,' Joel said. *Including mine.* 'Well, I've got to be going. I'm only next door but one, give me a shout if you need anything.' He put his hand in his pocket and fished out a card. 'Here's my number.' He looked around. 'You do have a phone, don't you?'

'Yes, I've got a mobile,' Lloyd told him. 'Thank you for your help.'

'You're welcome.' Joel nodded at Lexi. 'Bye, Lexi. I'll let you know about the tree.'

'Thanks.' She handed Sweetie, who she had been stroking, to him. 'I hope she doesn't keep you awake tonight.'

'Me too. I'm exhausted.'

'Well, remember, pop her around to me when you have to go to work, or out anywhere. I'm happy to look after her,' Lloyd told him.

Joel nodded. 'I will, thanks.' It would be a relief to know that Sweetie was happy and being looked after, and he thought the little dog would be good company for Lloyd too. The old man was obviously lonely.

Lexi waited until Joel had gone, then turned to Lloyd. 'That's really sad about your son. It would be lovely if you could both make up for Christmas.'

'It would, but there's not much chance of that. I have no idea where he's living now and he's washed his hands of me. I'll be spending Christmas alone, as usual.' Lloyd brushed the tinsel off his jumper. 'Thank you for today, Lexi. You've really cheered me up.'

This was her cue to invite him for Christmas dinner. She had to word it carefully, she didn't want Lloyd thinking it was charity.

'Why don't you join us for Christmas dinner. You'd be very welcome. All the family will be there – my brother Jay and his wife are coming over from Canada on Wednesday, and my brother Ryan and his girlfriend will be there, and my gran, too. We'd love to have you join us.'

'That's very kind of you, and don't think I don't appreciate it, but I'm happy here with the TV and my memories.' Lloyd smiled at her. 'You enjoy Christmas with your family and don't be worrying about me.'

'Are you sure? You'd be very welcome.' Lexi hated to think of the old man sitting on his own eating his dinner in front of the TV. She wished she knew where Lloyd's son was and could persuade him to visit his father for Christmas. That would be the perfect Christmas present.

'Absolutely positive. Now, would you like another cuppa before you go?'

When Lexi finally arrived back home, her mother was in. She'd said she was taking the afternoon off from the bakery to get a few jobs done. 'Did Lloyd like the Christmas tree?' she asked. 'Your gran said that you'd given it to him.'

'Yes, he did. Joel came round with some logs for him, too, and he helped put the lights up in the window.' She looked around. 'Where's Granny?'

'She's still out. She sent me a text to say that she's gone for coffee with her friends this afternoon, and she hasn't come back yet. I hope she comes back before it's dark. I know that the roads are fairly clear and the snow has stopped now, but I still worry.'

Lexi wondered if her gran was still at her yarn-bombing meeting. 'I'm sure she'll be back soon,' she said.

Sure enough, a few minutes later, the front door opened and in walked her gran, wrapped in a thick coat, hat and scarf. 'Hello, love, did Lloyd like the tree?' she asked Lexi.

'Yes, and . . .' She looked from her mum to her granny. 'He's going to be on his own for Christmas so I invited him over for us, he said thank you but he was happy on his own.'

'That's a shame, he would have been welcome. He might have kept Ma out of mischief,' her mum said.

Granny Mabe threw her a look of mock-indignation. 'What mischief? I've just been for a coffee with my friends.'

When Granny Mabe had taken off her coat and boots and they were all sitting in the lounge, Lexi filled them both in about the latest developments with the Christmas tree. 'Joel's going to see if he can get permission to cut off the dead branches and save the tree, or at least persuade them to postpone cutting it down until after Christmas.'

'Good,' Granny Mabe nodded, taking her knitting out of the bag she kept by the armchair she always sat on

Lexi looked at her suspiciously. 'Are you and your friends planning something, Granny?' she asked, when her mother had left the room. 'What was that secret you were going to tell me?'

'Secret? I don't have any secrets,' her gran replied. 'You worry too much, Lexi. It'll all be fine. Now, can you get a darning needle out of my bag and help me stitch these squares together? I need them sewn four squares wide, like a long scarf.'

Like a long scarf! Lexi thought of the long scarf-like yarn-bombs she'd seen wrapped around the trees and lamp posts in the village. 'What are you going to yarn-bomb with this?'

'Never you mind.' Granny Mabe refused to meet her eye and concentrated on her knitting.

The big secret. Suddenly it all made sense. 'You're going to yarn-bomb the fir tree on the green aren't you?'

Granny Mabe looked up and peered defiantly over her spectacles. 'Yes, we are. If it's still standing that is. Every year that tree is decorated for Christmas and this year isn't going to be any different. We might not be able to put lights on it, but we can brighten it up. We're going to hang knitted garlands and baubles on it.'

'Granny, you can't! Joel said that tree is dangerous, branches could fall off it at any time. That's why it's all cordoned off.'

Granny Mabe peered through her glasses at Lexi. 'Don't look so worried. The council are exaggerating about the tree being dangerous. They just want an excuse to chop it down.'

Lexi could hardly believe it. Her gran seemed to have no sense of the danger she and her friends would be putting themselves in. She had to do something to stop this before someone was seriously hurt. Or killed. Then she remembered her dad saying that he was going to get people who came into the shop to sign a petition to save the tree. She could start one online too.

She went upstairs and logged onto her laptop, then selected the website to set up an online petition and started one to save the Christmas tree.

Save the Lystone Christmas tree! For decades the big fir tree on the village green has been the focal point of a communal

carol service. Every Christmas Eve, the lights are switched on
and the villagers gather around to sing carols. Except this year.
The council are planning to cut down the tree. We've only got a
few days to save it. Please add your signature below.

She posted the link to her Facebook page, the Lystone Facebook page and as many other relevant pages as she could, as well as emailing the link to the local newspaper. Could she possibly get enough signatures in the next twenty-four hours or so to make the council listen and agree to Joel saving the tree?

Chapter Fourteen

Tuesday, four days before Christmas

'Have you seen the petition to save the village tree?' Andy asked as soon as Joel answered the phone.

'What petition? Joel asked, surprised.

'It's online. It's got a thousand signatures already and it only went up last night. There's a big spread about it on the *Lystone News* page.'

Joel grabbed his tablet and keyed in a search for *Lystone News*. 'Council threatening to cut down healthy tree,' announced the headline. He frowned as he read it and discovered that Lexi had started the petition. The newspaper had interviewed her and she had told them that the tree could be saved but the council wanted to cut it down. 'Word has it that they want to build some houses on the green,' she was quoted as saying. Apparently a local conservationist group was already involved and the numbers signing the petition were growing every minute.

'You still there?' asked Andy.

'Yeah, I got the article up and was reading it. It doesn't

mention us, thank goodness.' He paused. 'I know the woman who started the petition, she's passionate about saving that tree.' He briefly filled Andy in about his encounters with Lexi.

'Well she certainly knows how to drum up support.' There was an edge of admiration in Andy's voice. 'What do you think Martin will say?'

'I don't think he's going to be very happy, but we're not the only company that's looked at the tree, so one of the others could have leaked that it could be rescued,' Joel pointed out. 'Hopefully he'll get back to us this morning. You still okay to work with me for the next couple of days if he gives us the go ahead?'

'Sure, let me know later.'

Joel had just ended the call when his doorbell rang. *Well, today looks like it's going to be a busy day.* Could it be Lloyd needing help?

Sweetie had already jumped up. She barked and ran to the door. When Joel opened it, he was surprised to see Lexi standing on the front step.

'I'm sorry to disturb you, but I wondered if there was any news yet from the council.'

'I'm afraid not. I would think your petition and newspaper article has stirred them up a bit.' He folded his arms and levelled his gaze at her. 'You're a quick worker, I'll give you that.'

She raised her chin defiantly. 'I am if I need to be. It's important that the tree is saved.'

'I get that you feel that.'

Suddenly Sweetie squeezed between his legs and jumped up to Lexi.

Lexi stooped down to make a fuss of her. 'Hello, darling,' she cooed, picking her up.

'I'm not sure that it was the wisest thing to get the press involved, but at least you didn't mention us,' Joel said, still bristling. 'That would have cost us the contract and put us on the council blacklist.'

'Of course I didn't. I would never do that. I'm not vindictive. I just want to save the tree,' she retorted.

He ran his hand through his hair in exasperation. 'Look, Lexi, you do realise that even if we manage to save the tree, it will be too late for the carol service to go ahead? There's no way the council will be able to get the lights put on it in time. There will have to be a meeting about it, it's not a decision just one person can make.'

'Of course I know that,' she snapped. 'I'm just worried that someone will get hurt.' She stopped and clamped her mouth shut as if regretting the words that had just escaped.

Joel narrowed his eyes. 'What do you mean?'

'Nothing.'

'Lexi?'

She dropped her gaze. 'I can't tell you, I'd be breaking a confidence, but it is important that the tree is made safe.'

Joel's landline started to ring and he glanced towards it then back at Lexi. 'Come in a moment, that could be Martin from the council now,' he said. He'd given Martin his landline number as a backup, the signal was bad in the cottage because of the granite walls.

Lexi hesitated then nodded. 'Okay.' She stepped inside and Joel indicated for her to go into the lounge as he picked up the telephone receiver in the hall.

It wasn't Martin, it was someone for Al. Joel explained that he was away for a few months, then went in to see Lexi. She was sitting in the armchair by the window, with Sweetie curled up on her lap.

'Sorry, it wasn't Martin.' He sat down in the chair opposite her, noting that she looked a bit anxious. 'What's this about saving someone from getting hurt?'

She twisted a strand of hair around her finger and was silent for a moment as if wondering what to do. Then she took a deep breath. 'If I tell, you must promise not to say anything to anyone. I'm breaking a confidence here, but I really don't know what to do.'

'This sounds serious.' Joel waited for her to talk.

'Gran belongs to a group called the Yarn Warriors . . .'

'What's that, a knitting group?'

'Yes, but more than that. They're yarn-bombers. They're responsible for all the yarn-bombings around the village. You know, the knitted figures and baubles that are decorating the postbox and lamp posts.'

He shook his head disbelievingly. 'And how old is your gran?'

'Eighty-four. She's a bit of a rebel. Likes to live life to the full.'

'So it seems.' He couldn't help but smile to think that Lexi's gran and a bunch of probably equally elderly villagers were responsible for the controversial yarn-bombings. He quite liked yarn-bombings himself, he'd seen quite a bit of it in Glasgow and Yeovil, but he knew that the council was annoyed by it and had threatened to fine the culprits. No wonder that Lexi was worried, but he wasn't sure what she wanted him to do.

Lexi raised her eyes to his as she fiddled with the sleeve of her coat. 'The thing is, they're planning on yarn-bombing the fir tree on Christmas Eve.'

'What?' Joel sat forward and clasped his hands together, leaning his elbows on his knees. 'But it's dangerous and the tree is cordoned off to stop people going near it.'

'I know, but Granny Mabe won't listen. She reckons a few woollen baubles dangling from the branches won't do any harm. And that cordon tape won't stop them.'

This was serious. Joel kept his tone even. 'You do realise that you've put me in a very difficult position by telling me about this. I really should mention it to the council. These old folks will be in danger. Now I know they're planning that, I will be responsible for not preventing it.'

Lexi glared at him. 'You promised not to tell anyone! Anyway, you have no proof,' she added. 'Granny and her friends will just deny it. And so will I.'

She was right; he had no evidence. 'Then let's hope that the council agree to me saving the tree before Christmas. If they don't, then I'm sorry but I think the safest option is to make sure that the tree is cut down quickly, as Martin wants. Then no one can yarn-bomb it or do anything else to it.' They were a stubborn lot in this village, he thought.

'That's why I started the petition, to make some noise, then the council might save the tree,' said Lexi. Her deep-brown eyes looked pleadingly into his and Joel felt a stir deep inside him. 'Please try and persuade them to.'

'Well, you've certainly got a lot of interest already, but what the council will do is anyone's guess.' He could see that she was worried but her attitude had softened now. Pleased that they were on a friendlier footing and wanting to keep it that way he said. 'I was about to make a cup of coffee. Would you like one?'

She nodded, accepting his symbolic olive leaf. 'Yes, please. Perhaps you'll hear from our contact on the council while we're drinking it.'

After checking whether she took milk or sugar, Joel went into the kitchen to make the coffee. When he came back, Sweetie was fast asleep on Lexi's lap.

'She's taken to you. Mind, she's happy to let most people fuss her, it's being alone she doesn't like. I can't understand it, Hazel and Al said she's happy to be left for a few hours.'

'Dogs like routine. I guess it's because everything's strange. Her doggy parents have gone, and you're here, and the life she was used to has changed,' Lexi said.

'Do you have a dog?' Joel asked as he handed Lexi her mug of coffee, then sat down in the chair opposite, cradling his own mug.

'Not now, but we did when I was a child. We had a collie called Tess, she was gorgeous.' She took a sip of her coffee.

'Is there enough milk in it?' he asked.

'Perfect.' She took another sip before saying, 'I feel so sorry for Lloyd losing touch with his son, and being on his own for Christmas. I wish I could find Rocco and get him to come and visit his dad – or at least contact him – for Christmas.'

'That would be a tough one when we have no idea where he is. Besides, maybe Lloyd wouldn't want anyone to interfere.'

Lexi seemed to mull this over. 'I don't think he would mind. He seems desperate to see him, and Christmas is the time for families to get together. I'll see if Granny Mabe or my parents have any idea how I could contact Rocco. They've lived in this village for years.'

'When did you move away?' asked Joel.

'When I went to university in Exeter. I trained to be a teacher and got a job at a school in Gloucester. I've been there ever since. How about you? I can detect a slight Scottish accent.'

'Yes, I was born and grew up in Glasgow, my parents are still there. I worked for the Forestry in Scotland for a while, then moved down to Somerset and met my soon-to-be ex-wife.'

'So, how did you end up in Lystone?' she asked, idly stroking the still-asleep dog's head.

'Toni, my ex, found someone else and left me to live with them. I remained in the house to sell it. The sale had just gone through when Hazel told me about her and Al being offered work in Dubai by the hotel group they worked for. They needed someone to look after the house, and Sweetie, while they were away, and asked me to do it. It seemed like a good opportunity to sort myself out, and find out what I wanted to do with my life and where I wanted to live.'

'I'm sorry your wife cheated on you. Ben, my boy— ex-boyfriend cheated on me too. I only found out on Friday. This would have been our first Christmas together.'

Joel could see from the look in her eyes that this was still raw. 'That's rough. So you've only been split up a few days.'

'Yes, but he'd been seeing this other woman behind my back for ages. I didn't have a clue until I went to meet him from work and caught them snogging.' She shrugged, but the wobble in her voice showed that it still hurt. 'Love eh, who needs it? I'd much prefer a good friend. I never want to fall in love again.'

'I'll drink to that.' He held out his mug.

'Single's best,' she said and they clinked mugs.

Later, as she was leaving, Lexi gave her phone number to Joel and he promised to phone her as soon as he heard from the council.

She hoped she'd done right telling Joel about Granny Mabe and her friends' plan to yarn-bomb the tree, Lexi thought as she walked up to the bakery to see if her parents needed a hand.

'Hello, love, have you come for a cuppa?' her mum called as Lexi walked into the bakery.

'Thanks, but I've just had one with Joel. I called in to see if he'd heard from the council yet about saving the Christmas tree, but he hasn't.'

'I hope they allow him to. It would mean such a lot to us all. I know that Jay really wanted Sonia to experience all the Christmas traditions, and was looking forward to taking her and Toby to the carol service. I haven't told him that it's been cancelled yet. I keep hoping something will come up to save it.'

'People have come in talking about your petition, and we've got one on the counter, too.' Her dad nodded at a clipboard on the counter, where Lexi could see several signatures. 'I know there isn't much time, but even if we can get them to postpone cutting down the tree until after Christmas then we might be able to stop it altogether.'

Lexi was tempted to tell them about Granny Mabe's plans, but what was the point of worrying them? She'd just have to keep an eye on her gran and make sure nothing happened to her.

'Anyway, I've come to help out and I'm not going to be fobbed off,' she told them. She went through to the staff quarters, took off her coat and hat, put on an apron, tied her hair back, washed her hands and came back in. 'What do you want me to do?'

Her father and mother exchanged a smile. 'Stubborn, like you,' her mother said.

'Like the two of you,' Lexi replied. It was true: both her parents could be very stubborn and neither of them liked to give in if they were having a disagreement over something. Lexi and her brothers had often mediated when they were younger, and she suspected that Granny Mabe did now. Although, her gran was stubborn too. In fact, it was a family trait, she acknowledged.

'Could you give the tables in the tearoom a wipe, please, love? We'll have our regulars coming in for elevenses soon. Then maybe you can give me a hand making some sandwiches, her mother called.

'Sure.' Lexi picked up a cloth and some antibacterial spray, and set off for the tearoom. The tables were all clean and tidy, but she gave them an extra spray anyway. Everyone was still extra careful about cleansing after the worldwide Covid outbreak.

'Do you know anything about Lloyd's son Rocco?' Lexi asked when she'd returned, washed her hands again, donned latex gloves and was buttering bread ready for her mother to put in the sandwich fillings.

I can't remember much about Rocco, but I could ask the ladies in my group. Someone might know something. I'll ask Granny, too.'

Lexi buttered the last slice of bread. 'I'd love to get them back together. It would be wonderful if Rocco could visit his dad on Christmas Day.'

'It would, love, but we've only got a few days to go, so it's highly unlikely. And maybe Lloyd wouldn't want you to inter-fere in his life,' her mum warned her.

Joel had said the same, Lexi thought. 'It's not interfering, Mum, it's helping. Sometimes people need a gentle push to get them back together,' she replied.

Chapter Fifteen

Hazel had replied to Joel's messages about Sweetie, she was concerned that her pet was so unsettled, and said she was happy for Lloyd to look after her while Joel worked, rather than the little dog be left barking but she reminded him that Sweetie was used to being left for a couple of hours and he wasn't to spoil her by taking her everywhere with him. She wasn't pleased about her sleeping in Joel's room (he hadn't confessed that Sweetie shared his bed, too). *I don't want her getting into bad habits, Joel. We never let Sweetie upstairs. She's playing you. You must be firm. What if you get a girlfriend and want to bring her back?*

Joel read the message with amusement. 'Be firm.' Hazel obviously didn't know how stubborn her little dog could be. And, yes, she probably was playing him, but he couldn't let her bark all night, could he? Apart from the fact that he needed his sleep, and didn't want her to disturb the neighbours, he hated Sweetie to be upset. And he knew that Hazel wouldn't want her to be, either; his sister and her husband adored the little pooch. Obviously, Sweetie was much better behaved with them than she was with him.

As for bringing back a girlfriend, that was laughable. The last year of his marriage and the divorce with Toni had been far too draining for him to want to get involved with anyone else for a long time. Joel liked a quiet life and wasn't one to talk about his feelings. He got on with things, did what he had to do. That's how he'd always been. But apparently that meant he was emotionally inadequate and too self-centred, according to Toni, anyway.

He sent Hazel a quick reply back then checked his emails to see if there was a reply from Martin. If the council decided to take him up on his ridiculously low offer to make the tree safe in time for Christmas he had some hard work ahead of him and little time to do it in. The amount he'd agreed to do the job for would just about cover costs and Andy's cut, which would mean that Joel was working almost for nothing. He must be mad. He still couldn't believe that he'd offered to do it so cheaply, but after what Lexi had told him that morning, he was glad he had. He didn't want people to get hurt, and that's what would happen if the tree was left as it was and Lexi's gran and her knitting group went ahead with their plans to decorate it on Christmas Eve.

He should report them, but that would mean betraying Lexi's trust – and, as she'd said, they would only deny it. Besides, he liked the sound of Lexi's gran and her friends, still living their life to the full and fighting for a cause. He admired that.

Admit it, Lexi's somehow sneaked into a corner of your heart and you want to please her, he told himself. Yes, he could admit that he found Lexi attractive – who wouldn't? – and her love of Christmas was starting to rub off on him, but that was as far as it went. She was only here for Christmas, and he didn't want or need another relationship. And neither did she. They had both toasted to that this morning – even if it was only with coffee.

* * *

Martin phoned Joel just before lunch. 'I asked you for a quote for cutting the tree down, not pruning it,' he said.

'I know, but do you really want to antagonise the villagers when you can make the tree safe and let them have their traditional Christmas Eve carol service? I've kept the cost right down for you, as a special festive concession,' Joel pointed out. 'If you still want to cut the tree down later on in the year, you can, but to do it this close to Christmas is causing a lot of bad feeling. I presume you've seen the petition?'

'Yes, I have, I've had the newspaper on the phone wanting a comment too. I could do without this.'

'Christmas traditions mean a lot to people. Especially after the restrictions of last year.' Joel couldn't believe how much like Lexi he was sounding. 'Why not let it carry on for this year, at least?'

Martin was silent for a moment. 'I guess you're right,' he agreed. 'We couldn't cut it down this side of Christmas anyway, because the boss wants an inquiry thanks to that darn petition. And I have to admit your quote is a good one. Are you sure that you can make it safe enough?'

'I can,' Joel assured him. 'As I put in my email, I've checked out the tree and the ivy is only affecting the lower branches. It's choking them, which is why they are dying back. I can cut it off and the tree will be fine. I could start it tomorrow and should be finished on Thursday morning.' He knew that the council offices were closed from Thursday afternoon until Monday.

'Okay. I need to call a meeting and get formal permission first. I've arranged one for this afternoon, so I'll let you know how it goes. There's a couple of members who want to keep the tree cordoned off until the inquiry in the new year. I'll let you know the decision later today.'

So, not cut and dried yet then, Joel thought, although Lexi's petition had definitely caused a few waves. He had to admire her fighting spirit.

As soon as the phone call was finished, Joel phoned Andy. 'Fingers crossed, we're saving the tree, starting tomorrow,' he said.

'Blimey mate, you've actually pulled it off.' Andy sounded surprised. 'How did you manage that? I thought that petition might persuade the council to postpone things until after Christmas, but I didn't think they'd fork out money to save the tree.'

'I gave Martin an offer he couldn't refuse. We have to wait for the committee to make a final decision this afternoon, but I reckon it will go ahead. It's caused too much uproar. It's even been on the local news,' Joel told him.

'And what was the offer he couldn't refuse?'

Joel told him the sum he'd quoted and Andy whistled. 'We're not making much on that, good job we've got the necessary equipment between us.'

'Don't worry, you'll get your fee. I'll take the fall.'

'Bloody hell, mate. What's happened to you? Not only are you caring about a village Christmas tradition, but you're practically working for free.'

'I know. I have my reasons. Are you still in?'

'Sure. No way am I going to miss Joel Dexter working on a "save the Christmas tree" project. I'll be there tomorrow.'

'Thanks. I'll give you a call later when I've got the all-clear.' Joel let out a sigh of relief as he put the phone down. It would have been awkward if Andy hadn't wanted to do the job, he wouldn't be able to do it on his own in such a short time.

He dialled Lexi's number to give her the good news, but it went straight to answerphone, so he sent her a quick text saying that Martin had agreed to put Joel's quote to save the tree to the council and he should have a final decision later that day.

Now, he had another job to finish today – the removal of a tree trunk in a neighbouring village. *That should be simple, thank goodness.* He'd have to start on the fir tree as soon as it got light tomorrow. He wondered if Lloyd would mind him leaving Sweetie with him tomorrow. He'd be working all day and didn't want to leave the dog on her own. He'd pop in on his way home from work and ask him. He could perhaps leave Sweetie at home for a couple of hours in the morning, then take him over to Lloyd's after lunch, that would give Lloyd time to go out to get some shopping if he wanted to.

He really did have to sort this dog out, he thought, as he picked up his car keys. He looked over at Sweetie, who was fast asleep in her basket. Should he leave her or take her? He'd already cleared it with the owner of the tree stump who had said that it was fine for Sweetie to run around her large garden while Joel worked. Apparently she had a fenced-in area so Sweetie would be safe from the equipment, but he couldn't keep taking the Maltese everywhere with him. Or expecting Lloyd to look after her.

He put his keys in his pocket and headed for the door. Sweetie immediately shot out of her basket and followed him, barking at the door. He paused, then picked her up, and sighed. 'Okay, you can come with me, but only for today.'

Sweetie snuggled into his arms and woofed happily.

It was hectic at the bakery all morning, with villagers dropping in to talk about the newspaper article, sign the petition and ask if there was any news from the council yet. Lexi was so busy serving and waiting on the customers in the tearoom that she didn't have time to check her phone until after lunch. Her heart skipped a beat when she saw a missed call and a text from Joel. She opened the text anxiously, wondering what the council's decision was.

'I've got an update on the fir tree!' she shouted. A hush fell on the bakery as they all waited to hear what the news was. Lexi read out the text telling her about the council's change of plans to cut down the tree and the meeting that afternoon. A loud cheer rang out.

'We won't know until later if the council will let Joel trim off the damaged branches to make the tree safe,' she reminded everyone.

'At least there's been a reprieve for the tree. That gives us more time to protest in the new year if they do decide to cut it down,' her mum said. 'It would be lovely if we could go ahead with the carol service, though. I know we can hold it in the square, but it's not the same. Jay really wanted Sonia and Toby to see the tree lights switched on and sing carols around it like we always do.'

'Even if the council let Joel save the tree, there won't be time to put the lights on it,' Lexi reminded her. 'But we could carry lanterns and candles. That would look really pretty.'

'I've got some large Christmas inflatables in the loft, we can put them in front of the tree, too,' her dad said.

'You know, that's a great idea,' her mum agreed. 'We can still have a good carol service without the Christmas lights.'

More and more people piled into the bakery throughout the day, wanting news about the tree and thanking Lexi for starting the petition, and crediting her for saving the tree.

'It's Joel, the tree surgeon you have to thank,' she told them. 'He's just moved into Lystone and is practically doing it for nothing because he knows how much it means to the village.'

Granny Mabe came in with a group of women. They were all delighted with the news and made straight for the tearoom, then huddled together over tea and cakes. Lexi watched them. They looked like a bunch of sweet little old ladies meeting for a chat, but the snippets of conversation that came floating over from their table suggested that they were all part of the Yarn Warriors. She decided to go over and see what they were plotting, under the pretence of wiping a table that some customers had just vacated.

'We need time to do it on Christmas Eve so that the council don't have time to take it down,' a woman said.

'Good idea. The council offices are shut by lunchtime on Thursday, so even if they realise what we've done there's no way they'll have time to send anyone out to remove it,' another woman added.

'And if Joel doesn't get permission to save the tree, we'll do it anyway!' Granny Mabe added. 'That cordon tape won't stop us.'

Lexi listened worried. It seemed that Granny Mabe and her friends were determined to go ahead with their plans to yarn-bomb the tree no matter what. She hoped that Joel could save it. She didn't want one of them to get hurt.

Chapter Sixteen

He was finished, thank goodness. The roots on the tree trunk were strong so he'd had a bit of a job removing it, but it was all done now thanks to the stump grinder. Joel took the small towel that was tucked into his back pocket and wiped his forehead with it, then checked his phone. No message from Martin. It was almost 4 p.m., surely the council had finished their meeting now. Maybe they were finding it difficult to come to a decision.

He shoved his phone back in his pocket and made his way over to the house, pausing for a few minutes outside the garden to watch the Fishers' young daughter play with Sweetie. She was throwing a ball for the Maltese to chase. Sweetie bounded after it, picked it up in her mouth and came trotting back with it. They both seemed to be thoroughly enjoying their game. Mrs Fisher came to the door and waved to him. 'All finished?'

'Yes, but I tell you, those roots were buried deep. How's Sweetie been?'

Sweetie's ears pricked up at the sound of Joel's voice, and she turned around, then came bounding over to him, wagging her tail happily.

'Hello, girl.' He stooped down to give her a fuss.

'Would you like a cool drink?' Mrs Fisher asked him. 'We've got shandy or Coke?'

He would have loved to say a shandy, but he had a strict rule never to drink and drive. His parents had drummed that into him after all the accidents they'd dealt with. 'Coke, please.'

He was in the van, just about to drive off, when his phone rang. He glanced at the screen and saw that it was Martin, so he swiped to answer.

'The council have agreed to allow you to make the tree safe,' he said.

'That's great! We'll start on it first thing in the morning.'

'As I said, there won't be time to decorate the tree, but that can't be helped. At least they can still gather around and sing some carols. so that should keep them happy.'

Joel sensed that Martin still wasn't pleased with the idea and was sure that he would still be pressing for the tree to be cut down, but at least it was safe for now.

'Remember that I need confirmation that the tree is safe emailed to me by lunchtime on Thursday. I can't let the carol service go ahead without it.'

'You'll get it,' Joel promised him.

He finished the call and then dialled Andy's number. It was engaged, so he left a voicemail to let him know the job was on. Then he texted Lexi. Her reply came straight back. *Well done! And thank you!*

He smiled as he read it. This was going to be a tough job, and they'd be working against the clock with only a few hours of daylight, but it felt good to know that he was doing something that meant such a lot to the villagers.

And to Lexi.

'Come on, Sweetie, let's go home,' he said to the little dog.

The tearoom was heaving, people had been coming in all afternoon, asking if there had been any news, stopping to have a drink and sandwich or cake while they waited. Lexi and her parents hadn't stopped serving in the bakery, while Claire waited on the tables in the tearoom. Even Lloyd had popped in to enquire. Granny Mabe had called him over to join her and her friends at their table.

Lexi had kept her phone on her, anxious not to miss Joel's call. When it finally rang, just before the bakery was due to close, everyone went quiet.

'He's done it! Joel's got permission to save the tree!' Lexi shouted as soon as she'd ended the call with him.

Cheers rang out from the customers.

'That's marvellous!' her mother said. 'Now we can go ahead with our plans for the carol service.'

Her parents declared that the bakery was staying open for another hour, and more cups of tea and coffee were made as Lexi's parents, members of the WI (Women's Institute) and various villagers, all gathered together to sort out who was doing what.

'We won't be able to do anything until Christmas Eve itself because by the time Joel and his partner clear away the branches and their equipment on Thursday, it will be dark,' Lexi reminded everyone. 'And I know most of you will be busy on Christmas

Eve with your Christmas preparations, so there will be no time to decorate the tree, but we can all bring a lantern or candles.'

'I've got a couple of big lanterns. I'll bring them with me,' Lloyd said. He was looking very animated, and Lexi noticed that he and Granny Mabe seemed to be getting on really well. Maybe he'd change his mind about coming to them for Christmas dinner. She hoped so. She hated to think of him being on his own.

The tearoom was buzzing with excitement. Joel had really saved the day. And to think that she'd accused him of hating Christmas! Her cheeks flushed as she remembered how angry she had been with him, but then he had been really dismissive of their concerns about the tree at first. She wondered what had changed his mind.

Her phone vibrated in her pocket and she took it out to check the message. It was from Ben.

Please talk to me. I love you. I made a mistake and I'm sorry. Please give me another chance and I'll drive down right now. We can spend Christmas together. Our very first Christmas.

Less than a week ago, it had been what she had wanted more than anything, to spend Christmas with Ben.

Lexi thought about Christmas Day with her parents, Jay and Sonia, Ryan and Nell – everyone partnered up except for her and her gran. Only last week, she thought that she and Ben had a future together.

Should she forgive him? Was everyone entitled to one mistake?

When the bakery was closed and everyone finally went home, Lexi declined her parents' offer of a lift, deciding to pop in and thank Joel personally instead. He really had gone out of his way for them, and although it was work for him, he probably would have earned more money cutting down the entire tree.

She was pleased to see that Joel's van was outside, so he was home. She rang the bell and waited for the familiar little yap that announced Sweetie was on the other side of the door. Then she heard the key turn in the lock, and the door opened. Joel stood in front of her, clad only in a pair of jeans, his feet bare. He was rubbing his hair dry with a towel. He'd obviously got straight out of the shower.

Her eyes darted to his broad shoulders, toned body and those abs . . . Realising she was staring, she quickly averted her gaze to his face.

'Hello, Lexi. Is everything okay?' Joel asked, looking a bit concerned.

'Everything is perfect. I've been helping out in the bakery today and everyone has been waiting for the council's decision. You should have heard the cheers when you phoned to say that they had agreed to let you save the tree. Thank you so much for persuading them.'

'I think it was your petition that pushed it,' Joel told her.

'Well, we all really appreciate what you're doing.' She felt a bit awkward, realising that Joel probably wanted to finish drying his hair and get dressed. It was chilly for him to be standing on the doorstep half-naked. 'Anyway, I'll leave you to it,' she said, turning away.

'I was about to pour a glass of wine, would you like to join me? To celebrate saving your Christmas tree?'

She turned back. 'That would be lovely.'

He stepped aside, grabbed Sweetie's collar to stop her running off, and opened the door wider. 'Come in. Please take off your coat and go into the lounge. I'll nip upstairs and grab a jumper and put a comb through my hair and then I'll be right with you.'

Lexi stepped inside and bent down to make a fuss of Sweetie and stop herself from staring at Joel's very fit body as he raced up the stairs, two steps at a time.

She slipped out of her coat and hung it on the stand in the hall, then headed for the lounge. Sweetie followed her and jumped on her lap as soon as she sat down.

The lack of Christmas decorations struck her again. She might have persuaded Joel to save the Christmas tree, but she certainly hadn't changed his mind about celebrating Christmas.

'Pinot Grigio or Sauvignon?' Joel stood in the doorway. He was now wearing a thick, dark-green, zip-up-the-neck jumper that clung to his broad shoulders, and his hair was combed and almost dry. His feet were still bare.

'Pinot, please. And do you have any lemonade?'

'I do. Do you like it half and half?'

'Perfect.'

Joel returned a few minutes later with two glasses and handed one to Lexi. She thanked him and raised it. 'To you, for saving the Christmas tree,' she said.

He lifted his glass. 'To you, for persuading me to. And for starting that petition.'

She grinned and took a sip of her wine. 'It's going to be a busy day tomorrow, then, you're on a tight deadline, aren't you?'

'Yes, but we can do it. Luckily, we've got the equipment we need between us, so we don't have to pay out to hire any.'

'What sort of equipment do you need?' she asked.

'A hoist, although I may be able to do it all with the

127

platform – Andy's got one – a wood-chipper and chainsaw – I've got those – and then we both have protective clothing.'

'Gosh.' This sounded a lot more complicated than she had realised. Although, to be honest, she hadn't really thought about what it would involve for Joel to cut the deceased branches off the tree. 'Did you have your own business in Somerset, then?'

'Yes, although I was contracted to the Moreton Estate and didn't have to fish for work. So, I'm basically starting from scratch down here. Luckily, I know Martin from way back and Andy has some contacts so we're hoping to eventually form a business together, but until then, he's continuing with his land-scaping business and working with me when he can.'

She could see why this contract was important to him and appreciated even more that he had cut his costs so that he could save the tree for them.

'Will Sweetie be okay tomorrow if you are leaving her all day?'

'She's settling down, and Hazel insists that I be firm and leave her a while, she said I'm going to spoil her for when she comes back. Apparently, if I leave the radio on, Sweetie will feel more secure. So, I'm going to leave her here in the morning, then pop home at lunchtime and drop her around to Lloyd's for the afternoon. I've already asked him and he said that's fine.'

'That's great.' Lexi watched as Joel lightly stroked Sweetie as he talked. He really was a kind man. She was glad that they had sorted out their differences and that he and Lloyd had become close.

I'm going to miss them all when I go back home, she thought. *Especially Joel.*

Chapter Seventeen

Wednesday, three days before Christmas

At eight thirty in the morning Joel pulled up at the green and got out of his van. He'd hitched the chipper onto his tow bar, and the rest of the equipment was in the back of the van. Andy pulled up behind him, a mobile platform to reach the upper parts of the tree attached to the back of his truck. 'At least it's not snowing or raining,' he said.

'Yep, it's nippy, though. I reckon we're in for more snow.' Joel rubbed his hands together. 'Let's get this done, shall we?'

They both set about removing the cordon tape around the tree and then securing the whole site by placing cones around the edge of the green, finally putting red-and-white tape across and placing some yellow danger signs about.

Andy walked over to the huge conifer, craning his neck to look up at the top. 'It's a big tree!' he observed.

'Tell me about it!' Joel joined him.

Andy walked around the tree, looking at the trunk. 'How bad's the ivy?'

'Bad, but I'll be able to saw it off,' Joel told him. 'It's choked a few of the lower branches, so I'll have to remove those, but the rest of the tree looks okay. It's a good job it was caught now; if it had been left much longer, the tree would probably be unsalvageable.'

'Do you think that's what the council were hoping? I hear that there's plans to build a few houses here.' Andy looked over at the row of houses each side of the green. 'It's a good spot, property here would fetch a lot I reckon. They could probably build them around the other trees too.' There were a couple of small oak trees on the green.

'I was thinking that myself. In fact, I wouldn't be surprised if they don't go ahead and cut the fir down later in the year, but I guess that's not our business.' Joel wiped his hand across his forehead. 'Best get going, we haven't got that many daylight hours.'

He felt exhilarated as they both rigged themselves up in chainsaw boots and trousers then put on protective helmets with ear guards and visors. His work excited him. He knew that there was always a risk, but it was a calculated one and he always took the safety precautions seriously, ensuring his harness was clipped correctly to the ropes on the platform.

Lexi slipped the two cottage pies – one huge enough to feed the seven of them and one small – into the oven. She'd insisted that she would prepare the dinner for tonight. Jay and Sonia were due to arrive about seven, so it was a quick meal for them all, and cottage pie was a Forde favourite. She'd made a smaller one thinking that it might be nice for Joel to come home to a ready-cooked meal that he only had to warm up, seeing as he was working on the tree all day. She thought she'd pop back for it when she'd finished serving at the bakery – she'd promised to go and help out for a couple of hours this afternoon. While the pies were cooking, she booted up her laptop and checked her Etsy site and LexiKnits page, and then the petition, which had now exceeded four thousand signatures. There was also a piece in the online version of the *Lystone News* about the council agreeing to allow a local tree surgeon to save the tree. She'd still got some lesson planning to do too, but had taken to doing that either first thing in the morning or in the evenings before she went to bed.

The timer alerted her that the pies were cooked, so she took them out, and covered them up while they cooled, then went back to her laptop to see if she could find anything about Lloyd's son. Lloyd's surname was Winston, her granny had said. Rocco, his son, was a painter and decorator and had married and moved to Somerset years ago. So, the first thing she did was a Facebook search on Rocco Winston, Somerset. There was no one with that name. Then she did an Internet search on 'painters and decorators in Somerset'. There were no Rocco Winstons but there was a Winston and Drake. That could be him; he could be in partnership with someone else. She clicked on the company's webpage and read the information. Richard Winston and Terry Drake. She clicked on the photos, Richard Winston had blond hair, very pale skin and looked about forty. Definitely not Lloyd's son, then.

She sighed. This was going to be more difficult than she thought. She wondered whether to pop in on Lloyd and ask him a few more questions about his son, but then that would seem as if she was being nosy. She would like to see him, though, and persuade him to change his mind about coming for Christmas dinner.

Her thoughts went back to Joel, he'd be working on the tree now. Impulsively, she did a Facebook search on Joel Dexter, arborist. There wasn't much personal stuff on his page but there were a lot of photos and videos of him working. She selected a video and watched – fascinated – as Joel, togged up in protective gear - felled a huge tree. Then there was another video of him, harnessed up, cutting branches off the top of a very tall spruce. He'd obviously climbed all the way to the top! Heck, this looked dangerous! She watched another video, her heart in her mouth at Joel on a hoist, hanging high up on a sky-scraping pine. He said he'd worked for the Scottish Forestry, so these videos must be from then, she thought.

She closed the laptop down, and decided to go and check on how Joel and Andy were getting on before she started work at the bakery.

A text pinged in and she reached for her phone and looked at the screen. It was from Ben. Her hand shook as she read the words on the preview: *Please don't delete this.*

Well she was going to delete it. She didn't want to think about Ben, never mind read his message. He had no right to contact her, he'd made his choice.

Why would he even want to message her? Because he was feeling guilty and wanted to apologise and explain that he hadn't meant it to happen? Well, she didn't want to hear it. She pressed lightly on the unread message and went to select 'delete' when another thought occurred to her: maybe Ben had left something behind at the flat? He had packed in a rush. Or maybe he'd taken something of hers by mistake. She read the preview text again. *Please don't delete this.* Then she took a deep breath and opened the message.

I love you, Lexi. I'm sorry for treating you like this. Please give me another chance. What we had was too good to throw away over a stupid mistake. Can we please meet up and talk about this? Love you forever, Ben. Xxx There were a couple of heart emojis too.

That stunned her. He must be really missing her to be so persistent. For a moment, she imagined Ben holding her in his arms, kissing her, telling her how much he loved her and regretted cheating on her, vowing that he would never hurt her again. And yes, part of her, a really big part of her, wanted to take him back, for life to go back how it was. She had felt so comfortable with Ben, they had got along well, rarely argued. But they hadn't spent much time together over the last few months to have chance to row, had they? she reminded herself. Ben always seemed to be out working. Or rather, seeing Rosa.

And if she did take him back, would she ever be able to trust him again? Whenever he said he was working late, she would be wondering if he was seeing someone else. She couldn't live like that. She'd seen what a partner having an affair did to people. She didn't want to turn into a suspicious, jealous person, checking Ben's texts, going through his pockets. She shook her head. No, there was no going back. The perfect relationship she'd thought they had had never existed. Ben had stayed with her because it was easy, but as soon as someone more exciting had come along, he had been off.

Yet he wanted to come back.

And she wanted him back. But was that because she loved him, or because she wanted the familiarity of their life together?

She closed the message and put her phone back in her bag. She wasn't going to answer yet.

She walked into the kitchen and poured herself some orange juice. She'd just taken a sip, when her phone rang. She glanced at the screen, wondering if it was Ben – or Joel – and panicked when she saw it was from her friend, Fern. *Oh no!* She'd forgotten that she'd arranged to meet Fern for a coffee and catch up this week, back in Gloucester. She checked her watch. Today, actually, and in half an hour's time.

'Hi, Fern …'

'So sorry, Lex, but I'm running a bit late. Can we make it one instead of twelve?' Fern said in a rush. 'You wouldn't believe the morning I'm having. Polly got hold of the flour and threw it everywhere. It's taken me ages to clean up and now she's fallen asleep and if I wake her, she'll just be grouchy all day.' Polly was Fern's toddler.

'Oh, Fern, I'm so sorry. I forgot we were meeting …' Lexi felt terrible. She knew that sometimes Fern found it a struggle to get out of the house with Polly, and she would have felt really bad if her friend had turned up at the café they were supposed to be meeting at only to find no sign of Lexi.

'That's okay. Look, why don't you pop around instead? We can have a chat while Polly sleeps.'

'I can't. I'm in Devon.'

'Devon?' She could hear the astonishment in Fern's voice. 'But I thought you and Ben were going down on Christmas Eve?'

'There is no me and Ben. We're finished.'

'What?' Fern squealed. 'It's only been a few days since I spoke to you. What the hell has happened in that time?'

'It's a long story …'

'I've got time. If you have.'

Lexi took her orange juice into the lounge and settled down on the sofa for a long chat.

'The rat!' Fern exclaimed when Lexi told her about Ben cheating on her and how she'd decided to come down to Devon early rather than stop in the flat moping by herself. Lexi then filled her in about the Christmas tree and Granny Mabe's yarn-bombing.

Fern giggled. 'Your gran sounds a real character. And this Joel sounds a hunk. I could fancy a tree surgeon myself – don't tell Tim that – I bet he's dead sexy!'

An image of Joel the previous night, shirtless and barefooted, flitted across her mind. 'He is,' she admitted. 'And kind, too. Although, we did get off to a bit of a bad start.' She told Fern about their first meeting when Sweetie had escaped, and how Joel had said Christmas was overrated.

Fern laughed. 'I can imagine your reply to that!'

'I did kick off a bit. I wanted us all to have a real family Christmas, just like we used to have, and the carol service around the fir tree is a big part of it.' She could feel her voice break. Why was she getting so upset?

Because last Christmas had been so difficult with the Covid restrictions and then Ben had destroyed her dream of their perfect first Christmas so she desperately wanted a nostalgic family Christmas to replace that.

'It's not just the tree making you sad, it's Ben too, isn't it?' Fern asked softly.

'Yes. I miss him so much.'

'He's a scumbag and he didn't deserve you.'

'He said he's sorry and he wants me back,' Lexi confessed tearfully. 'I had a message from him this morning.'

'Please tell me that you're not going to take him back.'

'No. I don't think so. I don't know.' On Friday evening, after she'd just found out about Ben and Rosa, she'd been adamant that she wanted nothing to do with Ben, but now she was wondering if she was being hasty.

'Don't go all soft just because it's Christmas, Lexi. If you give Ben another chance, you'll never be able to trust him again.'

'I know.'

'Honestly, hunny, you deserve better ... Oh, Polly's up! I've got to go, but let's have another catch up soon. After Christmas. And please don't take Ben back. Bye.' Then she was gone.

Lexi sat on the sofa thinking about Fern's words. Was she just being sentimental because it was Christmas? Because this was the season that made you want to be happily coupled-up? Fern was right, though, how could she trust Ben again? As Granny Mabe would say, you can't turn back the clock. What's done is done, and you have to deal with it and move on.

Her thoughts went to Joel and the 'single's best' toast they had made. It had only been a light-hearted toast, showing solidarity for each other's pain, but it made her stop and think. She might still love Ben, but that didn't mean she should give him chance to hurt her again. She was getting over him. She'd lived without Ben before, and could do it again.

She typed a reply back to him.

It's over, Ben. I don't want you back. Rosa is welcome to you.

Then she pressed 'send' before she could talk herself out of it.

She put the now-cooled-down cottage pies into the fridge, then pulled on her coat and boots. She decided to take her car today, then she could nip home and get the cottage pie for Joel when she'd finished at the bakery.

She pulled up on the other side of the green and got out of the car. The noise of the chainsaw was deafening. A man in protective gear was standing on a platform as he sawed off a branch. Was that Joel? She hurried over for a closer look. Another man – who was definitely not tall enough to be Joel – was putting the branches into a machine that was making loads of noise. That must be Andy, his partner.

Lexi walked over and stood outside the barrier of tape and cones, anxiously watching Joel in action. Until she'd checked out his Facebook page that morning, she hadn't realised just how dangerous his work was. Thankfully, this tree wasn't as tall as the ones she'd seen him climbing up in the videos online, but even so he was pretty high in the air, and that chainsaw looked hazardous. If he slipped – or if one of those branches hit him – he could be killed.

He's harnessed to that platform. He does this all the time.

Her heart raced as she saw his hand go to his face. Was he hurt?

Chapter Eighteen

Lexi strained her eyes, trying to see what had happened. The platform was descending now. Joel was coming down! Why? Was he injured?

She bit her lip as, gradually, the platform lowered. Joel stepped off, then took off his helmet and gloves before walking over to a box on the floor. He took something out of the box and dabbed his eye. Andy saw him, switched off the machine and walked over to him.

She waited anxiously; both men were turned away from her, but Andy seemed to be dabbing something on Joel's face. Had he cut himself? Then Joel turned around, noticed Lexi watching and walked over to her. 'Is anything wrong?'

Relief flooded through her as she saw he was okay, apart from his eyes looked a bit sore. 'I saw you put your hands to your face. I thought you were injured.'

'I got some sawdust in my eye. I came down to get it out. It'll be fine in a minute.'

'It looks dangerous up there.'

'Not if you follow the safety procedures, which I do.'

Of course he does. Even so. She swallowed. 'Have you got to go much higher than that?'

'No, that's the highest bit. Luckily, the ivy that's causing the damage hasn't reached the top branches yet. It's a pig to saw off, though.'

'Please be careful.' The words were out before she could stop them.

His eyes met hers. 'I will.'

Feeling a bit embarrassed, she shoved her hands deeper into her pockets. 'Will you be able to do it in time?'

He pushed his helmet back and some of his thick red-brown hair flopped over his forehead. 'I promise that it'll be done by tomorrow afternoon.'

'That's great.' She hopped up and down with the cold. 'It's freezing out here. Would you both like a coffee? I can fetch one from the bakery. I'm doing a shift there later.' She glanced over at Andy who was still feeding branches into the noisy machine.

'I'd love one, thanks, we're about to take a break. Black, one sugar, for Andy . . .'

'Black, no sugar for you,' she finished.

Joel grinned. 'You remembered.'

'Any cakes? We do a big variety.'

'Do you have bread pudding?'

'We do.'

Joel's eyes lit up. 'Bread pudding for me, then. Andy likes Danish pastries.' He looked a bit awkward. 'Can I pay you later, though? I can't get to my money with this gear on.'

'My treat, for saving the Christmas tree,' Lexi told him. 'I'll be back shortly.'

139

'Thanks, Lexi.'

Her parents both looked surprised when Lexi walked in. 'Hello, love, we weren't expecting you for another couple of hours. Is anything wrong?' her mother asked, glancing up from the table she was wiping down.

'No, I came out early to check how Joel and Andy were getting on with the tree. I'm taking some refreshments for them,' she said. 'Shall I serve myself? I'll pop the money in the till. I told them it was my treat.'

'No it's okay, and no need for money. Your gran is so happy that the carol service can go ahead, and I know that Jay and Ryan will be pleased, too. It's a shame there isn't time to decorate the tree and have it all lit up, but the lanterns will make it look festive.'

Her dad looked up from the baguette he was buttering. 'They will. I've got a couple of other ideas too. I'll tell you all about it later.'

Knowing her dad, he'd find a way to string some lights up somewhere, Lexi thought. It was the kind of thing he would do. What with Granny Mabe and her Yarn Warriors, and her parents, she reckoned the green would look pretty festive even without the usual decorations and lights. Although her parents had no idea about her gran's involvement with the yarn-bombers yet, or their plans for the tree.

'Do you want coffee and a cake, too?' her mother asked.

Lexi looked at the tempting array of freshly made cakes and pastries. 'Yes, please, a bread pudding.'

'You know, love, we've got Claire and Brad coming in this afternoon, so we're covered if you want to do a bit of Christmas shopping instead of helping out,' her mum said.

'Are you sure?' She could do with a trip to the shops. 'Is there anything you need?'

'Now you mention it, there are a couple of things.' Her mum took a piece of paper out of her pocket and handed it to Lexi. 'Only if you have time. I'm off work tomorrow, so can do it then.'

'It's no problem, the supermarket's open until late.' Lexi slipped the cakes in her bag, put the coffees into a cardboard-cup holder and took them out to her car, then put them securely in the box she kept in the boot to place shopping in.

When she got back to the green with the coffee and cakes, Joel and Andy had taken their helmets off and were both leaning against the van, well away from the tree.

'Come and join us,' Joel called. He opened the van door. 'Take a pew inside.'

'Thanks.' She walked over and placed the coffee-holder on the top of the van, then handed the two men their cakes before sitting down in the passenger seat.

'I'd better introduce you two properly. Lexi, this is Andy, my business partner. Andy, this is Lexi, the Christmas fanatic who's been nagging me to save the tree.'

Is that how he sees me, as a Christmas fanatic?

'So, you're the one who persuaded Mr What's-all-the-fuss-about-Christmas to not only save the village Christmas tree, but practically do it for free?' Andy unwrapped his Danish pastry. 'Good to meet you, Lexi.'

Lexi looked worriedly at Joel. 'I didn't realise you'd reduced your fee. That was very kind of you.'

'He's suddenly found his Christmas spirit. You'll be getting him wearing a Christmas jumper next,' Andy quipped.

141

Joel gave him a look of mock-horror. 'Absolutely no way!'

As they drank their coffee and ate their cakes, Joel talked Lexi through what they were doing. 'Some of the branches are choked and have to come off, but most are okay and the tree itself hasn't been damaged. We caught the ivy just in time.' He popped the last bit of bread pudding into his mouth and munched it before saying, 'That was delicious. Do your folks make the cakes themselves?'

'Not entirely. They're all homemade but there are a couple of people who live in the village who bake some of them. And my gran makes the bread pudding. It's a secret recipe, which she won't divulge. We have persuaded her to write it down, though, and she's sealed it – and a few other recipes – in an envelope, which we're forbidden to open until she dies.' She took the last sip of her coffee.

'Hopefully that's a long way off. Does she live with your parents?'

'Yes. Granny Mabe's eighty-four, but my mum says it's like having a teenager in the house,' she told him.

'She sounds a character,' Andy said. 'My gran's in her seventies and she acts like she's in her forties. They don't make grandparents like they used to, do they? None of them want to sit by the fire and knit anymore.'

'Well, my gran knits, but it's not your traditional stuff,' Lexi told him.

'She's a yarn-bomber.' Joel's eyes twinkled.

Andy nearly choked on his last piece of cake. 'Blimey,' he spluttered.

Lexi grinned. She'd really enjoyed this chat. It had been good to see Joel relax.

142

'Well, I'd better go. My brother and his family are arriving from Canada this evening, and I'm going to do some last-minute shopping.' She stood up and dusted a few crumbs from her coat. 'I'll see you later.' She went to walk off, when she remembered Sweetie. 'Ah, I almost forgot. Where is Sweetie today? Do you want me to go and check on her?'

'I was going to pop home and get her in a few minutes as Lloyd's having her this afternoon for me, so it would be great if you could take her round there for me. Would you mind? Then I can carry on here – it gets dark so early, we need to make the most of the daylight.'

'Happy to help,' she assured him.

He shoved his hand in his pocket and took out a bunch of keys, searched through them, then took one off the ring. 'This is for the front door. I've got another one, so just pop it through the letter box when you've finished.'

'Will do.' She waved and set off.

She parked her car outside Joel's house and listened. She couldn't hear Sweetie barking. Maybe she'd settled down now, she thought. That would make life easier for Joel. She opened the door, shouting the little dog's name, expecting her to come running. She didn't.

'Sweetie! Where are you, Sweetie?' she called.

She expected the Maltese to appear at any moment, but there was no sign of her.

How strange. She checked the kitchen – noting that Joel had left the radio on, probably for company – and the lounge. The back door was safely shut, so the dog couldn't have escaped, but she wasn't anywhere to be seen. What had happened?

Chapter Nineteen

'Sweetie!' Lexi called again, listening for an answering bark. None came. She frowned worriedly. Could Sweetie be trapped somewhere? Maybe upstairs? She paused at the bottom of the stairs; it didn't seem right to go up there, but she had to find Sweetie. She could be ill or injured. And she couldn't phone Joel to ask his permission to go up the stairs, he wouldn't hear his phone ring over the noise of that chainsaw and the wood-cutting machine. Surely he wouldn't mind, he would want Sweetie to be safe.

'Sweetie!' She shouted loudly as she started to walk up the stairs. 'Sweetie! Are you up here?'

'Yap! Yap! Yap!'

Thank goodness! Relief flooded through her. She'd reached the top of the landing now and could tell that the yapping was coming from the door in front of her. Was that Joel's bedroom? And how had Sweetie got trapped in there?

'Sweetie, it's only me, girl,' she said softly as she slowly opened the door. Sweetie squeezed through the gap in the door and ran out, yapping and wagging her tail happily. Lexi picked up the little dog and cradled her in her arms. 'Have you been scared, locked in here?' she asked softly.

Her eyes widened as she noticed some feathers on the floor by the door. Oh no, what had Sweetie done? She pushed the door open wider and looked in dismay at the feathers all over the bed, the curtains, the carpet, and oozing out of a very-chewed-up pillow on the bottom of the bed. The poor little dog must have got really distressed when she realised she was trapped. Joel had said she'd chewed a couple of cushions up when he'd left her before. She glanced around the room to see if there was any more damage.

She could see a pair of jeans sprawled over the back of a chair – feathers were scattered over them too – the door to the en suite was open, and a feather-covered towel lay on the floor. Joel had obviously left in a hurry this morning.

It looked like Sweetie had been on the bed, she had probably fallen asleep on it after finally exhausting herself with barking and pacing around her, which is why she hadn't heard Lexi come in. How had she got trapped in here, though?

Sweetie nestled into her and whimpered softly.

'You're okay now, girl. Were you frightened?' Lexi murmured, stroking her. She wondered how long she'd been trapped in here. Had Joel left the bedroom door open, and Sweetie had come up to look for him, then somehow knocked it shut behind her?

She turned around and gave the door a slight push. It immediately slammed shut. Yes, that's what must have happened. She glanced around the room. *Apart from the chewed-up pillow, Sweetie doesn't seem to have done any damage.* She walked over to the bed to check that the little dog hadn't done anything there – after all, she'd been trapped in there all morning. She guessed that the

Maltese had gone upstairs looking for Joel then got trapped in his room.

It all looked fine. Her eyes rested on the other pillow, where she could still see the slight indent left by Joel's head. An image of him lying there, naked, flashed across her mind and she batted it away immediately. Where had that come from? She had no romantic interest in Joel at all.

Sweetie yapped and squirmed in her arms. She must need to go to the loo, Lexi thought. She went out of the room, pulled the door closed, and went downstairs into the garden. As soon as she put Sweetie down, the little Maltese terrier hurried over to a patch of soil and crouched down to do her business.

Rubbing her arms to keep warm, Lexi stood outside for a few minutes to let Sweetie have a bit of exercise, then took her back inside. The kitchen showed more signs of Joel having left in a hurry that morning: two plates and a couple of mugs were in a bowl in the sink – she guessed the larger plate was left from last night – and an opened loaf of bread was on the side, beside a toaster.

Sweetie ran over to her dog bowl at the side of the fridge and eagerly lapped up some water, then grabbed a biscuit bone from out of her food dish and trotted out with it dangling from her mouth. Lexi followed her out into the lounge where the little dog climbed into her basket, lay down and continued chewing her bone.

The room looked bare without any Christmas decorations or a tree, she thought. There weren't even any Christmas cards. She wondered if Joel would be sitting here, all alone, on Christmas Day, whether he would even bother with a turkey dinner, or any of the festive traditions.

He might be having dinner with a friend. Andy, perhaps.

Her eyes rested on a small table beside the chair in the corner. *Just the right size for the remaining Christmas tree in the attic.* And there were plenty of baubles left, too.

Should she? She had enough time to do it before she went shopping.

She pondered over it. Joel seemed to have enjoyed putting up the lights for Lloyd and she had the feeling he wasn't as anti-Christmas as she'd first thought. He might not want the fuss of putting up a Christmas tree, but if he came home and found one already up he couldn't fail to be delighted, could he? She'd do it.

She crouched down and patted Sweetie on the head.

'Let's feed you, then take you around to Lloyd. Then, I've got a surprise to do for when your daddy comes home.'

Sweetie obviously recognised the word 'feed' and trotted over to her food dish, wagging her tail happily.

Lexi phoned Lloyd to check that he was home now. He was, and said to bring Sweetie straight around. 'I'll leave the door on the latch and put the kettle on. You will stop for a cuppa, won't you?'

'Of course,' Lexi told him. She didn't want to spend too much time chatting, though, she had plans for this afternoon.

Lloyd was all smiles when Lexi and Sweetie arrived. Christmas carols were playing in the background, and the lights of the Christmas tree were already on.

'Hello, lass,' he said, bending down to fuss Sweetie. 'Have you been a good girl this morning?'

'She got trapped in Joel's bedroom and chewed up a pillow,' Lexi told him. 'I guess that's not really her fault.'

'Oh dear. Joel said that he wanted to leave her on her own this morning, so she would get used to it, and I had to go to the doctor's. Only a check-up,' he added hastily. 'I'm very healthy for my age, the doctor said.' He handed Lexi a mug of tea. 'Your gran was there, too. We had a nice chat. She's quite a character, isn't she?'

'She didn't say she was going to the doctor's,' Lexi said worriedly.

'Looking at the worry on your face, that's probably why. The doctors like to keep a check on us old folks, you know. It doesn't mean anything is wrong, but we all seem to be on some medication when you get to our age and it needs to be monitored.'

Granny Mabe was on medication? That was the first Lexi had heard of it.

'Blood-pressure pills, that kind of thing,' Lloyd said as he sat down. 'You know, there's a lot of social clubs in this village that I had no idea about. Mabe's been telling me all about them. I think I'll join a few in the new year. It'll get me out and about a bit.'

'That sounds a great idea. We were worried about granny when Grandpa died, but luckily she'd always had an active social life, they both had, and I'm sure that's really helped her.' She liked the thought of Lloyd getting out and about with Granny Mabe and her friends. It would be good for them both. Maybe Lloyd might even be a calming effect on her gran.

Or Gran might be a bad influence on him.

She smiled at her thoughts. She knew what her mother meant by saying that having Granny Mabe around was like having a teenager in the house! Lexi hoped she was as outgoing and adventurous as her gran when she got to that age, though.

148

'Thanks for the tea. I need to get going now.' She said when she'd finished her tea. She got up and fussed the little dog who was now lying on Lloyd's lap. 'Be good for Lloyd.'

'She'll be fine.' Lloyd assured her. 'Mabe said your brother is arriving from Canada today. You must all be excited to see him.'

'We are. I'm going to do some last-minute Christmas shopping later, so let me know if you need anything.' She paused, wondering whether to tell Lloyd what she had planned that afternoon, then decided to, as she wasn't sure whether to go ahead with it or not. 'But first, I want to put a Christmas tree up in Joel's house, as a surprise for him when he comes home. What do you think?'

'I think that's a splendid idea. My Christmas tree has cheered me up no end.'

'I was a bit worried that he might not like it, but his house seems so bare. And we've got another one in the loft, I can decorate it in half an hour or so. I want to clear up all the feathers from the ripped pillow, too. Joel's working so hard cutting the branches off the tree that I don't want him to come home to that mess.'

'That's very kind of you, I'm sure Joel will appreciate it. I love my Christmas tree, it really brightens up the lounge.'

Lexi was so pleased to hear him say that. Saying her goodbyes again, she set off home to pick up the Christmas tree.

The house was empty, so her gran was still out. *No surprise there!* Lexi went straight up to the loft, picked up the little tree and some red and gold baubles, then stopped off at the kitchen to grab the smaller cottage pie from the fridge, before going back out again.

Less than an hour later, the cottage pie was in Joel's fridge,

149

with a sticky note on the door telling him it was there and how to heat it up, and the tree was in place on the small coffee table, adorned with its baubles and with a gold angel on the top. It looked so pretty. Joel couldn't help but love it, surely. She would tell him it was a thank you for saving the Christmas tree on the green.

She looked around for the vacuum, found it at the back of the cupboard under the stairs, and carried it up to Joel's bedroom to clear up the feathers, taking a plastic bag to put the torn pillow in. When she'd done that, she sent Joel a text to say that she'd found Sweetie trapped in his bedroom, but she was fine. She explained about Sweetie ripping up the pillow, that she'd cleaned it up and that the dog was now with Lloyd. Then she closed the door and popped the key through the letter box. Now she needed to get to the shops.

Chapter Twenty

When she drove home later that afternoon, Lexi was surprised to find the green lit up by floodlights, and Joel still on the platform. He had a head torch on his helmet that lit up the branches he was cutting with his chainsaw. Andy was on the ground, a light on his helmet too, illuminating the machine he was feeding them into. A chipper, Joel had said it was called. She felt guilty that they were working so late. It was dangerous, surely, to work in the dark.

She pulled up and got out. She walked across the green, calling to them, but of course they couldn't hear her, not with the noise of the equipment and the ear protection they both wore. She moved closer to the tree.

Then, she was aware that the chipper had stopped and she heard Andy yell. 'Lexi, get out of the way!'

Horrified, she looked up and saw a branch heading towards her. She stepped back just in time as it crashed to the ground centimetres away from her. God, that could have landed on her.

'Are you okay?' Andy was beside her in instant.

She was literally shaking, so could only nod.

Joel was down now and running over to her. 'What the hell do you think you're doing? You could have got killed! What do you think all those bloody cones and signs are for?'

Lexi backed away. 'Sorry.'

Joel pulled off his helmet, his face furious. '"Sorry!" Bloody hell, Lexi! If that branch had hit you . . .'

She bristled at the tone of his voice, but knew that he was right to be angry. It had been stupid of her. So, she simply apologised again and turned to walk back to her car.

'Lexi!'

She turned around.

'I'm sorry. I shouldn't have yelled like that but . . .' Joel thrust his hand through his hair.

'I know. It was stupid of me. I should have been more careful.' She looked at Andy. 'Thank you for warning me.'

'What are you doing here, anyway?' Joel asked.

What, indeed? How could she explain that she had been so worried about him up there cutting branches when it was so dark – even if they did have floodlights – that she had come to tell him to leave it until tomorrow?

'I wanted to make sure everything was okay. You're both working so late and it's been a long day.'

'She's right. We should wrap it up for tonight, mate, it's almost six,' Andy said. 'We'll come back first thing tomorrow.'

'Is there a problem?' Lexi looked from one to the other of them worriedly.

Joel's face relaxed a little. 'The ivy has been tougher to cut off than I initially thought. It's wound itself like tight tendrils around the tree trunk and several of the lower branches and I haven't made as much progress as I'd hoped,' he admitted.

152

'We'll come back early tomorrow morning. We'll get it done,' Andy said.

'I'm not so sure we'll do it in time. I have to email the assurance that the work has been completed, and the tree is safe, to Martin by midday tomorrow. And I've no way of knowing how tight this ivy is around the lower branches of the tree until I start tackling it.'

He looked exhausted, Lexi thought. And the shock of the branch almost landing on her hadn't helped. She dreaded to think what would have happened if it *had* hit her. Why had she got so obsessed over saving the tree? She knew that the other villagers were upset about it, too, but she was the one who had started the petition, who had almost forced Joel into taking on the job. He'd even cut his rates. And for what? To work himself to exhaustion.

'I don't want one of you getting hurt, just to save this tree. You've both tried your best. I'm sure everyone will understand that.' Joel had got sawdust in his eye that morning, what if that happened again and he couldn't see clearly, then he cut his hand instead of the branch. She shuddered. She remembered Joel's words that some things were more important than Christmas traditions. She had been so annoyed with him, but he was right.

'The villagers will be disappointed,' Joel told her. 'We've got their hopes up now. And what about your gran and her mates?'

'You were the one who told me that safety was more important than Christmas traditions,' she reminded him. 'And you were right.' Her gaze swept earnestly over them both. 'If you can't make the tree safe in time then it doesn't matter. At least you've saved it from being cut down.' Her gaze swept from Joel to Andy then back to Joel again. 'Thank you both. I'm sorry

153

for being stupid enough to walk over here and almost cause an accident. I won't do it again.'

She turned and walked off, tears springing to her eyes at the shock of her near-accident and Joel's rebuke.

Joel stared after her. He felt like a right heel. But she could have been killed. He turned to Andy, who was standing silently beside him.

'Was I a bit over the top then?'

'Yep. But you had a point, mate, she could have been badly injured or worse. It was stupid of her to come here, in the dark, and with no protection. We've both seen enough bad accidents to know how dangerous this job is.'

Even so, he could have been a bit kinder. Fear had made him react so angrily.

'I know. Let's call it a day now, and be here at six tomorrow to see if we can get this finished.' He was sure he would feel a lot better once he'd got over the shock of that branch heading for Lexi and had a shower and something hot to eat.

'We'll get it finished, even if it takes a bit longer than midday. I know that we have to have the paperwork over to Martin by then, and we'll do that. If it takes another couple of hours to actually make the tree safe, then that's fine.'

'You'd be okay with that?' It was both their reputations at stake.

'Joel, if you assure me that you can make that tree safe in time for the carol service to go ahead on Friday, then I believe you.'

Joel considered this for a moment. 'I can do it. I promise. And I'll try to make it for midday. Now, let's clear up here and get home.'

Right now, all he wanted was to collect Sweetie from Lloyd, go home and have a shower. Or maybe he should have a shower first, rather than turn up on the doorstep like this. Lloyd was bound to ask him if he wanted to stay for a cup of tea, and it would be rude of him to refuse when he'd looked after Sweetie all afternoon. So, he sent Lloyd a quick text to say he'd be there shortly.

As he opened the door, he saw a big black bag in the hall. He peered inside and saw the ripped pillow. Sweetie had certainly shredded that. The bedroom must have been a right mess; it was good of Lexi to clean it all up. He'd hoped Sweetie would be all right this morning, she'd seemed so much more settled. He'd left the radio on in the kitchen, and taken her for a walk to tire her out before he went to work. He should have made sure that he closed the bedroom door, though. Goodness knows what damage she could have done, and the mess he would have come home to, if Lexi hadn't popped in to check on her. He always kept a litter tray in the kitchen in case Sweetie needed it, but she couldn't use it if she was trapped upstairs, could she?

He groaned as he walked into the bedroom and saw the unmade bed and clothes strewn about. He'd been running late and thought that taking Sweetie for a walk was more important than tidying his room. Thank God he hadn't left his dirty underwear on the floor! Lexi must have walked in to a right mess but she had cleared up the feathers the only sign of Sweetie's damage was that there was just one pillow on the bed.

He undressed and went straight into the shower, feeling himself relax as the warm water cascaded over his skin. Then he pulled on clean jeans and a sweatshirt and went back down the stairs, pausing as he noticed the lounge door was open. Had he left it like that, or had Lexi gone in there, maybe looking for Sweetie? She must have been in a panic when she couldn't find her. He stepped inside, switched on the light and gasped in surprise as his eyes rested on the Christmas tree in the corner, its green branches shimmering with red and gold baubles. Lights were draped around the tree, too, although they hadn't been switched on. Lexi must have done it when she came to check on Sweetie that afternoon. She seemed determined to thrust Christmas on him.

He walked over to the tree, and stared at the baubles hanging from the branches, his head a mix of emotions. This was the last thing he'd expected. And it was a bit of a liberty, to be honest. But he knew that Lexi had meant well, that it had come from a good place in her heart. Then he saw a white envelope on the table with his name written on the front. Had she left him a Christmas card as well?

He put the mug down and picked up the envelope, the blue handwriting was clear, the letters exquisitely formed. Curiosity got the better of him and he opened it up. The card had a robin on the front, with 'Merry Christmas' across the top, and inside she'd written:

I hope you don't mind me giving you this Christmas tree. It seemed a shame for it to be unused and forgotten in our loft when it could brighten up your room. Lexi x

Joel put the card down and surveyed the tree. Then he bent down and switched the lights on, they twinkled on the branches like little silver stars, reflecting in the baubles. He remembered putting up the tree with his sister, he and Hazel always had the job of decorating the tree. They enjoyed doing it. They used to have a big tree, it stood in the hall, and was a magnificent sight when you walked in. But it was the little tree his grandparents had in the lounge that he had loved the most. It stood on a sheet of Christmas paper on the sideboard, twinkling away, the Christmas lights playing 'Jingle Bells' until either his gran or grandad had enough and switched it off. He and Hazel had loved those lights, and often begged to switch them back on again. Christmas Day had been fun, with presents to open, turkey, homemade Christmas pudding, cake and an evening of playing games. Now he was older, he realised what a wonderful job his parents did and how selfless it had been of them to give their Christmas Day up to keep other people alive, but also make sure that he and Hazel had a wonderful time by sending them to stay with their grandparents. Maybe he had become too cynical about Christmas. Yes, it wasn't the be all and end all, and not worth drinking yourself stupid or getting into debt for, but he did have some fond memories of past Christmases, and it did bring a lot of happiness to people. Look how delighted Lloyd had been with his tree, and how much the traditional carol service meant a lot to the villagers. And he had to admit that this tree certainly brightened up his lounge.

His phone buzzed to announce an incoming message. He took it out of his pocket and looked at the screen. Lexi. He slid his finger across to open the message. *I hope you don't mind about the Christmas tree. I just wanted to cheer you up. Enjoy the cottage pie. And I can't tell you how sorry I am about earlier. It was stupid of me.*

'Enjoy the cottage pie?' Puzzled, Joel went into the kitchen and looked around. Then he saw the note on the fridge. *I was making a cottage pie for our tea and thought you might appreciate one, too. Saves you cooking after your hard day. x*

He opened the fridge and looked inside. On the bottom

157

shelf was a silver-foil pie dish with a ready-cooked cottage pie. All he had to do was warm it up.

Now he felt even more of a heel. She'd done all this for him, and he'd repaid her by yelling at her and almost making her cry. He'd seen the tears in her eyes when she'd turned and walked away.

She could have been killed.

Joel took a deep breath and tapped out a reply. *Thank you for everything. It's very kind of you. I'm sorry for yelling at you, it was just the shock of what could have happened.* He paused, then added '*x*' on the end and pressed send.

Lexi bit her lip as she opened Joel's reply. She hoped that she hadn't annoyed him even further. She read and reread the message. He hadn't specifically mentioned the tree, so she wasn't sure if he was annoyed or not, but he had thanked her. And apologised for his rant.

'He liked the tree, then?' Granny Mabe asked.

Lexi nodded. 'I'm not sure if "liked" is the word, but he's thanked me for it and not blown his top. I did wonder if he would think I'd overstepped the mark.'

'Nonsense, you were simply spreading the Christmas spirit,' Granny Mabe told her. 'Good on you, girl.'

'I thought the message might be from Ben saying that he could come down after all,' her mother said

Granny Mabe and Lexi exchanged a quick glance.

Her mother stiffened. 'Okay, I know that look. What's happened?'

Lexi guessed she would have to tell her parents at some

point. And it didn't feel so raw to talk about it now. 'Actually, we've split up. Ben's been having an affair. I only found out last week, that's why I came down early.'

'Some men, eh. Take notice of their loins instead of their heads.' Granny Mabe shook her head.

'I'm so sorry, love. That's an awful thing to have happened. Is he serious about this other woman?' Paula replied.

Lexi pushed a strand of hair from her eyes. 'He said not. He keeps messaging asking me to forgive him.'

Now it was her mum's turn to exchange a look with her gran.

'And will you?' Granny Mabe peered at Lexi over her glasses.

'No,' Lexi said firmly. 'The thing is, although I'm really upset about it, I can see now that it was me who made all the effort. Ben, he just went along with everything because it made life easier. I thought that he loved me, but I can see now that he didn't.'

'And do you still think you love him?' her mother asked.

'I don't know.'

'Well, if you don't know, take it from me, dear, you definitely don't,' Granny Mabe told her.

Chapter Twenty-one

Thinking about his family reminded Joel of what Lexi had said about Lloyd being estranged from his son and being on his own for Christmas. He knew that Lexi's parents had invited Lloyd to their house for Christmas dinner, but the old man had refused, probably the idea of joining in a family gathering with people he didn't know – apart from Lexi and her gran – was off-putting. It would be for him, too. Christmas was for families and he'd have felt an intruder, which is why he'd refused Andy's invitation to join him and his family. He intended to cook the turkey crown Hazel had left him and was planning on having a lie-in, cooking a late dinner, then watching a movie. But that was before Lexi had sneaked in and put up a Christmas tree for him, decorated with glitzy baubles and twinkling lights. Just as she had for Lloyd. Now he felt bad about Lloyd being on his own. *I'll invite him around for dinner*, he decided. *It's the least I can do, when he's looking after Sweetie for me.*

He pulled on his jacket and went around to pick up Sweetie. Lloyd greeted Joel with a big smile when he opened the door.

Sweetie came dashing to him and wagged her tail. 'Come in, come in. The kettle's just boiled. Will you have a cuppa with me?'

'A cup of tea would be lovely, thank you,' Joel said. Lexi was right, Lloyd was lonely. He hoped that he could persuade him to agree to share Christmas Day with him. As he followed Lloyd into the kitchen, with Sweetie trotting at his heels, he realised that his 'sharing Christmas dinner' idea had now extended to sharing Christmas Day. *Steady on, think about this*, he warned himself.

Lloyd made a cup of tea for them both and they took it into the lounge. Joel paused at the doorway, thinking how festive it looked. Lexi had brightened up Lloyd's home, as she had done his.

'It looks pretty, doesn't it? Really cheers me up,' Lloyd said as he made his way over to his chair, while Joel put the two mugs down on the table. 'I never usually bother with Christmas decorations, but now, well, I think I'll put them up every year.' He smiled at Joel. 'Lexi's so full of Christmas cheer and joy, it's infectious.'

'She certainly is. I gave her the key to my house so she could check on Sweetie today, then arrived home to discover that she'd put a Christmas tree up. And left me a cottage pie in the fridge to reheat.'

Lloyd shot him a look. 'How did you feel about that?'

Joel sat down and took a sip of his hot drink. 'If you'd have asked me beforehand how I'd feel if someone snuck into my house and put a Christmas tree and lights up, I'd have said *fuming . . .*'

'And now?'

Joel shrugged. 'After the initial shock . . . well, like you said, it brightens up the place. And the cottage pie is very welcome.'

'She's a kind lass.'

Joel was quiet for a moment, wondering how to phrase the words to ask Lloyd his question. He was out of his comfort zone here. He had never invited anyone to have Christmas dinner with him. He and Toni had always eaten out on Christmas Day, she was even less into cooking than he was, although, she was very much into a commercial Christmas. And Lloyd had already turned down Lexi's invitation. Joel didn't want it to sound like charity, as if he was feeling sorry for the old man.

'She is. And I think a bit of her Christmas spirit is rubbing off on me. So, I was thinking . . . how do you fancy joining me on Christmas Day? We could have dinner together and watch a film?' He tried to gauge Lloyd's expression. 'I know Lexi asked you, and you refused, but I figured that might be because she'd got all her family there. Whereas it'll be just you and me and Sweetie. And you'll be doing me a favour. It'll be nice to have company,' he added quickly.

Lloyd's face broke into a big smile. 'In that case, thank you. I'd love to.'

So, that was it, he was cooking Christmas dinner and had a guest. Lexi Forde had certainly changed his life.

Jay, Sonia and Toby arrived just after seven, Toby clinging sleepily to Jay. 'He fell asleep in the car on the way from the airport,' Jay said, as Paula ushered them into the lounge. 'He'll be okay in a minute, as soon as he wakes up properly.'

'I think this might help,' their dad said, switching on the little Christmas village he'd placed on the table by the window. Immediately, it started playing 'Jingle Bells' and a tiny train came out of the station and started puffing around the village. Toby's eyes opened wide and he stared at it in wonder, then wriggled out of his father's arms and ran over to the table.

'Don't touch it!' Sonia warned.

'He's okay, love. Let him enjoy it,' Craig said as an enraptured Toby knelt down to watch the train.

Sonia's gaze went from the musical village to the huge, twinkling Christmas tree, then over to the lights sparkling around the window. 'It's like a grotto in here!'

'I reckon it will be the same in our bedroom, won't it, Dad?' Jay said with a grin.

'Every bedroom!' Lexi replied.

They all laughed, then they were hugging, and everyone was introducing themselves, welcoming Sonia and talking over each other. Then Paula served dinner – Lexi's cottage pie with steamed vegetables, followed by Granny Mabe's apple crumble and custard. It was a noisy, happy affair.

It was a wonderful evening catching up with her family. Jay and Sonia regaled them with anecdotes of their life in Canada, where Jay was an engineer and Sonia a nurse, and little Toby was so sweet – they all adored him.

'Well, this is lovely, and when Ryan and Nell come on Friday, I'll have my whole family round me for the first time for years,' Paula said with a smile of contentment as Craig went into the kitchen to heat up mulled wine on the stove.

'I thought your boyfriend was going to be here, too, Lexi,' Jay said. 'It would be good to meet him.'

Lexi hesitated, wondering whether to tell everyone the truth. Seeing her brother happily coupled up made her own split seem raw again, and no way did she want to sound emotional and ruin everyone's Christmas. Besides, she still hadn't decided whether to get back together with Ben, so the fewer people who knew about the split, the better.

'He's working until tomorrow, so he's decided to spend Christmas Day with his mum,' she lied. 'We'll celebrate New Year together instead.'

Paula and Granny Mabe exchanged a glance, but said nothing.

Suddenly, a message pinged into her phone. *I hope that's not Ben again*, she thought, taking her phone out of her pocket to look. To her surprise, it was Lloyd.

You've been working your magic on Joel. He loves the Christmas tree and has invited me to spend Christmas Day with him.

Lexi grinned. *That's marvellous.* She'd been worrying about them both spending Christmas Day on their own, and now that was the perfect solution. She could hardly believe that people-make-too-much-fuss-of-Christmas Joel had invited Lloyd to Christmas dinner. *Wow!*

'It's from Lloyd. Joel has asked him to have Christmas dinner with him,' she told her mother, as she texted back to Lloyd.

That's fantastic. Make him wear a Christmas hat and send me a photo!

'Who are Lloyd and Joel?' Jay asked. Lexi related the story of how they all met, and how she'd managed to persuade Joel to save the Christmas tree.

Jay whistled. 'So, the carol service can still go ahead Christmas Eve?'

'Hopefully. There was a lot more ivy twisted around it than Joel realised, but he and Andy are starting again early tomorrow, so it should be finished in time. If not, at least they've managed to persuade the council not to cut the tree down before Christmas.'

'Fingers crossed, then. I really wanted Sonia and Toby to join in the carol service,' Jay said.

'It's very good of Joel to try, and apparently he kept his costs really low to persuade the council to accept the quote.' Paula turned to Lexi. 'I know you asked Lloyd to Christmas dinner and he politely refused, but why don't you ask him and Joel to come over on Boxing Day? It's a lot more relaxed then, and if Joel was there too he might feel more at ease.'

'Yes, I agree. Joel's tried his best to save the traditional Lystone carol service, we'd like to show our appreciation,' Craig agreed.

'What a lovely idea. I'll ask them both tomorrow,' Lexi replied. She'd been planning on going over to the green – keeping well behind the barriers this time – to see how Joel was getting on. She hoped both Lloyd and Joel would agree to spend Boxing Day with her and her family, it would be fun and she hated to think of them spending it alone. How she wished she'd been able to find Lloyd's son in time for Christmas. *You only had a few days*, she reminded herself. And she'd be back home soon. Maybe his son would turn up at some point in the new year.

'When will Ryan and Nell be here?' Jay asked. 'I can't wait to see my little bro again.'

'They won't be here until Friday afternoon, they're both working in the morning on Christmas Eve,' Paula told him. 'And they're back at work on Tuesday, but at least we will be all together over Christmas.'

'So, tell me about this Joel, who's rescuing the fir tree,' Sonia said, her eyes fixed on Lexi. 'Is he single?'

'Divorced,' Lexi told her. 'Why?'

Sonia smiled. 'Because your face lights up when you talk about him, more than it does when you talk about Ben.'

165

Lexi flushed. 'That's because I'm grateful for him coming to our rescue. He's not much of a Christmas person, so it's a big thing for him to do this.' She sighed. Why keep pretending? 'Look, I didn't want to tell you, because I didn't want to put a dampener on everyone's Christmas, but Ben and I, we've split up. He's been cheating on me.' As she said the words, tears sprang to her eyes, and she batted them back. She wasn't going to get upset over this.

'Oh, love, I'm so sorry.' Her dad immediately pulled her into a big hug. 'So, that's why you came down early?'

Lexi nodded. 'Ben's moved out – I threw him out, actually.' She was proud of herself for that. 'And I'm fine, really, I am.' She glanced around at her family's anxious faces and gave them all a watery smile. 'I don't need you to all feel sorry for me. It was a shock, but I know I'm better off without him.'

'You are that,' Granny Mabe agreed.

Lexi picked up her glass of mulled wine. 'Now, let's forget about me and Ben and toast to us all having a wonderful, family Christmas.'

They all raised their glasses and chorused, 'To a wonderful family Christmas.'

Lexi was determined that nothing was going to spoil this Christmas for her. Tomorrow, first thing, she would go and see how Joel was getting on with the tree and invite him to spend Boxing Day with them. Then she'd go and invite Lloyd, too. She hoped both men accepted; she was really looking forward to it. As she got into bed that night and settled down to sleep, she refused to think about why the idea of spending Boxing Day with Joel meant so much to her.

Chapter Twenty-two

Thursday, two days before Christmas

Jay, Sonia and Toby were suffering from jet lag, so were having a late morning, then going Christmas shopping in the afternoon. Her mum wasn't working in the bakery that day, both Claire and Brad were coming in, but Brad couldn't make it until midday, so Lexi had offered to work until then. As she drove up the hill, she could see Joel and Andy hard at work over on the green. *I'll take them a coffee and sandwich a bit later*, she thought.

'Oh, Lexi, you're a lifesaver!' her father said as Lexi stepped through the door. To her astonishment, the café was packed and both her dad and Claire were rushed off their feet. 'Would you mind serving in the tearoom for a while? I was tempted to ask your mother to come in, but I know she's got lots to do at home.'

'Of course.' Lexi had her coat off, hands washed and apron on in a flash. She picked up a notebook and pen from the counter and went to take orders from the tearoom.

Every table was full, and she soon found out that most of the gossip was about the fir tree being rescued. 'We hear that it was thanks to you, dear,' one of a group of women said as Lexi went over to take their order.

'It's Joel – the tree surgeon – and his partner Andy who've saved the tree,' she said.

'But you're the one who persuaded him.' This was from a man.

'I pointed out how important the carol service was to people in the village, yes, but Joel was the one who agreed to do it at such short notice. And for a reduced fee, too,' she added.

'Well, we're all very pleased. It won't be the same without the Christmas lights, but at least we can still have the carol service,' someone else said.

'Exactly.' Lexi gave them all a big smile. 'Now, what can I get you all?'

It was two hours later before the rush subsided. 'Thanks for your help, love,' her dad said. 'Now, why don't you sit down and have a break. I'll make you a cuppa, and grab yourself a cake.'

'Thanks, but can I take it out? I thought I'd take a coffee and a cheese and ham roll to Joel and Andy – they're still working on the tree. Unless you still need my help?'

'Brad will be here in a few minutes, so we're fine. You go and take refreshments to those two men, we all appreciate what they're doing.'

'Thanks.' Lexi made two rolls, poured three coffees, and set off.

She parked opposite the green and walked over with the coffee and rolls, then stood outside the barrier, waiting for one of the men to notice her, pleased to see that Joel was now working on the lower branches, so was standing safely on the ground. Andy spotted her first and waved. He turned off the chipper and called to Joel, who glanced across and waved, too.

Andy walked over and took the coffee-holder off her. 'Thanks so much. This is really appreciated.'

'You're welcome.' She looked over to see that Joel had now downed tools and was also making his way over. 'Is it safe to come round?'

'Yep.' Andy looked at her thoughtfully. 'It's not like Joel to lose his rag, but he was worried.'

She nodded. 'I know. It was entirely my fault.'

They moved away from the equipment, and both men removed their helmets when they were a safe distance from the tree.

'How's it going?' Lexi asked. She knew that Martin needed assurance that the tree was safe to be emailed to him by noon, and it was almost twelve now.

'Almost done. I've emailed Martin.' Joel took a swig of his coffee. 'Thanks so much for this.'

'So the carol service can definitely go ahead?'

'Yep.'

'Thank you, both of you. You've made a lot of people happy. Everyone's talking about it,' she said sincerely, wanting them to know how grateful she and the villagers were.

'You're welcome.' Joel unwrapped his roll. 'I was thinking, I might even come to the carol service myself.'

Andy was about to take a bite out of his roll, but he paused, mouth open, to stare at Joel. 'You, go to a carol service?' He sounded astonished. 'Who are you and what have you done with Joel?'

Joel grinned. 'There's a first time for everything.'

Seeing that Joel's attitude to Christmas had softened, Lexi seized the moment to mention her family's invitation for Boxing Day.

'Lloyd told me you'd invited him around for Christmas Day. That's really kind of you.'

Joel chewed some of his roll and nodded. 'Seemed a shame for him to be on his own, and he's been great with Sweetie. I figure I owe him.'

Lexi bit the bullet. 'My folks have asked me to invite you and Lloyd over for Boxing Day,' she told him. 'Fancy it? It'll be really relaxed: a buffet and a few drinks.'

Andy looked at Joel with amusement. 'Sounds like you're definitely celebrating Christmas this year, mate.'

Joel looked a bit wary. 'Thank them for me, please, but I think I'll have a quiet Boxing Day on my own.'

Lexi tried to hide her disappointment. 'Of course. I hope Lloyd still comes, though. We told him that we were inviting you too, we thought that he might feel more comfortable if you were there.'

Joel looked a bit guilty. 'Oh, well, maybe I could pop in for an hour? If it means Lloyd will accept.'

'Great. We won't pressure you to stay, I promise.'

Joel's eyes met hers, and she felt a shiver of awareness. Feeling awkward, she switched her gaze to the tree and all the needles, branches and pine cones underneath it. 'Is there anything I can do to help? Perhaps I could rake up some of the needles?' She knew that they'd both been working since early that morning and must be exhausted. And they were doing it all for a reduced fee, too.

'That would be very helpful. If you're sure you don't mind?' Joel said. 'I've got spare protective gear in my van.'

'I'd be happy to help. Let me text my dad first to let him know the carol service tomorrow is definitely on. So many people have been dropping into the bakery this morning to ask.' She took out her phone, and sent a quick text to her dad. Then she picked up the empty coffee cups and other rubbish. 'I'll put these in the bin, then I'm all yours.'

Joel's eyes met hers again, there was a spark of amusement there at the double meaning of that remark, and she turned away quickly so that he couldn't see the flush she could feel heating up her cheeks. She really had to choose her words more carefully.

Joel got a spare helmet, gloves and hi-viz jacket out of his van and gave them to Lexi to put on then continued sawing off the diseased branches at the bottom of the tree, while Lexi raked up needles and cones from the branches he'd pruned earlier, and Andy put them in the chipper. The sawdust then came out of the spout and sprayed into the box attached to the back of his van.

'That's clever,' she said.

'It saves a lot of work,' he told her. 'Sawdust is a lot easier to get rid of.'

Joel had finished now, and was using a leaf blower to clear the grass, while Lexi did a final sweep up. She raked the branches over to Andy to put in the chipper, then gasped in horror when she saw sawdust all over the road. What had happened?

'Andy, there's something wrong with the machine!' she shouted.

Andy came running over to investigate. 'The spout on the chipper has come loose and it's all going onto the road instead of into the box!' he said with a groan.

Joel sprang into action, placing cones and danger signs around the heap of sawdust on the road, to warn any traffic. Then they set to cleaning it up.

Finally it was all clear, and the cones, signs and tape were all in the back of Andy's van. Joel pushed his safety helmet back and wiped the back of his hand across his forehead. 'That's it. All done' He turned to Lexi. 'Thanks for your help.'

'You're welcome.' She took off her protective gear and handed it to him. 'Best be off, my brother and his family arrived from Canada last night and I promised to go shopping with them this afternoon. Have a good Christmas, Andy. You too, Joel, if I don't see you beforehand.'

'I reckon you're in there, mate. You've even had an invite to the Boxing Day family get-together,' Andy said as Lexi walked over to her car.

'Rubbish, Lexi's like that with everyone. She thinks Christmas is the most wonderful time of the year, and wants everyone else to be caught up in its spell, too,' Joel told him.

'She's definitely interested in you, and I reckon that you're interested in her, too. Why fight it? She seems lovely. You could do a lot worse.' He pulled off his hat. 'Actually, you have done a lot worse.'

Yes, I have, Joel thought, his mind drifting to Toni and their messy marriage and even messier divorce. 'She's nice, but she's only visiting. And even if she wasn't, I wouldn't want to get involved. I've had enough of relationships to last me a lifetime.' Not that he thought that Lexi was the slightest bit romantically interested in him. She was one of those people that was naturally friendly and drew others to her. She treated him the same as she treated Lloyd, and probably everyone else she met. Besides, he had a feeling she wasn't over that cheating boyfriend of hers yet.

Chapter Twenty-three

Joel was relieved that he couldn't hear any barking coming from the cottage when he parked his van outside. He had left Sweetie at home, not wanting to wake Lloyd up so early, and she hadn't whined at the door this time after he went out. Was she finally settling down? As he put his key in the door, he heard her bark, and she was waiting, tail wagging, when he went in. He made a big fuss of her, then thought that maybe he should have checked around and made sure she hadn't chewed anything first. Luckily, she hadn't. He let her out for a few minutes, then showered and got changed. He had one more job before Christmas, and this one was a lot easier as it didn't involve any climbing up trees and cutting branches. A man called Jim Robinson, who had recently taken over a local country estate, had contacted him to ask for advice on what kind of trees to plant in a wooded area they were planning. Joel really enjoyed this sort of work and after a bit of a discussion with Jim had agreed to go over today, asking if it was okay to bring his dog with him. Jim had agreed so Joel securely fastened Sweetie in the passenger seat of the van and set off.

As he pulled into the driveway of the house, he saw a van parked outside. It looked like a workman's van – not surprising as Jim was having a lot of renovations done.

As Joel walked past the van he noticed 'R.Winston & Co, Painters and Decoraters' written across the side in big black letters. He paused. Lloyd's surname was Winston and his son was called Rocco. He was sure Lloyd or Lexi had said that Rocco was a painter and decorator. Could it possibly be his van?

The front door opened and two men came walking out, chatting. Joel took one look at the black curly hair, brown eyes, big smile and mocha-toned skin of one of them and knew he was Lloyd's son. There was no mistaking the resemblance. Should he say something?

If Lexi was here, she would go straight over to the man and ask him if he was Rocco. Joel wasn't as impulsive as that, but he knew how much Lloyd wanted to see his son again and felt that he had to at least try to make that happen.

'Wow, you've got to be related to Lloyd Winston, you're almost his double,' he blurted out, in what he hoped was a light-hearted way.

The man stopped and stared at him. 'You know my father?'

So, he *was* Lloyd's son, then. 'Yep, I live next door but one to him. Lovely man. He sometimes looks after this one for me when I'm working.' He indicated Sweetie who was now pulling at the lead and sniffing at some flowers. 'You must be Rocco. He's talked about you.'

'He has?' Rocco looked surprised. 'How's he keeping?'

'Good. He gets a bit lonely, though.' Joel put a smile on his face so that Rocco wouldn't take his words as a dig. 'Look, it's none of my business, but I know you two had a bit of a disagreement and he'd love to see you.' He held up his hand, palm outwards. 'Just thought you might want to know.'

Rocco narrowed his stare. 'Did he tell you what we argued about?'

'Nope and I didn't ask. Not my business. I've only mentioned it in case you were missing him, too, but didn't want to make the first move because you didn't know what your reception would be – well, it would make his Christmas.' He nodded and walked inside to talk to Jim. He'd done all he could. It was up to Rocco now.

'Good to see you, Joel.' Jim shook Joel's hand. 'Let me tell you what I'd like done and you can tell me how feasible it is, and what trees I should plant, and then give me a quote for the job. I'd be looking at you starting in the new year. Can you do that?'

'I sure can,' Joel replied.

When he returned from talking to Jim, the decorator's van was gone. Would Rocco take any notice of what he'd said? Joel wondered. All he could do was hope. He said goodbye to Jim, promising to have the quote to him in a few days – allowing a break for Christmas – then put Sweetie in the van and set off back home.

On the drive home, his thoughts drifted to the carol service the following night. He knew that the villagers were planning on taking some of their own decorations, and hoped that none of them were intending to climb the tree and put them higher up. Someone could get hurt. An idea occurred to him. As soon as he got home he dialled Andy's number.

'Are you free tomorrow afternoon?'

'Don't tell me you've got another job for us?'

'It's a freebie, but it won't take long.'

Andy listened in stunned silence as Joel explained what he had planned. 'Have you had a personality transplant, mate?' he asked.

Joel grinned. 'Are you in?'

'You bet I'm in,' came the amused reply.

Lexi was feeling tired now. It had been fun Christmas shopping with Jay, Sonia and Toby. Toby had been fascinated by the Christmas lights, and Sonia and Jay had enjoyed browsing around the big stores, as had Lexi. It was wonderful to spend time with her brother again. She remembered him as being a bit of a lad in his early twenties, but he really seemed to have settled down and become a proud family man. When little Toby said he was too tired to walk, Jay had lifted him up on his shoulders until Toby was ready to get down again. He pointed out the decorated Christmas trees and the festive yarn-bombings to Toby who gazed at them with an expression of sheer delight.

'This is the first Christmas he's really been aware of what's going on. I can't wait to see his face on Christmas Day when he opens his presents,' Sonia told Lexi. 'I love it now he's growing up. Babies are adorable, of course, but my favourite time is when they become toddlers and start to explore the world and develop their own little personality. I can already tell that he's going to be into mischief like Jay.' She grinned at Jay.

'And he likes his own way, like you,' Jay said good-naturedly.

'How about we take him to see Santa before we go home?' Lexi suggested, spotting a sign saying, 'Santa's Grotto'.

'Oh, yes, he would love that.' Sonia crouched down to talk to Toby. 'Do you want to see Santa and get a present off him?'

Toby nodded.

'I bet he only understood the word "present",' Jay told her. 'He's got no idea who Santa is yet.'

'He will by the time he goes home. You know Dad, once Christmas Eve arrives he'll be wearing his Santa outfit non-stop until Boxing Day ends,' Lexi told her brother.

'Does your father dress up as Santa? How cute,' Sonia exclaimed.

Lexi and Jay exchanged a grin. Sonia had no idea what a Forde family Christmas was like yet, but they were sure that she would enjoy it. And that little Toby would be spoilt rotten.

As they joined the not-too-long queue to see Santa in his grotto, Lexi thought how glad she was that the carol service around the tree could go ahead the following night. It wouldn't be the same without the tree being all lit up, but they would still enjoy it.

A message pinged into her phone. She took it out of her pocket and glanced at the screen. It was Joel.

I've got some news about Rocco. Fancy popping around later?

Had Joel found Rocco and managed to persuade him to come and see Lloyd? This really was turning out to be a special Christmas. She quickly replied.

Love to. Still shopping with my brother and family. About 8 p.m. OK?

Joel sent a thumbs up as a reply.

Lexi put her phone back in her pocket. She was looking forward to seeing Joel tonight and finding out about Rocco. Thank goodness they had got over that awkwardness and become friends again. She really did enjoy his company.

Toby squealed with excitement beside her as the gate opened to let them into the grotto and Lexi smiled at him, sharing his joy. It had been so special to spend the day with Jay, Sonia and Toby, and Ryan and Nell were coming tomorrow. It was great to have her family around her, she hoped that Joel's text meant Lloyd would have his family around him, too. That's what Christmas was all about.

Another message pinged in. Thinking it was Joel again, she took her phone out of her pocket and glanced at the screen. Ben.

She quickly shoved the phone back in her pocket. She wasn't going to read his message. She didn't want to think about Ben. Not now. Not ever.

Chapter Twenty-four

They all piled home much later, laden with goods. Sonia and Jay had treated themselves and Toby to some new clothes, a new suitcase, explaining that they'd booked an extra case in for the return trip as they had intended to go shopping, and presents for the family. Lexi treated herself to a new dress, bought another couple of gifts for the family and a cute squeaky toy for Sweetie.

'I was thinking, why don't we all go out for a meal tonight?' Craig suggested. 'I've checked at the Lystone Arms and they've got a table free. Anyone fancy it?'

'That sounds great.' Jay turned to Sonia. 'You'll love it there. It's a typical old English pub, with lots of character.'

'Can I meet you there?' Lexi asked. 'I need to pop in to see Joel for a few minutes.'

'Give him our thanks for saving our Christmas tree,' her dad said.

'I'll meet you there about eight thirty. I'll just pop my shopping up to my bedroom and quickly get changed.' She hurried upstairs, put the shopping bags on the floor by her bed, changed her jumper, refreshed her make-up and was off. She took the car, she was happy to have a soft drink with her meal and it would save time.

She could hear Sweetie barking as soon as she rang the bell.

'I swear she knew it was you,' Joel said, answering the door.

Lexi scooped up the little dog, who was running around her legs, yapping excitedly. 'How's she been today?' she asked as she cuddled Sweetie. Joel had said last night that he wasn't leaving Sweetie with Lloyd as it was too early.

'Really good. I took her with me this afternoon; someone wanted me to give them a quote for work they needed done, she was good as gold. I was going to take her for a walk in a minute, fancy joining us?'

Lexi followed him into the lounge, still holding the little dog. 'Oh, sorry, I can't. I'm meeting my family at the Lystone Arms in a little while. We're having a meal.'

'That's great. You must be pleased to see your brother again, and to meet his wife and son.'

'I am. And everyone said to thank you for saving the Christmas tree. The village is buzzing with excitement for tomorrow night now.'

'You're welcome.'

She paused. She didn't want to be rude after all Joel had done, but she really did have to go soon. 'So, what's the news about Rocco?'

'I saw him today.' Joel explained what had happened that afternoon.

Lexi was so pleased she could have hugged him. 'Do you think he might get in touch?' she asked.

'I hope so. I guess there isn't much time for him to do it before Christmas, but he did ask about Lloyd.'

'Thank you so much for talking to him. Do you think we should mention it to Lloyd? Did you get the number of Rocco's company? We could give it to him.'

'I took a note of it but I think we should wait to see if Rocco turns up first. Give him a couple of weeks, then I'll mention it to Lloyd and give him his number.'

She'd have gone home by then, Lexi thought. She was going to miss Lloyd. And Joel.

She nodded. 'Good idea, I'll have to leave that to you, then, as I won't be here.' She gave him a little smile then put Sweetie down on the floor. 'I'd better go and join my family now, then. Were you serious about coming to the carol service tomorrow?'

'I was.'

'Great. I'll see you there, then.'

The pub was crowded when Lexi walked in. She peered around trying to locate her family, then saw Jay stand up and wave, in the corner on the right. So, she made her way through the crowd to join them. They were all seated around a big table with a covered bench seat under the window which spread around into the corner, and chairs on the outside. Jay, Sonia, Toby and Granny Mabe were sitting on the bench seat, leaving the chairs for Lexi and her parents.

'You don't mind us sitting here, do you?' Sonia asked. 'We thought it would better for Toby. He can lie down if he feels sleepy, he'd be out of the way in the corner there.'

'Of course not,' Lexi assured her.

'I never thought, you could have asked Joel to join us,' Paula said. 'He would have been very welcome.'

182

'It's okay, he looks tired anyway – he and Andy had an early start this morning.' She took off her coat and put it on the back of her chair before sitting down next to her mum. 'Guess what, Joel saw Lloyd's son today.'

'Really? Where?' Granny Mabe leant forward, anxious for more news.

'What's all this?' Jay asked. Paula filled him and Sonia in, then Lexi related what Joel had told her. 'You mustn't say anything to Lloyd, Granny. We don't want to get his hopes up in case Rocco doesn't show up.'

'Oh, I hope he does, that would be marvellous,' Granny Mabe said. 'I feel so lucky to have all my family around me. So many old folk are on their own. It's sad.'

'You'll never be on your own, Ma,' Craig told her, giving her a hug.

Lexi felt a warm glow as she saw her granny and her dad exchange a loving look. Her family had their ups and downs, like everyone else, but they were always there for each other.

'How long does it take to travel here, Lexi? Do you come down to Lystone often?' Sonia asked.

'My flat in Gloucester is about two hours away. And no, I don't. Not as often as I should, but you know what it's like with work and everything,' Lexi replied.

'I can't wait to meet Joel and Lloyd at the carol service tomorrow,' Sonia said. 'And Sweetie, of course. Will Joel be bringing her on Boxing Day?'

'I actually hadn't thought of that. What do you think?' she asked her parents.

'I think he must, we all want to meet her now,' her dad replied.

Amidst more laughter, and chatting, they picked up the

menus and ordered their meal. Throughout the night, people came over to say hello to Jay, and to Lexi, and were introduced to Sonia and Toby. Some of them joined their table, once they'd eaten, so more and more chairs were added.

As she sat, talking to her family and friends, Lexi thought that Granny Mabe was right. They were so lucky to have family around them. She was going to miss them all when she went back home. To her empty flat.

You'll have your job. And Fern. And you can come down at weekends. Every weekend if you want, she reminded herself. She was determined that, in the future, she was going to make more of an effort to spend time with her family.

Joel felt restless. He'd spent most of his adult life ignoring Christmas as much as he could. The traditional Christmas of decorating the tree, singing carols, exchanging presents and spending time together as a family was a nice idea, but Toni's ideal Christmas had been a consumer one. She had paid the housekeeper to decorate the tree, they'd eaten Christmas dinner out in an expensive restaurant with friends, exchanged expensive presents, gone on to a party. It had been enjoyable, but empty, in a way. Their whole life had seemed superfluous. It had been a life he'd drifted into. When he and Hazel were growing up, they had stayed with their grandparents in rural Scotland during the summer holidays while their parents worked, which meant they'd helped out a lot on the farm. Hazel had hated farm life and had gone into hotel management, then met Al, who also worked at the same company. Joel, on the other hand, had loved the farm. As he'd got older, he'd helped his grandad more, especially with caring for and felling the many trees that grew on his land. When he left school, he'd taken a university course in Arboriculture, while volunteering whenever he could for the Woodland Trust, then had got a job working for the Forestry, where he met Andy. He'd loved that job; climbing and felling those sky-high pine trees was dangerous but also exhilarating – and the view! Andy had been a climber too, back then, but after an accident that resulted in them both having to be aerial rescued and Joel's arm in plaster, Andy hadn't wanted to climb anymore and had worked as a groundsman instead although he didn't mind going on the platform. They'd seen the damage falling branches could cause, which is why they'd both been shaken up at Lexi's near miss. Then Andy had moved away, and eventually Joel had become restless, ready for a change, so had applied for jobs in England. He'd been delighted when he was offered the job of looking after the vast woodland on the Morton Estate.

Then he'd met Toni, fell head over heels in love, and to his eternal regret, married her within the year. Once they were married, Toni wanted him to do something more lucrative, where he had to wear a suit instead of coming home 'filthy', as she often complained. Joel hated the thought of an office job, he liked working outside, liked the thought of doing his bit to help nature. Lately, though, since the divorce, he'd been feeling a bit restless again, and had been thinking about a change of direction once more. He was thirty-three, and in his prime, but could he see himself climbing and felling trees in another ten or twenty years? Although, his job did involve a lot more than that. The trouble was, he didn't know what else he wanted to do. When he left university his grandfather had wanted Joel to take over running the farm, but Joel had gently declined, knowing how hard that life was, so his grandfather had sold it. Now he wondered if he had made the right decision, if he should have stayed in Scotland. If he had, he would never have met Lexi, though. Somehow Lexi's love of Christmas had wrapped him up and pulled him along. It was because of her that he was planning this big surprise tomorrow. Yes, it was for the villagers, too, and he couldn't wait to see their faces when they turned up for the carol service.

But he was looking forward to seeing Lexi's face the most.

Chapter Twenty-five

Christmas Eve

When Lexi got up the next morning, the kitchen was bustling. Toby was at the table, eating some cereal that her mum had bought especially for him, her parents were drinking a mug of tea each, Sonia was making toast, and Jay was ironing a shirt. Lexi did a double take at the previously never before seen sight of her brother ironing.

'Wow! How did you manage that miracle?' she asked Sonia, remembering how Jay used to pay her to iron his clothes when she was a teenager. Her parents had always insisted that Lexi and her brothers did their share of the chores and their own ironing, but while Jay was happy enough to wash up or put the vacuum around, he hated ironing with a vengeance.

'Jay always irons,' she replied, surprised.

Jay grinned at her. 'I finally mastered how not to get the cord tangled up and now I find it quite relaxing. Look, I'm even ironing Sonia's top for her.'

'Fancy doing some of my ironing, too?' asked Lexi.

Jay smoothed the creases out of the sleeve of his shirt. 'Sure. Pass it over, but there's a three-garment limit.'

She was surprised he said yes. 'I was only kidding.'

'Morning everyone,' Granny Mabe said as she came in, still wearing her dressing gown. 'What are you all up to today?'

'Morning, Granny. We're going out for a drive around. I want to show Sonia and Toby some of the pretty Devon villages,' said Jay. 'Anyone fancy joining us?'

'Thanks, but I'm going to help out in the bakery again today so that mum can have a few hours off and be here to welcome Ryan and Nell,' replied Lexi. She wanted to do a bit more lesson planning, too, if she had time.

'You don't have to do that love,' her mum protested.

'I want to. Please, Mum, let me do this for you. You work so hard, and it's Christmas tomorrow. You must have lots to do.'

She was rewarded by the beam on her mother's face. 'I do. Thank you, love, that's very kind of you.'

'I'll enjoy it. It's nice to be back in the village again.'

'Would you ever move back down here, Lexi?' Sonia asked. 'With your job, I'm sure you could get work anywhere. Teachers are always needed. You could even join us in Canada.'

'I'd love a trip there to come and see you both, but I'm a homebody. I'd miss England,' she said.

'I did at first, but now I've got Sonia and Toby, Canada feels like home. Although, it's been great to come back to England and see you all. We were saying to Mum and Dad that we would absolutely love it if any of the family were to come over and see us.'

'We're definitely planning to at some point, we just need to arrange cover for the bakery,' Craig said.

'I know we've got Claire and Brad but we'll have to get a manager in if we go away for a few weeks,' Paula added.

Granny Mabe sat down at the table and poured herself a cup of tea. 'I might come and see you too. I fancy a trip to Canada. As long as I can bring a friend with me. I don't feel like doing a long trip like that alone.'

'Of course you can. That would be wonderful, wouldn't it, Jay?' Sonia said.

Jay nodded. 'You go for it, Granny M. Would it be a female or male friend you'll be bringing?'

'Now, that'd be telling,' Granny Mabe said with a twinkle in her eye. She finished her tea. 'Right, I'm off to get ready now, I'm off out in a bit so I'll see you all later.'

'Your gran is out so much. She must have lots of friends,' Sonia said when Granny Mabe had gone.

'She's hardly ever in. Drives herself around, too,' Paula said. 'It wouldn't surprise me at all if she did come to visit you both. There's no stopping her.'

Lexi could imagine her gran flying to Canada. It was just the sort of thing she would do.

'Right, I have to go,' her dad said. 'Shall we both go in my car, Lexi?'

'Sure.' She pulled on her coat, double-bobble hat, gloves and scarf. It was a bit chilly today, although she knew the bakery would be warm and cosy. She was hoping it would snow. That would make Christmas Day perfect.

The bakery was busy for the first couple of hours, with people popping in for the Christmas cakes, puddings and other odds and ends they'd ordered, but by midday it was quiet.

'You get off, love. I'll tidy up here,' said her dad.

'Are you sure? I don't mind helping?'

'Positive. Providing you don't mind walking home. It's a bit nippy. I think it might snow again.'

'I hope so. That would make Christmas perfect.' Lexi fetched her coat, hat and scarf. 'Don't worry about me being cold, I'm all togged up,' she said, taking her gloves out of her coat pocket and pulling them on. She wanted to check whether her gran and her friends had started their yarn-bombing yet.

As she turned the corner, she glanced over at the green. The tree looked so majestic, standing in the middle. She walked over the road, onto the green and looked up at the dense branches with their needle-like leaves and cones. *Joel has made a really good job of this*, she thought. She knew that he had removed quite a lot of branches, but the tree still looked thick and healthy. It would be safe enough now for Granny Mabe and her friends to hang baubles and things on the branches, she thought. She hoped they stuck to the lower ones and didn't bring a ladder so they could reach higher up. She wouldn't put anything past them, though.

When Lexi arrived home, Granny Mabe was about to drive off in her car again. She wound the window down and called, 'Want to come and help? We could do with another pair of hands?'

Lexi glanced into the back of the car and saw the bag of knitted baubles. 'Are you going to yarn-bomb the tree?'

'I am that. Hop in. Jay, Sonia and Toby are still out and your mum's popped to the supermarket to get some last-minute odds and ends. Ryan phoned to say they won't be here until teatime, they've got a bit delayed.'

Lexi hesitated. 'Gran, if you get caught doing this, you'll get fined.'

'Bah, who's going to report us? The villagers are pleased that the tree has been saved and the council offices are closed now. But if you're worried, you stay here.'

She *was* worried, but her gran was right it was highly unlikely any of the villagers would report them. And at least if she helped them, she could keep an eye on them and make sure that none of them attempted to climb on ladders – or even, heaven forbid, the tree! – to hang their glittery creations higher up.

'Okay.' She opened the passenger door and clambered in beside her gran.

'We're going to Cynthia's first to gather all the things together,' Granny Mabe said as she started up the car, then pulled away so fast that Lexi was thrown back in her seat – it was a good job she'd managed to fasten her seatbelt. 'Take it easy, Gran!' she said. 'I don't want to be spending Christmas in A&E.' She glanced at her grandmother. 'Perhaps I should drive?'

'You will not! This is my car, and I haven't had a serious accident in the fifty years I've been driving,' Granny Mabe said as they headed off down the street.

Lexi didn't find the words 'serious accident' very comforting, but she had to admit that the drive to Cynthia's house – on the other side of the village – went smoothly. And she was quite excited to meet all of the yarn-bombers.

To her surprise, one of them was just a little older than herself, and there were two men in the group, too. She wondered if Granny Mabe would persuade Lloyd to join them.

Lexi couldn't believe all the things they'd knitted: tiny snowman and Santa baubles; tinsel, squares with Christmas trees, snowmen and Santas knitted in them. They were beautiful and would make the tree look really festive. She was worried about the safety aspect though.

191

'You are only going to hang these on the lower branches, aren't you, Granny? The ones you can easily reach? I don't want anyone getting hurt.'

'We've got it all sorted. Stop worrying,' Granny Mabe told her.

Lexi sighed. There was no way her gran or any of her friends were going to listen to her. She was going to keep a close eye on them, and make sure no one did any climbing on ladders – if necessary, she would do it. She wasn't risking one of the elderly folk getting hurt. The least they would do was break a bone. She didn't want to think of the worst damage.

Lexi spotted Andy's truck parked on the road as they approached the green. Had he come to check on the tree? Then she saw the platform parked beside the tree, and two men in hard hats, goggles and wearing high-viz jackets, draping lights over the tree.

'Well, would you look at that! The council must have decided to put the lights on the tree after all. Isn't that wonderful,' Granny Mabe exclaimed, as she pulled up on the kerb outside the shops opposite the green.

'It's not the council, it's Joel and Andy.' Lexi opened the car door and stepped out.

'Are you sure?' Granny Mabe asked, surprised.

Although she couldn't see the men clearly, Lexi was sure it was them. One was tall and broad, the other smaller. And that was definitely Andy's truck. What was going on? Had they managed to get permission from the council to decorate the tree?

Everyone else was piling out of their cars and staring over at the tree. The man on the platform had finished arranging the top of the tree now. He dismounted to help the other man drape the lights over the lower branches. Then he bent down and fiddled with something and the tree lit up with hundreds of sparkling white lights.

'Hooray!' The watching crowd cheered and clapped.

He switched off the lights and turned to watch as they all walked over the green towards the tree.

It was Joel. He greeted Lexi with a big grin. 'Like it? I was just testing that they worked. I'll keep them off now until the lighting-up ceremony.'

'How did you manage to get permission off the council to do this?' she said. She guessed that Joel and Andy had offered to put on the lights because the council employees were off work now.

'I didn't. I sort of took it upon myself. The tree is safe, the lights are outdoor ones and I've got a generator. I can't keep them on here for long, just a few days, but I didn't like to think of you all having your carol service around a bare, unlit tree.'

'Well, that's splendid, young man, splendid,' Granny Mabe told him, patting his arm.

Joel suddenly became aware of the crowd of people. 'What are you all doing here anyway?'

'We came to yarn-bomb the tree,' Granny Mabe said. 'We thought that if the council weren't going to decorate it for us, then we'd decorate it ourselves.'

'We can still do it, can't we?' someone asked. 'It'd be nice to have a few baubles and things on the branches as well as those lovely lights.'

Andy and Joel looked at each other.

'Yarn-bombing is illegal,' Joel said.

'I'm pretty sure those lights you've just put up are, too,' Granny Mabe told him firmly.

Joel shot Lexi a glance and she grinned. Granny Mabe had him there.

'Okay, but only on three conditions.'

They all waited.

'You promise not to wrap anything around the tree. Tree-wrapping can lead to disease and insect problems. Second, you agree to me taking down the baubles Tuesday at the latest, and third, you only do the lower branches. Me and Andy will hang the stuff higher up. Agreed?'

'Agreed!' they all chorused.

'We had brought a stepladder with us, but your platform looks more useful,' Granny Mabe said, handing Joel a box of knitted baubles. 'Hang these on, will you, dear?'

It was such a cheerful afternoon. While Joel hung the colourful knitted baubles high up the tree, Lexi, Andy and the others hung them on the lower branches. They also wrapped the gold-and-silver glittery squares that had been stitched together in a long scarf around the nearby lamp posts. It all looked very jolly and festive.

Word was spreading around the village that the tree was being decorated, and more and more people arrived, wrapped in their coats, scarves and mittens, to watch. Lloyd had joined them, too.

'What time does your carol service usually start?' Joel asked Granny Mabe.

'Six thirty,' she told him. She turned to the crowd that had gathered. 'Light up time will be at six thirty, followed by the carol service. Spread the word! Let's have as many come as we can. Remember, the tree has only been saved temporarily. It might still be cut down in the new year. A big turnout could convince the council not to do that.'

Cheers and clapping greeted this remark. Then people crowded around Joel and Andy, patting them both on their backs and thanking them, before going home.

'Thanks so much for helping with this,' Lexi told Andy.

'I wouldn't miss it for the world. I'm going to bring my missus and kids to the carol service tonight, so I'd better get off.' He turned to Lexi. 'There's just one thing, though.'

'Yes?'

'How did you manage to convince Christmas-is-no-big-deal Joel to do all this?'

'I have no idea.' She was completely stunned herself. 'But I'm glad he's finally found his festive spirit.'

Chapter Twenty-six

Jay, Sonia and Toby were already back from their sightseeing drive when Lexi and Granny Mabe returned home. Then, a few minutes later, Ryan and Nell arrived. There were lots of hugs as they all greeted each other and the brothers introduced their partners.

'What was all that going on at the green?' Ryan asked, when the greetings were over. 'We saw a crowd gathered there when we drove past. Is it to do with the carol service tonight? I've been telling Nell all about it.'

'I'm really looking forward to going,' Nell said.

Lexi filled them in about the latest events, with Granny Mabe adding a bit now and again, finishing with how they had gone over to yarn-bomb the tree and found Joel and Andy putting up the lights.

Lexi's parents were dumbfounded. 'You're one of the yarn-bombers, Ma? I thought you were knitting blankets?' her dad said incredulously.

'You do know you can get fined, don't you?' her mum looked concerned.

'They've got to catch me first,' Granny Mabe said with a grin.

Ryan and Jay both burst out laughing. 'Granny the rebel!' Ryan said. 'I can't believe it!'

'Well, I think it's a lovely thing to do,' Nell butted in. 'I love yarn-bombing. It really brightens up the place. And this Joel sounds very kind.'

They all chatted for a while, exchanging news, then Granny Mabe made some of her 'special' dumplings and popped them into the stew that she and Paula had prepared that morning and had been cooking in the slow-cooker all day. Half an hour later, they all sat down to eat. They'd decided to have their meal early, as Toby would be too tired to eat after the carol service.

'This is delicious,' Jay said. 'I've missed your stews, Mum, and Granny's dumplings.'

'Me too,' Ryan agreed, helping himself to another dumpling from the stew pot in the middle of the table. 'You must give us the recipe so we can make some ourselves.'

'I will not. Those dumplings have a special ingredient in them and I won't be divulging what it is until I'm dead.'

This remark was met with a roar of laughter.

'You can't tell us when you're dead, Granny!' Jay reminded her.

'I've written it down and sealed it in an envelope which is not to be opened until after my funeral. And only Paula and Craig can know it.'

'We'll be old men before it's passed on to us,' Ryan said to Jay.

'We'll ply her with wine tomorrow and she'll tell us then,' Jay replied.

'Trying to get your poor old Granny drunk so you can prise secrets from her.' Granny Mabe tutted, shaking her head in mock-disapproval. 'So, this is how they treat the elderly nowadays.'

'Elderly!' Jay spluttered. 'If we dared to call you that, you'd give us a clip around the ear.'

Lexi smiled as she listened to the banter between her brothers and her gran, remembering the times Granny Mabe had done just that for some misdeed they'd done, or for cheeking her. She loved being back with her family, and was so pleased that they'd all managed to get together for Christmas.

'If the lighting-up ceremony is at six thirty, we need to get going,' Paula said when the meal was finished. 'Have you sorted out the inflatables and lanterns, Craig?'

'They're all in the boot of the car,' he told her.

Craig, Paula and Granny Mabe went in the car, but Lexi and the others walked, Jay carrying Toby when he got tired. The little boy loved looking at all the Christmas decorations in the houses they passed. When they arrived at the green, Craig and Paula had added the Forde's contribution of an inflatable snowman and Santa, a big Santa on a sleigh, and several lanterns, to the decorations already around the tree, and it looked really festive.

Quite a crowd had gathered by now, all wrapped up in thick coats, scarves and gloves, rubbing their hands and stamping their feet as the cold night air bit through them. Lloyd came over to join in and was greeted warmly by Granny Mabe and her crowd. A couple of people came with musical instruments – an accordion and a trumpet – and someone else handed out carol sheets. The atmosphere was building.

'It looks like it might be cold enough for snow,' Ryan said.

'Oh, I wish it would. A white Christmas would be perfect,' Lexi said, wrapping her scarf tighter around her neck. She checked her watch. Twenty past six. She had thought that Joel might come a little earlier. And there was no sign of Andy yet.

Then she saw Joel hurrying over the green, Sweetie on a lead beside him. 'Sorry, Sweetie refused to be left, so I had to bring her,' he said. He looked around. 'Is Andy here yet?'

Lexi shook her head. 'Want me to hold Sweetie while you turn on the lights?' she asked.

'Thanks.' Joel passed the lead over to her.

'It's six thirty!' someone shouted.

'Can we hang on a few more minutes, please? The man who helped me do all this is on his way to join in the carol service. I don't want to do it without him.'

There was a chorus of yes. People were chatting to each other and the minutes were ticking by. Lexi looked at her watch. Twenty to seven.

'Here he is!' Joel shouted as Andy walked over the green with a woman and two young children.

There was a cheer and Andy bowed. 'Sorry, folks, someone hid my car keys.' He pointed to his little daughter who looked a bit guilty.

This was greeted by laughter.

Finally, Andy was by Joel's side, his two children next to him. Joel called Toby over, too, and the children pressed the switch to turn on the lights. There was a cheer as the Christmas tree blazed alight.

'Merry Christmas!' everyone shouted.

Then Craig stepped forward. 'First, can we give a big round of applause to Joel and Andy for saving our carol service.'

'And Lexi, she was the one who persuaded me,' Joel said.

Lloyd took Sweetie from Lexi and gently pushed her forward to join Joel and Andy. Then everyone clapped and cheered. Lexi felt her cheeks go hot, but wasn't sure whether it was because Joel had his arm around her shoulder or because she felt a bit awkward at being the centre of attention.

Then her dad raised his hands. 'And now, let's start with our first carol. Number three on the carol sheet. "Ding Dong Merrily on High!"'

Everyone sung at the top of their voices, accompanied by the accordion and trumpet players.

As Lexi joined in, looking at the happy crowd, the sparkling tree, and all her family together, she thought that she had never felt happier.

Joel caught her look and smiled at her. Impulsively, she gave him a hug. 'Thank you,' she said, wrapping her arms around him and kissing him on the cheek. 'You've saved Christmas for us all.'

Chapter Twenty-seven

As the carol singers started a rendition of 'O Little Town of Bethlehem', Lexi stepped away from Joel quickly, embarrassed. She hadn't meant to kiss him, the excitement of them being able to have the traditional Christmas carol service had got the better of her. She went over to join her family, who were all singing with gusto. Her mum, her dad, Jay, Sonia with Toby in her arms, gazing in awe at the tree, Ryan and Nell, their arms around each other's waists, Granny Mabe and Lloyd, chatting away like old friends. Ben should have been here, too. She wondered briefly what he was doing. *Stop thinking about him*, she told herself. *You're over him.*

The Christmas tree lights twinkled and sparkled as they sang one carol after another, then, as they started the chorus of 'Hark! The Herald Angels Sing', a flutter of snowflakes started to fall.

'It's snowing!' someone shouted.

Lexi turned her face up to the sky, and let the soft flakes fall on her skin. *Snow.* Now Christmas really would be perfect.

They sang louder, now, and the snow fell faster and faster. By the time the carol service had finished, the snow had covered the ground.

'Merry Christmas!' rang out the shouts of the carollers. 'Merry Christmas!'

'Right, who's coming on to the pub?' someone shouted out.

Jay looked down at Toby, who he had taken off Sonia a little while ago and was already fast asleep in his arms. 'I think I'll give it a miss, this little lad needs his bed. You go, though,' he told Sonia, but she shook her head. 'I'm ready for a hot chocolate and bed.'

Ryan and Nell said they were ready to go home, too, and Lexi decided to join them. It wasn't often the whole family was together for Christmas Eve, and she wanted to make the most of it.

'Thank you again for doing this. And everything else,' she told Joel. Then she delved into her bag. 'I've got a little something for Sweetie tomorrow. I hope you don't mind,' she said, handing the squeaky toy that she'd wrapped earlier to him.

Joel looked surprised. 'Thanks. That's very kind of you.'

'I guess it's time for us to leave, too,' Lexi's father said. He turned to Lloyd, who was talking to Granny Mabe. 'Look forward to seeing you on Boxing Day, Lloyd.'

'Me too. I can't thank you enough for the invite.' Lloyd patted Granny Mabe's mittened hand. 'It's been a pleasure to meet you all. A real pleasure.'

'Would you like us to walk home with you? It's a bit slippery underfoot,' Jay offered.

'Don't worry, I live by Lloyd,' Joel said. 'I'll make sure he gets home safely. We're spending Christmas Day together, too.'

Lexi was pleased that they wouldn't both be alone. It was good to think that Lloyd would still have Joel when she'd gone back home, as well. And hopefully his son would come and visit him, too, some time over the Christmas period.

'We'll see you both on Boxing Day,' Paula said. 'Any time after two. And please don't bring anything with you. We have plenty to go around.'

Joel nodded. 'I look forward to it.'

'Merry Christmas!' they all called as they walked away.

'Merry Christmas!' Joel shouted back, his eyes seeking Lexi's. She held his gaze and smiled at him. Then she turned and walked away.

'What a lovely evening,' Sonia said, as she and Jay walked home hand in hand. Toby was already asleep on Jay's shoulder. 'It's a wonderful start to Christmas, isn't it?'

Ryan and Nell both linked their arms through Lexi's. 'You okay, sis? I know it's rubbish that you've split up with Ben right before Christmas,' said Ryan.

Lexi smiled at him. 'It's fine, spending Christmas with you all more than makes up for it.'

'If you ask me, you're well rid of him anyway,' Nell said. 'Now, that Joel really is something . . .'

'Hey, what are you doing, lusting after other men?' Ryan said teasingly.

Nell blew him a kiss. 'I'm happy with you, but a Christmas romance might be just what Lexi needs to get over her cheating ex.'

'I've got no intention of having a romance with anyone, thanks, my heart is a man-free zone,' Lexi told her.

She had to admit, though, she was glad Joel was coming over

for Boxing Day. He'd become a good friend, and she enjoyed his company.

As she walked back through the streets, twinkling with sparkling Christmas lights, alongside Jay and Sonia, Ryan and Nell, Lexi couldn't help feeling a little bit sad and lonely, everyone was paired up and happy, except for her. This was supposed to be her first Christmas with Ben. A special Christmas for both of them.

And until a week ago, she had thought that her and Ben had a future together. How wrong she had been.

Joel linked arms with Lloyd as they walked home together, his mind on a woman with long honey-brown hair, dark-brown eyes and a smile that lit up her face. Lexi. She had waltzed into his life, bringing her love of life and Christmas sparkle with her, and somehow he had got caught along with it all.

'Would you like to come in for a tot?' Lloyd asked. 'I've got some brandy in.' He glanced down at the little dog. 'And some treats for Sweetie.'

Why not? Joel thought. He could sense that the old man wanted some company, and if he was honest, he didn't want to go back to an empty house either. Especially a house that wasn't his. He still felt very much a lodger there. 'That would be lovely, thank you.'

They sat, chatting and drinking brandy in Lloyd's lounge, with the lights from the Christmas tree sparkling, while Sweetie gobbled up her treats. Then the little dog fell asleep on the sofa besides Joel.

'I haven't had company for Christmas for a long time,' Lloyd said as he took a sip of his brandy. 'I didn't mind either, I got used to it. Told myself that Christmas was just like any other day, but it isn't, is it? And Lexi, she's reminded me of that. Christmas is a special time, it's for friends and family.' He looked over the rim of his glass. 'I've decided that I'm going to find Rocco and make it up with him for next Christmas. I should never have let this rift between us go on for so long. What does it matter, who's right or who's wrong? We're family.'

Should he tell him that he'd found Rocco? Joel thought. But maybe the fact that his son knew he wanted to see him but hadn't been in touch would hurt him. I'll leave it until New Year, he decided. Maybe Rocco might get in contact. If not, I'll give Lloyd the number of his company and let him take it from there.

'That sounds a great idea,' he told him.

'So, how about you? Are you intending to stay in Lystone when Hazel and Al come back, or is it just a stopgap for you?'

Joel swished his brandy around in his glass for a moment, thinking about his answer. 'I don't know,' he said. 'It was just temporary but I'm not sure now.' He found himself telling Lloyd about his divorce and how he had come down here to try and sort himself out. 'To be honest, I was at a loose end. I'd got to that stage in my life where I wanted to do something different. So, I seized on the chance to housesit for Hazel, and I've only been here for a couple of weeks but already the village is growing on me. I could see myself making a home here.'

'There's something about Lystone that wraps its arms around you and makes you want to stay. It was the same with me and Ruby. We loved it as soon as we set foot in the place. And we had such a good life; when we retired, we were out and about on day excursions, we were so happy together we didn't need anyone else. Then, when she died, I was bereft and lonely. Ruby had been my world. I had no idea what to do without her. Rocco tried to persuade me to move, but I couldn't. I feel like while I'm here, Ruby is still with me in a way. Rocco told me I needed to live again. We had an argument. I yelled at him that he might be able to forget his mum and carry on with his life but I couldn't.' Lloyd's eyes filled with tears and he took another sip of his brandy. 'He said if that's how I felt, he was going. I told him not to come back.' His eyes were filled with sadness as they rested on Joel. 'I shouldn't have said that. It was grief talking, but still, I shouldn't have said it. I kept thinking that I would contact him, tell him I was sorry, but I kept putting it off. As the weeks turned into months, and then years, it seemed too late. Besides, I don't even know if he has the same phone number or if he's moved house.'

'Lexi would tell you that it's never too late.'

'I know. Well, things are going to be different in the new year. I'm going to get out, join a few of the clubs Mabe has told me about, and I'm going to find Rocco.'

Two more glasses of brandy later, Joel let himself back into his own house, a sleepy Sweetie in his arms. He gently lifted her out and put her in her basket, she'd done her business in Lloyd's garden half an hour ago, so didn't need to go out again. She wagged her tail, without even opening her eyes, and snuggled down. Well, it looked like he was actually going to have his bed to himself tonight. That would be a change.

As Joel settled down into bed, Lexi's image flashed across his mind. He went to sleep dreaming of her lips on his cheek.

Chapter Twenty-eight

Christmas Day

'Wake up, Auntie Lexi!' Toby shouted.

Feeling the mattress wobbling beneath her, Lexi rubbed her eyes sleepily and saw that Toby was jumping up and down excitedly on her bed. 'Mewwy Christmas!' he shouted.

'Mewwy Christmas, Toby.' She lifted herself up on her elbows and smiled at him.

Toby jumped off the bed, grabbed her hand and tugged. 'Santa's here. And Mrs Santa!' Toby's eyes were round with wonder.

Lexi grinned, her parents must have got up early to put their Santa outfits on. They always used to do that when she and her brothers were young. They must be really enjoying having Toby here. She glanced at the clock. Seven o'clock. That wasn't bad; when they were young, she, Jay and Ryan would often have their parents out of bed at five o'clock in the morning. Although Toby was probably still suffering from jet lag, and had gone to bed late yesterday, so she was actually surprised that he was up and looking so lively.

'I'm coming,' she said, swinging her legs out of bed. 'Can you pass me my dressing gown, please?'

Toby ran to the chair that the white fluffy dressing gown was draped over, and brought it to Lexi as she slipped her feet into her slippers and stood up. 'Thank you,' she said, taking it off him.

'Same!' Toby pointed proudly to his red pyjamas with white snowmen printed over them. Lexis pyjamas were red, too, and there was a big snowman on the front.

'We're almost twins,' Lexi said with a grin. She slipped on the dressing gown and tied the belt at the front. 'Is everyone else up?'

Toby shook his head. 'Not Gwanny.'

At least she wasn't the last one. She held out her hand. 'Come on, then, let's see what Santa has brought us.'

She'd placed her presents for everyone around the tree yesterday. Her parents always liked to pick up the presents one by one, then call out the name of the person the gift was for, and then everyone would watch as they opened it. It took ages for all the presents to be opened, but it was fun.

Her family were all in the lounge: her brothers and their partners with bed hair and sleepy eyes, all clad in dressing gowns and onesies, and her parents in their Santa and Mrs Claus costumes, ready for the grand present opening session.

'We're just waiting for Granny Mabe,' Paula said, passing Lexi a mug of tea when she came in.

'Thanks.' Lexi clasped the warm mug in her hands and sat down on the sofa, by Ryan and Nell, who both looked very sleepy.

'My Christmas doesn't normally start this early.' Nell yawned.

'It does when you have children,' Sonia told her.

If she was still with Ben, they would probably be tucked up in bed fast asleep, Lexi thought. Now, Ben was tucked up with Rosa instead.

She's welcome to him. Lexi pushed any thought of Ben out of her mind. She was with her family. She needed to stop letting him creep back into her thoughts. Especially today.

'Your parents look great in those outfits, though.' Nell gave another yawn. 'Do they always do this at Christmas?'

'They did when we were young,' Ryan told her. 'I'm sure they're enjoying making the most of Toby being here for Christmas.'

Lexi glanced over at Toby, who was sitting on Jay's lap, looking impatiently at the door and asking every now and again when Granny Mabe was coming. At last, the lounge door opened as she ambled in, dressed in a snowman onesie and nursing a big mug of tea.

'Hooray!' Toby cheered. 'Can we have our presents now, Santa?'

'Merry Christmas!' Granny Mabe said as she sat down in the armchair that had been left vacant for her.

'Merry Christmas!' everyone shouted.

'Right, are you all ready for your presents?' Santa Craig shouted.

'Yes!' they all chorused back.

He turned to the pile of presents placed around the tree and picked up one covered in Santa Clauses. 'This one is for Toby!' he called.

Toby clapped his hand. 'Mine!' he shouted, scrambling off his dad's lap and running over to retrieve his present. They all watched as he opened it, his face breaking into a huge smile when he saw the dinosaur game Lexi had bought him. 'Look!' he squealed, running to show his parents.

Mrs Santa Paula picked up another present and called out to Ryan. He was delighted when his present turned out to be a metal detector. Nell smiled at his delighted expression. 'I thought we could go detecting at weekends – you never know, we might find some treasure,' she said.

There was lots of fun and laughter as Santa Craig and Mrs Santa Paula took it in turns to call out the presents one by one, and lots of squeals of delight from little Toby.

'We were right to book an extra suitcase for the flight back,' Sonia said, looking at the pile of presents surrounding Toby, who was now sitting on the carpet playing with a very noisy fire engine.

When all the presents had been opened, they had breakfast and a glass of Buck's Fizz, then took it in turns to use the family bathroom to shower and get dressed. Everyone wore Christmas jumpers – apart from Paula and Craig, who kept on their Mr and Mrs Claus outfits. Even Toby had a cute Santa jumper.

'It's like a flashback to when we were all kids, isn't it?' Jay remarked as they sat around the table playing a noisy game of Monopoly whilst dinner was cooking.

'Exactly the same, none of you have grown up,' Craig jested.

'Who's the one dressed as Santa and sulking because he's losing?' Ryan retorted, and they all burst out laughing.

As Lexi looked around at her family, she thought that she hadn't been this happy for a long time.

The only thing missing was Ben. She'd received another text from him that morning, wishing her a Merry Christmas and telling her how much he missed her. She thought of the early

Christmas dinner she had planned for them, and the presents she had bought for him. She shrugged the thoughts from her mind. She would get over Ben. It would take a little time, but she would do it. Meanwhile, she was enjoying this break with her family.

When the game was finished – Sonia won, to her delight and the groans of the men – Lexi went upstairs and took out the Christmas jumper she'd knitted for Ben. Her brothers had already all got one, so she was planning on wrapping it up as a present for Joel and giving it to him tomorrow. She knew that he had jested with Lloyd that he would never wear a Christmas jumper but hopefully, he would join in as her brothers and her dad would be wearing their Christmas jumpers again. She also had a present for Lloyd, a new pair of slippers. She'd noticed that his current ones were wearing out and was worried about him tripping up, so had checked out his shoe size one day when he'd changed into his slippers and gone into the kitchen to make a drink. She'd been planning on giving the presents to them both tomorrow, not wanting to give them earlier in case they thought that they had to get her a present back.

She wondered how their preparations for Christmas dinner were panning out. *If only Rocco would turn up*, she thought, but he had probably got plans to spend Christmas Day with his own family. Perhaps he would come to visit Lloyd another day. She hoped so. She'd love it if he came before she went back home.

When she went downstairs, Ryan and Jay were out in the garden testing out the drone that Nell had bought Ryan for Christmas. Toby was asleep in the armchair, still clutching the cuddly penguin that Lexi had bought him, and Sonia and Nell were sitting on the sofa, chatting over a bottle of wine. 'Come and join us, we got a glass for you.' Nell pointed to the empty glass on the coffee table.

'Thanks, I will. I'll just check that Mum and Dad don't need any help in the kitchen first.'

'We've offered, but they've kicked us out,' Nell told her.

Lexi could believe that. The kitchen was her parents' domain on Christmas morning. 'In that case, pour me the wine.' She grinned, plonking down beside Nell. 'We'll gang up on them after dinner and make them sit down while we clean up the kitchen, deal?'

'Deal,' Sonia and Nell agreed.

Lexi picked up the glass of wine Nell had poured her. 'Now, how are you two coping with my brothers?'

'It's a work in progress,' Nell said with a grin. 'Mind you, the metal detector and drone will keep Ryan occupied for hours. They were genius presents, even if I say so myself.'

'Jay's got a drone, too, at home. I bought it for his birthday. They'll be taking videos with them and having a competition to see who takes the most unusual one.'

'That is so like them,' Lexi agreed, remembering how competitive her brothers had always been.

'Had you and Ben been together long?' Sonia asked her. 'Don't answer if it's too painful to talk about.'

'Over a year,' Lexi told her. 'We met in September last year and video-called each other every day during lockdown. We got on so well that Ben moved in after lockdown eased, so we'd been living together for a few months.'

'So, it was a fairly new relationship, then. It's awful that he's cheated on you like that, but you really are better off with-out him.'

'I know. We were "comfortable" together, we jogged along okay, but there was no real passion. I can see that now. I guess that's why he went off with Rosa.' She turned to Sonia. 'Now, do tell us more about Canada. I'm already planning my visit for next year.'

'So are we,' Nell told her. 'You could travel with us. It'd be fun.'

'Thanks. I'd like that. And by the sound of it we might have Granny Mabe joining us, too, if she gets wind that we're going over.'

'As long as she doesn't start yarn-bombing the airport,' Nell said.

They all laughed.

It had been a long time since he'd looked forward to Christ-mas, Joel thought. He'd got up and switched on the lights on the Christmas tree, then given Sweetie her present from Lexi to unwrap. It had surprised him when Lexi had given him a present for the little dog, but he had to admit that it was fun watching her opening it – a squeaky bone – then watch-ing her excitedly play with it. He wished Lexi was here to see it, too.

Joel picked up the Christmas wrapping paper that Sweetie had scattered all over the lounge in her eagerness to unwrap her present, and shoved it in the bin, then went to put the oven on to cook the turkey crown. He'd taken it out of the freezer and put it in the fridge to defrost yesterday morning. Lloyd was coming around for one o'clock, so there was plenty of time for the turkey to cook. He'd wrapped up a small bottle of whisky as a present for Lloyd, and had pulled up an armchair by the fire for him to sit on.

He wondered what Toni's Christmas plans were. When they were together, they had always got up late, opened their presents, then gone off for Christmas lunch, followed by a party at one or other of their friend's houses. And the same on Boxing Day. He was sure she would find some friend to put her up and a party to go to. Toni was one of those people who could always wrap people around her little finger. It had worked with him enough times. She might even have made it up with Drake. Even if he had agreed to give their marriage another try, Joel knew that Toni would have soon been off again. He wasn't going-getting enough for her. And he was past wanting to try. Life was a lot more peaceful without Toni in it. So was Christmas. He'd spent last Christmas alone, as had many other people, thanks to the Covid restrictions, treating it just like any other day. This year, though, he felt ready to have a bit of company. He was actually even looking forward to going around to Lexi's parents' house tomorrow. They were a friendly family, and as he was going to be in the village for a few more months it would be good to get to know people.

The snow had stopped falling now, but was quite thick on the ground. He didn't want Lloyd falling again, so Joel decided to go around and collect him. Just as he grabbed his coat, someone knocked on the door. Lloyd was standing on the doorstep.

'I was about to come for you. I was worried you might slip,' Joel said as Lloyd stepped into the hall and Sweetie bounded out to greet him.

'Mabe bought me some snow grips for my shoes,' Lloyd slipped off his shoes and turned them over to show him. 'She's got some herself, and said they're really good for gripping the snow and ice.'

Mabe really was a character, Joel thought.

Lloyd rummaged in the shopping bag he was holding and held out a parcel.

'Merry Christmas!'

'Merry Christmas and thank you.' Joel took the present off him and closed the door. Lloyd took a pair of worn slippers out of his bag and slipped his feet into them, then felt in his bag again and took out another present. 'And this is for Sweetie.'

Sweetie danced around his legs and barked, as if she understood what he had said.

'Thank you.' Joel held the door open. 'I've got a little gift for you, too. I'll give it to you in a moment. Do you want a cuppa or a tot? Dinner will be another half an hour or so.'

'I'll have a cuppa, thanks. I'll save the tot until later, otherwise I'll be falling asleep.'

'Go through into the lounge. You can give Sweetie her present if you want, while I make the tea,' Joel told him.

When he joined Lloyd with a mug of tea each a few minutes later Sweetie was chewing happily at a rubber bone, the Christmas paper it had been wrapped in now in the bin.

'That'll keep her occupied all day,' Joel said with a smile. 'And it's a lot quieter than the squeaky toy Lexi bought her, which she's been running around with all morning!'

The two men exchanged presents, Lloyd was delighted with the small bottle of whisky, as was Joel with the flask Lloyd had bought him. 'Just what I need,' he said.

'I thought you might appreciate it with you working out-side,' Lloyd told him.

They had a pleasant day, chatting easily and then watching a film on the TV. Lloyd fell asleep at one point, and Joel took the opportunity to go to the front door and check the street. It had suddenly occurred to him that if Rocco turned up and his father wasn't in, he might go away again.

You told him you lived next door but one, he'd give you a knock.

He kept an ear out for a knock on his door or ring of his bell all afternoon, but none came. It was only Thursday that he saw Rocco, very short notice, he reminded himself. Hopefully, the man would think about Joel's words and come to visit his father before New Year.

At just gone six, Lloyd rose from his seat, thanked Joel for a splendid day, and said he was off home. Joel suggested he call for Lloyd the next day so they could walk to Lexi's together, explaining that he didn't want to take the car as he would be having a drink.

'That's very kind of you,' Lloyd said.

'I'll walk you home now, Sweetie could do with a bit of exercise,' Joel told him.

Once Lloyd was safely home, Joel took the little dog for a short walk, then opened a bottle of beer, sprawled out on the sofa, and settled down for an evening in front of the TV. Sweetie jumped up beside him, snuggled up and went to sleep.

He'd enjoyed today, Joel thought, as he gently stroked the sleeping dog. And he was looking forward to tomorrow. And to seeing Lexi again.

Lexi texted later that night. *How did your Christmas lunch go? Did Rocco turn up?*

He replied: *Sadly, no. But we had an enjoyable day. And Sweetie loved her present, thank you.* Then he added: *Looking forward to tomorrow.*

Me too ☺

Joel smiled as he read Lexi's text. For the first time in years, he was actually enjoying Christmas.

Chapter Twenty-nine

Boxing Day

It had always been a tradition in the Forde household that the men in the family did the cooking on Boxing Day, while the women either went to the sales or put their feet up. No one fancied a trip to the shops today, so the women plumped for having a drink and catch up in the lounge instead.

'Remember, you're all banned from the kitchen. If you want something, you have to knock on the door,' Craig warned them as the men took to the kitchen to cook – Jay even took Toby with him, much to both Toby and Sonia's delight. 'I cook, too,' he said. 'Bye, Mummy!'

'Bye!' Sonia waved happily.

Paula reached for a bottle of wine. 'Anyone want a glass?'

'Yes, please!' Nell said with a smile.

'Me too! I must make the most of my child-free morning,' said Sonia. She took the glass of wine that Paula offered her. 'I'm so grateful that Jay was brought up to cook and do his share of household chores.'

'And me,' said Nell. 'Some men are hopeless, but Ryan's great at mucking in without even being asked.' She raised her glass. 'To well-brought-up sons.' She and Sonia clinked glasses.

'We were all raised to do that. Mum and Dad worked and we all had to muck in, but Ben's mum waited on him hand and foot and he wasn't great at doing stuff around the house,' Lexi said. In fact, Ben had expected her to do everything, and a lot of the time she had; as she got home from work before him, it made sense to her to cook the dinner or do a bit of housework. She bit her lip, realising that their relationship had had flaws in it long before Rosa came on the scene.

'It sounds like you're well rid of him,' Nell told her.

Lexi nodded. 'I think I am.'

It was a fun, lively morning. Roars of laughter were coming from the men in the kitchen, and Sonia and Nell couldn't resist poking their head around the door a couple of times, but they were immediately shooed away.

'No women allowed!' the men chorused every time the door was opened.

Nell reported back that the table was covered with pastries, cakes, quiches and sandwiches. 'They're cooking enough to feed an army,' she remarked.

'They always do,' Paula told her. 'If there's any left over, I'll take it to the bakery tomorrow and let the customers in the tearoom eat it.'

Lexi's parents never opened the bakery on Boxing Day, believing that it was important family time, but everything went back to normal the next day until New Year's Day, when the bakery was always closed again.

The morning flew by, and before they knew it, Lloyd and Joel were ringing the doorbell.

Lexi opened the front door. 'Merry Christmas!' she said.

'Merry Christmas!' they both chorused.

Sweetie peeped her head out from the neck of Joel's coat, which was wrapped around her. 'Woof!'

'Hello, girl!' Lexi stroked her head. 'Shall I take her?'

'Thanks. We've walked here. Lloyd insisted – your gran bought him some new grippers for his boots – and Sweetie didn't like getting her feet wet in the snow, so I had to carry her.'

He passed the little dog to Lexi, then wiped the snowflakes off his shoulders. 'I can't believe all these decorations you have up outside. You certainly do Christmas in a big way, don't you?'

'We do. Wait until you see inside,' Lexi told him, standing aside to let them both past, each of them carrying a bag of what she could see were wrapped Christmas presents. 'And you really shouldn't have bought all those presents. We didn't expect it.'

'It's been nice to have someone to buy presents for, that's one of the best parts of Christmas,' Lloyd told her.

'Thank you again for asking us,' Joel said. He looked at the lights twinkling in the hall, then up the stairs. 'I think I see what you mean about the decorations.'

'You will when you go into the lounge. Even the bedrooms have a Christmas tree and lights.'

'Really?' Joel's astonished expression made her giggle.

She led the way into the lounge. 'Joel and Lloyd are here,' she announced, still cradling Sweetie in her arms.

'Merry Christmas!' everyone chorused.

'Hello, Sweetie.' Nell stroked the little dog, who instantly wriggled in Lexi's arms.

'Do you want to go down?' Lexi put her on the floor and she ran around excitedly, from one person to the other.

'I think she's going to get thoroughly spoilt today,' Lexi told Joel.

Lloyd looked at everyone in their Christmas jumpers. 'Oh, it looks like we should have worn a Christmas jumper.'

'A Christmas jumper? I've never had one of those,' Joel replied.

'There's a first time for everything.' Lexi handed him his present.

Joel took it gingerly. 'It isn't?'

'It is,' she told him.

'And here's one for you.' Granny Mabe handed a parcel to Lloyd. 'I thought you might not have one.'

Lloyd's face broke into a huge grin. 'Thank you so much.'

Joel had taken off his coat and was now pulling his sweatshirt off, to reveal a black top that hugged his perfectly toned body. Lexi realised that she was staring, and tore her eyes away, only to catch Nell giving her a wink before mock-fanning herself. She grinned. Obviously, she wasn't the only one who thought that Joel had a very sexy body.

Lexi looked back at Joel and saw that he was now wearing the Christmas jumper which fitted him like a glove. He was the same height as Ben, but broader shouldered. The jumper would have been a bit looser on Ben.

'It fits you perfectly,' she said.

Joel grinned. 'It does and it's the same pattern as your cardigan so I presume you must have knitted it yourself?'

Of course! How stupid, she'd forgotten that! She was actually wearing her Christmas cardigan today, so now they both matched. 'Yes, it's my own design,' she admitted.

'It suits you,' Nell said to Joel, admiringly.

'Well it's the first time I've ever worn a Christmas jumper, but it is a very nice one. Thank you, Lexi.'

'You're welcome.'

Meanwhile, Lloyd had pulled on his Christmas jumper, too, a red one with a snowman on the front. 'Well, this is very festive,' he said with a grin. 'Did you knit it, Mabe?'

'No, I spotted it in the big supermarket yesterday and had a guess at your size. Looks like I made the right choice!'

There were a couple of presents for Sweetie, too: another squeaky toy, which she loved, and a biscuit bone.

Craig poked his head out of the kitchen door. 'You're just in time, the buffet's ready.' Then he whistled. 'Great, you've come in Christmas jumpers. Brilliant. Someone give them a party hat, too.'

Lexi picked up the two Christmas hats she'd put on the sideboard ready for them, and handed Lloyd and Joel one each. Her eyes met Joel's in an unspoken challenge to wear it. He grinned and put it on.

Joel gave Sweetie the biscuit bone, leaving her to chew it happily while they all piled into the kitchen, oohing and aahing at the laden table. Tiny quiches, pork pies, samosas, spring rolls, pasties, plates of assorted sandwiches, bowls of various salads, and, in the middle of the table, a cake stand with a selection of delicious cakes, as well as two bowls of trifle and a fruit flan. It was a scrumptious feast.

'This reminds me of spending Christmas with my grandparents,' Joel said. 'Gran and Grandad always did a spread like this on Boxing Day.'

'Tuck in, everyone, drinks are on the side here. Help yourself.

Me and the lads are off duty now, and we're going to celebrate.' Craig beamed at everyone. 'Anyone want a glass of my home-made wine?'

Jay and Ryan both exchanged a grin. 'No way, that stuff is lethal,' Jay said.

'I'll try it. What sort is it?' said Joel.

Jay looked at Joel. 'Seriously, mate, don't touch it. One glass and you'll be out of your head.'

'That's a bit harsh, lads,' Craig said, putting his hand on his heart as if he was deeply wounded.

'From what I remember of it, you lads drank a whole bottle ... each! No wonder you both had a hangover,' Paula chided them.

'Well, I'd actually like to try it,' Joel said. 'Just a small glass.'

Craig rewarded him with a beaming smile. 'I've got rhubarb, elderberry or parsnip.'

'I'll go for elderberry, please.'

Ryan patted Joel on the back. 'Good luck, mate. You can kip on the sofa if you can't manage the walk home.'

Lexi grinned at Joel's expression. 'Ignore them, they like to tease – but I would stick to only one glass,' she added, knowing first-hand how drunk some people had got after sampling too much of her father's seemingly harmless but very potent home brews.

'I think I'll pass on it and just have a cup of tea,' Lloyd said.

'I was about to put the kettle on,' Granny Mabe told him. 'I bet you like it strong.' She tilted her head to one side. 'One sugar. Am I right?'

'Spot on.' Lloyd rubbed his hands. 'Well, I must say, this spread looks delightful. Mind if I tuck in?'

'Please do. If this doesn't get eaten today, we'll be living off it all week!' Paula jested.

Sonia and Jay were already helping themselves. Lloyd picked up a plate from the pile on the end of the table and joined them.

The afternoon passed by so quickly. Lloyd and Granny Mabe chatted away, sharing their experiences of a childhood spent in Jamaica. Lexi smiled as she watched them both talking. She could see a budding friendship there, that would probably do both of them good. Hopefully, Lloyd would be a steadying influence on her impulsive grandmother – unless she led him astray!

Joel got on well with everyone. They were fascinated by his job as a tree surgeon, and he was particularly interested in hearing about Jay and Sonia's life in Canada. As Lexi watched him talking to Jay, sipping a glass of her dad's homemade wine, sporting the jumper she had knitted, she thought she had never seen him so relaxed. And for a man who didn't like Christmas, he certainly seemed to be enjoying himself.

'Time for the games now,' Craig suggested when everyone had eaten, drunk and chatted for a while. 'Shall we start with charades?'

Ryan jumped to his feet. 'Bags I go first.'

Lexi chuckled as she saw the expression on Joel's face. He evidently wasn't used to a noisy Christmas like this one. But he joined in eagerly when it was his turn, choosing to act out a film. Lexi guessed it straight away, when he hilariously opened his mouth wide and pointed inside. '*Jaws*!'

It was her turn next. She chose a book, *The Kite Runner*, which Lloyd guessed – to everyone's surprise.

'I've got a copy, it's a good read,' he said.

Everyone had a turn, even Toby, who mimed driving a car. '*Cars!*' They all shouted, and he beamed in delight.

After a couple more games, Toby was so exhausted he fell asleep and Sonia took him up to bed. With Toby now fast asleep, and Sonia assuring everyone he would sleep through anything, the fun got even more raucous, ending with a game of Balloon Body Pop. Everyone got into pairs, Granny Mabe with Lloyd, and Lexi with Joel, as the others were coupled up. A blown-up balloon was given to each pair, and they had to work together to burst it using just the pressure of their two bodies. As everyone was rather tipsy by now, it was hilarious. Joel and Lexi stood back to back, pressing the balloon between them, then Joel lost his balance and fell, and Lexi fell on top of him, and the balloon popped with a loud bang. Everyone clapped and cheered.

As they both scrambled to their feet, triumphant, Joel gave Lexi a spontaneous hug. 'We make a great team!'

His sexy green eyes looked into hers and she felt herself drown in the deepness of them. Then he was holding her closer, his lips brushing her cheeks, and she felt a tingle run down her spine. She pulled away, feeling her cheeks flush, conscious that the others were watching them. What was all that about?

Joel was looking awkward now. 'Well, it's been great, everyone. I've really enjoyed myself, but I'd better be off and sleep off this wine. If you're okay with leaving now, Lloyd?' He grinned at Jay and Ryan. 'You're right, it is toxic!'

'Fine by me,' Lloyd said. 'It's getting late now.'

'Don't walk home, get yourselves a taxi,' Lexi said, suddenly worried at the thought of the two men walking home in the snow. Joel looked unsteady on his feet.

'I'll phone one for you, we've got the number of someone

very reliable.' Paula picked up her phone and dialled for a taxi. It arrived a little while later, and Lexi and Ryan walked out with them to make sure no one slipped.

'Bye, Lexi. Thank you for a lovely day,' Joel slurred. He held out his arms and wrapped Lexi in a big hug, then kissed her soundly on the lips.

And for a moment, she kissed him back, then realised Ryan and Lloyd were watching, and stepped back.

Joel's eyes gazed into hers, and her stomach fluttered as if a butterfly was trapped inside it. Then he waved and got into the back of the taxi.

As Lexi lay in her bed that night, her thoughts drifted to Joel, the way he'd looked at her, how his lips had felt when he'd kissed her. How she had wanted to stay there in his arms and kiss him back.

It was the wine, she reminded herself. Her father's wine always was toxic. Joel would be embarrassed about it in the morning. Like she'd been after she'd spontaneously kissed him for saving the carol service.

It's Christmas, everyone is full of goodwill at Christmas, she told herself as she finally drifted off to sleep.

Chapter Thirty

Monday, the day after Boxing Day

When Lexi woke up the next morning, it was all quiet and she went downstairs to find the house almost deserted apart from Granny Mabe in the kitchen making tea and toast.

'Want some?' she asked.

'Yes, please. And some paracetamol.' Lexi sat down and massaged her temples. 'That was quite a night,' she said with a groan.

Granny Mabe grinned at her. 'It sure was. I can't believe that you got into a drinking challenge with Ryan and Jay. You know what your dad's wine is like.'

'I know but we'd already had a few drinks then Ryan challenged us all to see who could drink a glass of dad's wine the fastest ... and well it seemed a good idea at the time.' God her head was thudding. How many glasses had they drunk before she finally won? She took the glass of water and tablets that her gran offered her. 'Thanks.' She swallowed them down, then asked. 'Where is everyone? Surely I'm not the only one that's overslept?'

'Nope, they're all in bed fast asleep, apart from your mum and dad who are in the bakery.'

Of course, the bakery was open until midday. 'I'll go and give them a hand as soon as I've had breakfast and a shower,' Lexi said. 'I'm sure they're both tired, too.'

'We all went to bed and left you younger folk to it, once Joel and Lloyd went home. Let you all have a catch up.'

Lexi picked up the piece of toast her gran had made her, and took a bite, chewing it slowly. She couldn't remember much after Joel and Lloyd had gone home. A few snatches of conversation with her brothers. Talking to Ben.

Her eyes widened. When did she talk to Ben?

'Morning, or is it afternoon?' Ryan stumbled into the kitchen, hair standing on end, still looking half asleep. 'What a night!' He rubbed his hand through his hair. 'I've come to get a cup of coffee for me and Nell.'

'Sit yourself down and I'll make it,' Granny Mabe told him.

'Thanks, Gran.' He sat down by Lexi. 'How's your head?'

'Thumping,' she admitted. 'I can't believe I drank so much. I've never been one for drinking a lot.'

'You were on a mission, after that call with your ex . . .'

So she really had spoken to Ben. Lexi searched through her memory for some recollection of the conversation. 'Please tell me that I didn't call him.'

'Nope, he called you, don't you remember?'

'I remember talking to him, but I can't remember the conversation. My head is like fog.'

'Dad's wine!' they both said together.

'Can you remember what I said? Did I tell you what he said?' she asked.

'Not much.' Ryan frowned. 'You said something about having a new boyfriend called Joel.'

'I didn't!'

'Yup. Then you ended the call and put your phone in your bag. I think he was asking you to give him another chance. But don't worry, Joel had gone by then.'

'Thank God for that.' Lexi sunk her head into her hands. Ryan's words had flicked the memory switch in her brain and now the fog was clearing. Ben had messaged her a few times that evening, she recalled, and she had ignored him. Then he'd phoned. She didn't know what had made her answer, the wine probably. He'd been whispering, as if he didn't want Rosa to hear, telling her he was sorry and wanted her back. She remembered telling him that she didn't want *him* back, she'd moved on, got herself a new boyfriend. Had she really said his name was Joel? How embarrassing. Still, if it kept Ben from pestering her, and Joel hadn't been there to hear it, there was no harm done.

'Be careful with these, they're hot,' Granny Mabe said, passing two mugs of steaming coffee to Ryan.

'Thanks, Gran, I will.' Ryan nodded at Lexi. 'I thought there was something between you two, but I didn't realise you were an item. Good on you.'

'There's nothing between us. I was just trying to stop Ben from pestering me, and Joel was probably the first name that came into my head.'

'What? The way you two were gazing at each other all evening – and that kiss – there's definitely something brewing between the two of you, even it if hasn't actually taken off yet.'

He walked out of the room with the coffee, leaving Lexi to gaze after him, speechless.

'He's right, there was definitely a connection between you and Joel,' Granny Mabe told her. She wiped her hands on her apron. 'Right, I'm off now. People to see.'

'Not more yarn-bombing?' Lexi asked.

'Not today.' Granny Mabe winked. 'Just a coffee and chat with friends.'

Lexi finished her tea and toast, then went up to shower. She looked around for her bag, found it under the chair by the bed, where she must have put it last night, and checked her messages. There were several from Ben, telling her how much he loved her and begging for another chance, then a five-minute phone call, then another message.

I can't believe that you've moved on so quickly. Didn't you love me at all?

Lexi felt anger rising in her as she read the message. Who did he think he was? He'd been cheating on her for months, then he had the cheek to accuse her of not loving him because she'd moved on? Not that she had, but Ben didn't know that. And she was going to keep it that way. At least then he would leave her alone. She put the phone back into her bag, then went for a shower.

He'd kissed Lexi. And she'd kissed him back. The memory of that kiss before he got into the taxi was embedded in Joel's mind and kept replaying over and over. The softness of her lips on his, how his heartbeat had quickened.

It was the wine, he told himself. He'd been warned that Craig's wine was potent, and it was. His head felt like someone was kicking a ball around in there.

'Woof woof!'

Sweetie was standing on the bed, barking at him.

'Okay, girl, I'm getting up now,' he told her, glancing at the clock. *Ten thirty!* Goodness, he must have zonked out.

He let Sweetie out in the garden for a bit, fed her, had some breakfast, then showered. He'd go and check on Lloyd, he thought, then take Sweetie for a walk. He was starting another job tomorrow, so wanted to spend a bit of time with the little dog today. She was more at ease with him now and he hoped that she'd be okay to stay at home while he went to work. He didn't want to keep relying on Lloyd, the man had his own life to lead. And seeing how close he and Lexi's gran were getting, and how he'd been chatting with her group of friends at the carol service, he had an idea that Lloyd's life was going to become busier – which was a very good thing.

An hour later, he was showered, dressed and feeling more human, now. He knocked on Lloyd's door.

'Come in, come in.' Lloyd looked delighted to see him. He bent down to stroke Sweetie. 'Hello, again.'

'I wanted to check how you are and to tell you that I think Sweetie will be okay to leave at home when I go to work tomorrow,' Joel said as he followed Lloyd into the lounge. 'I don't want to tie you down with looking after her. You must have things you need to do, too.'

'Well, actually, I am going out for a while. But I could check in on her when I get back and bring her home with me, if you want. That's if you're happy to give me a key to the house.'

'That would be great, thank you. I've got a spare key and I'd feel much happier at work if I know that someone is checking on Sweetie. Could I pop the key around later this evening?'

Lloyd nodded. 'Now, do you have time for a cuppa or are you off?'

'We're going for a walk but, yes, a cup of coffee before we go would be great. Thanks.'

'I want to thank you for making my Christmas such a pleasurable one,' Lloyd told him as he put the kettle on. 'Inviting me for dinner, then coming to the Fordes' with me yesterday, well, it's the best Christmas I've had for years. I must thank Lexi, too, when I see her.' He got two mugs out of a cupboard. 'It's made me think, I need to get out more, mix with people, instead of sitting in here, moping, thinking over the past. My Ruby's gone, and Rocco, well, he's an adult and I'm sure he's happy. I will try to get in touch with him but I've got to build my life now.'

It was a shame Rocco hadn't come to see his dad for Christmas, but maybe he would at some point, Joel thought. And at least Rocco knew that Lloyd wanted to see him, so he would be welcomed if he did turn up. The old man certainly had a spring in his step today. 'Mabe told me about a few senior groups I could join, seems there's a lot happening in this village that I didn't know about.' Lloyd made the coffee and handed a cup to Joel. 'I'm going to start living my life again.'

'That's good to hear, but you be careful with that Mabe, she'll get you joining her yarn-bombing team next.'

Lloyd's eyes twinkled. 'Actually, I can knit, and there are a couple of male members ...'

Joel raised an eyebrow. Was he serious?

Lloyd chuckled. 'Only joking. She's a great character, though, isn't she? They're a nice family. You and Lexi seemed to be getting on well. Shame she's only here for a few more days.'

'We're friends, and like you, Lexi has drawn me into her love of Christmas and made me reassess my life. You're right, this is a lovely village. When Hazel and Al come back from Dubai, I might think about buying a house here myself.'

'Now that, I'm glad to hear.'

Sweetie yapped at their feet. Lloyd looked down at her and grinned. 'And I think Sweetie is, too.'

After his cup of coffee with Lloyd, Joel and Sweetie set off for a walk around the village, stopping in at the bakery, where he was surprised to see Lexi serving behind the counter.

'I've taken over to give Mum a couple of hours off,' she told him. 'What can I get you?'

'If Sweetie's allowed in the tearoom, I was going to have tea and a scone,' Joel told her.

'Sweetie is definitely allowed,' Craig said. 'Why don't you join Joel, Lexi? You could do with a break, too.'

There was nothing he would like more, thought Joel, although, he felt a bit awkward after that drunken kiss yesterday, and guessed that Lexi did, too. He smiled at her. 'If you could, that would be great.'

Her eyes didn't quite meet his. 'Okay, grab yourself a table and I'll bring it over.'

There were a few people in the tearoom, and they waved to Joel as soon as he walked through, he recognised them from the carol service the other night. They exchanged a few pleasantries, and made a fuss of Sweetie, then he strolled over to the table by the window and pulled out a chair. Lexi joined him a few minutes later.

'How are you feeling?' she said. 'I had a right hangover when I woke up this morning. Mum, Dad and Granny went to bed after you left, but the rest of us sat up playing drinking games – with

Dad's homemade wine can you believe?' She shook her head. 'I'm regretting it this morning.'

'I had a bit of a headache, too. Your dad's wine is lethal.' He raised a hand, palm outwards. 'I know I was warned.'

Lexi chuckled. 'Never mind, it's Christmas.'

Joel took the tops off the cartons of jam and cream as he considered his words. 'I popped in to see Lloyd, and he looked so . . . animated,' he said slowly. 'As if he'd got a new lease of life. He said it was the best Christmas he'd had for years. And –' Joel swallowed – 'It's been the best Christmas I've had for years, too. That's thanks to you, Lexi.'

Her eyes met his and his heart skipped a beat. Did she feel it too, this connection between them?

Chapter Thirty-one

For a moment, Lexi couldn't find the words to reply. It was as if her tongue had got stuck in her throat. She took a sip of her coffee while she composed herself, then asked, 'Does that mean that you're now a Christmas convert, and will be putting up a Christmas tree every year?'

'I guess it does.' He gave her a mock-grimace. 'What have you done to me?'

She smiled. 'Brought a bit of Christmas cheer into your life, I hope. Like you have done for us, by rescuing the tree.'

'You've definitely done that,' he said softly.

His gaze rested on her face and her heart stilled. Then he lowered his gaze and cut his scone in half, spreading the jam on it then the cream.

'That's the Cornish way,' she said.

Joel looked up at her in surprise. 'Pardon?'

'In Devon, we put the cream on first, then the jam, but in Cornwall, they put the jam on first,' she explained.

'Really? I had no idea there were two different ways of doing it.' He bit into the scone, waiting until he had swallowed it before asking, 'Do I owe you an apology?'

'Sorry?' For a moment she was surprised.

'I kissed you yesterday. Twice. I was a bit tipsy, and I'm sorry if it was inappropriate.'

'Oh, don't worry about that. It's Christmas. Everyone kisses everyone at Christmas,' she said flippantly, not wanting to admit, even to herself, just how much that kiss had affected her. She bent down to stroke Sweetie to give herself time to compose herself.

Lexi thought about Joel's words after he'd left to continue his walk. She was so pleased that she had helped make both his and Lloyd's Christmas a good one, and she'd enjoyed Christmas too. More than she had thought possible when she had discovered that Ben was cheating on her. That had hurt, but over the last week, while she'd been in Lystone, the hurt had lessened and now she was beginning to realise that her relationship with Ben hadn't been a good one. She had just got into a comfort zone with him, and they'd got on well together, but in truth, there was no spark between them. It had taken the kiss with Joel yesterday to make her realise that. She hadn't felt that way when Ben kissed her for a long time. If ever. And the way Joel had looked into her eyes today, she'd felt like their souls were meeting, and for a few moments had been transfixed, unable to tear her eyes away from his.

Had it been the same for Joel?

What if it had? She was leaving soon, going back to Gloucester, so there would be no future for them, even if she *was* attracted to him. But meeting Joel had shown her that whatever feelings she'd had for Ben hadn't been love, because if she truly had loved him, a kiss from another man wouldn't have had such an effect on her, would it?

'You seem a bit faraway, love. Are you thinking about Ben? He's been texting you, asking you to take him back, hasn't he?' Her dad's voice brought her out of her thoughts.

'Yes, but I don't want to go back to him. I could never trust him again.'

'Are you sure? He seems quite repentant. Perhaps it was a one-off?'

Lexi shook her head. 'No, it had been going on for a while. Besides, I don't love him, I realise that now.'

'Well, you're better off without him, then.' Her dad squeezed her shoulder reassuringly. 'Look, it's gone quiet and we're closing soon, why don't you get yourself off?'

'I will, thanks, Dad.' She went into the back, took off her hat, gloves and apron, and pulled on her coat. She'd walked up to the bakery, wanting some fresh air, and intended to walk the long way back so that she could stop and look at the Christmas tree. She had no idea how long the tree would stand for, Joel had told her the council still wanted to chop it down, but at least they had had one last special Christmas. It had been perfect.

When she got there, she was surprised to see Joel standing by the tree, hands in pockets, deep in thought.

'Great minds think alike,' she said.

He turned around, looking at her in surprise. 'Lexi. What are you doing here?' Then he clapped his hand to his forehead. 'Sorry, that sounded a bit off. I guess you just wanted to look at the tree, like me.'

'It's so pretty, isn't it? Even without the lights switched on.' Joel had taken the generator back home with him after the carol service on Christmas Eve, not wanting to risk it getting stolen. 'I hope the council change their mind about chopping it down.'

'Me too, but I'm not convinced they will. This is a prime spot, and more housing is desperately needed. Perhaps the villagers could find somewhere else for the carol service next year.'

'I guess they could, but it wouldn't be the same.' She looked at him. 'It won't be your problem then, though, will it? Your sister will be back by the summer and I guess you'll have moved on.' The thought of Joel not being in Lystone saddened her.

'Yes, but I've been thinking of staying in the village, buying a house here.'

'Really?' That surprised her and she felt her heart uplift.

'Yes, the place is growing on me.' His eyes held hers. 'So, you'll probably bump into me when you come down to see your parents.'

She hoped so. She hated the thought of not seeing Joel again.

'Well, this is cosy! So this is Joel, your new fancy chap, is it?'

Lexi swung around at the sound of Ben's voice. He'd pulled up by the green in his car and was shouting out of the window. He opened the door and got out, hurt and anger written all over his face.

'Ben! What are you doing here?' she asked.

'Charming! That's a nice way to greet your boyfriend.' He strode over the grass to join them. 'I came to see you. I missed you. It looks like you didn't miss me.' He looked from Joel to Lexi. 'That didn't take you long, did it? You were supposed to be going away to spend Christmas with your family because your brother was coming over from Canada, and here you are, all over another man. Is this the one you told me about on the phone last night?'

'Now, look, Ben . . .'

'I don't think you should be talking to Lexi like that,' Joel said levelly.

'I'm not bothered what you think, mate. I'm her boyfriend. We live together. Hasn't she told you about me?'

'We're not living together, Ben, we're finished,' Lexi reminded him. 'You decided you preferred someone else.'

'So, you thought you'd pay me back and get someone else too.' Joel's expression hardened. 'You've got this all wrong.'

'So, you're not Joel?'

'Yes, I am, but you've jumped to the wrong conclusion. Lexi and I are just friends.'

Ben frowned. 'That's not what Lexi said last night.' He glared at her. 'So, you told me you and him were together just to make me jealous?'

'You told him we were together?' Joel was staring at Lexi in disbelief.

'Err . . .'

She saw the expression change in Joel's eyes to one she couldn't fathom.

'I love you, Lexi. That's what I came to tell you,' Ben said, coming towards her, his arms outstretched.

Joel looked from Ben to Lexi. 'Look, I think I'd better leave you two to sort this out,' he told her, then turned and walked off.

Lexi was so outraged, she felt like hurling something at Ben. 'How dare you! How dare you make out that we're still together when you've left me for someone else?'

'That was a mistake. It's you I want. Please give me another chance. I'm begging you. I love you,' Ben pleaded, standing right in front of her now.

Then he knelt down in front of her and held out a small, velvet box.

'Lexi, will you marry me?'

Lexi couldn't answer, couldn't speak. She was staring over Ben's head at Joel, who had turned back and witnessed everything. His gaze met hers, before he continued across the road.

Chapter Thirty-two

'Lexi!'

She realised that Ben was still kneeling at her feet, holding out the little box, which he'd now opened to reveal a sparkling diamond ring.

'Please say yes. I love you. I'll never hurt you again, I promise.'

He was looking at her so devotedly, his tone so earnest. *He really means this.*

'I love you, Lexi. And you love me, I know you do. Please don't let my stupid mistake split us up. I'll spend the rest of my life making it up to you, I swear.' His voice quivered with emotion. 'We were so good together once. We can get that back. Be even stronger. I realise how much you mean to me. How much I love you.'

She had loved him too, at least, she thought she had. She knew now, though, that whatever it was they'd had between them had gone.

'Lexi?' Ben's face was upturned, pleading.

She slowly shook her head. 'I'm sorry, Ben, but I can't marry you. I don't love you.'

He looked stunned. He scrambled to his feet and reached out for her. 'You do. I know you do.'

'No, I don't. I thought I did, but being here and having some space to think has made me realise that I don't. And you don't love me either. Not really. We were just comfortable together. Go back to Rosa.'

'I can't.'

'What? Why not.'

He fidgeted, his eyes not quite meeting hers. 'We've finished. Because I realised that I loved you,' he added quickly.

'Or did she kick you out?'

She knew by the look on his face that it was true. Thank goodness she'd turned down his proposal.

'Goodbye, Ben,' she said. Then she walked off, head held high.

'Lexi!' Ben shouted. 'It was all a mistake. It's you I love!'

She ignored him and walked over the road, fuming all the way home. Ben obviously thought that she would jump at his proposal, forget about him and Rosa, and be happy to go back to how they were. Did he think she was stupid? She thought back to their relationship. She liked a quiet life and had never questioned it when Ben had been working late, or gone out with his friends. Had she been too trusting? Too much of a walkover? But what was the point of being with someone if you didn't trust them? She was still furious when she arrived home.

Her mum looked up from the sandwich she was buttering as Lexi strode in. 'You look like you need a strong cup of tea.'

'I do.' Lexi bit her lip, trying to find the words to tell her mother what had happened. 'Ben turned up and he proposed to me.'

Her mum paused and met her eye. 'And that's a bad thing?'

'Very bad.'

Lexi sank down at the table, and buried her head in her hands. She couldn't believe that Ben had turned up like that, completely out of the blue, and at the most awkward moment ever. Joel had looked really taken aback. She remembered him telling her that his ex had cheated on him, and hoped he hadn't thought she was intending to do the same to Ben. She'd told him that she'd broken up with Ben though, she reminded herself. And there was nothing between her and Joel, was there, apart from a quick hug and thank-you kiss on Boxing Day. Why on Earth had she told Ben that Joel was her new boyfriend when he'd phoned her last night? She groaned. How embarrassing. She'd have to call in on Joel later and explain.

'Want to tell me about it?' her mum sat down beside her. 'The others are upstairs packing,' she added.

Lexi raised her eyes to hers, still stunned by the events. 'I went to see the Christmas tree and Joel was there. We were talking . . .'

Her mum waited.

Lexi licked her lips. 'Then Ben pulled up and shouted at me, accused me of cheating on him. The nerve of him!' Anger was taking over from the shock now. 'Next thing I know, Ben is getting down on one knee and proposing. And Joel saw it all! He walked off. He was obviously embarrassed.'

'I take it you told Ben where to go with his proposal?' her mum said gently.

'Yes, I did. As if I'd marry him after what he's done. It's not working out with that Rosa, so he's decided he wants to come back to me. Well, I don't want him back.'

Her mum patted her hand. 'Good for you. You deserve better. So, has Ben gone now?'

Lexi nodded. 'I think so. I walked off and left him there. I'm going to block him, so he can't phone me. If he comes to the house, will you tell him that I don't want to see him, please?'

'Of course I will.' Paula leant forward and asked her intently, 'And what about Joel?'

'Joel?' Lexi asked, a little embarrassed. Was it that obvious that she was developing feelings for him?

'You seem upset because he witnessed the proposal. Are you going to explain things to him?'

'Yes, I will later. It's a bit embarrassing, though.' She told her mother about Ben accusing her of cheating on him with Joel because of what she'd told him on Boxing Day.

'I'm sure he will understand that you were just saying it because you wanted Ben to realise that it was over and you've moved on,' her mum reassured her. 'Unless you do have feelings for Joel?'

Do I?

'I hardly know him.' She flicked her hair back behind her ears. 'I can't believe the cheek of Ben, though. I hope he isn't going to be a nuisance when I get back home.'

'Don't let him be. There are laws to protect you,' her mum told her. 'Seriously, Lexi, if you definitely don't want anything to do with him, make that loud and clear and slap it down if he still persists.'

'Don't worry, I will,' she promised. 'I was thinking, maybe I should stay a little longer? Give Ben time to get used to the situation? He can't come round to the flat if I'm not there, can he? He'll have to sort himself out.'

'Stay as long as you want, love. I was going to talk to you about it later. Jay and Sonia are going to London for a couple of days, then coming back to see the new year in before they go travelling.'

Jay had said that he wanted to show Sonia more of England, so they planned on going to Stratford and York before returning to Canada, Lexi remembered.

'Ryan and Nell are coming back down for New Year's Eve, too, so it will be lovely for you to be there,' her mother added.

Lexi liked the idea of seeing the new year in with her family. 'I'll stay until the weekend, then. I start back at school on Tuesday, so I can go home on Sunday afternoon,' Lexi decided. That would give Ben time to realise that she was serious. And time to explain things to Joel.

Or take things further with Joel?

She pondered the thought. She liked Joel, he was a softie under that strapping exterior, but she wasn't sure she wanted to take things any further. She probably needed a break from relationships for a while, to sort out her own life. Besides, she lived in Gloucester and Joel lived in Lystone and was thinking of making the village his permanent home. And, while it was only a couple of hours' drive away, it just made things more complicated.

That was assuming Joel was interested in *her*. And judging by his expression and how quickly he'd walked off when Ben had proposed, he wasn't.

That Ben seemed a right jerk, he hoped that Lexi didn't accept his proposal. In Joel's opinion, if someone cheated on you once, they'd do the same again. That's why he hadn't given Toni another chance. That, and the fact that he no longer loved her. It had taken him a while to get over her, but now he could see her for what she was. If she'd said she'd made a mistake and wanted him to take her back within the first couple of months, would he have? He wasn't sure. Ben and Lexi had only recently split up, so she must still be heartbroken. Would she give him another chance? He hoped not. She deserved better.

Lexi was such a warm-hearted person, though, that he was sure she believed in second chances and might just say yes. He hated to think of her getting hurt all over again. Not that it was any of his business. They were merely acquaintances.

That kiss on Boxing Day didn't feel like we were only acquaintances.

He shouldn't read more into that, or the kiss and hug she'd given him for rescuing the Christmas tree, than she had meant. She was simply saying thank you.

He remembered her boyfriend's words. 'So this is Joel, your new fancy chap, is it?' Evidently, Lexi had told him that she was seeing Joel. Was that to make Ben jealous, or to make him keep away from her? Whatever it was, despite Ben's initial outrage, he'd got down on one knee and proposed to her. Lexi had seemed stunned, and, feeling like an intruder as well as an idiot, Joel had walked away and left them to it. He guessed that was probably the last time he'd see Lexi. Her boyfriend – fiancé – would surely be whisking her back home, after celebrating their engagement with her family, of course.

Maybe that was a good thing, he was getting too fond of Lexi. After Toni, he'd promised himself that he would take his time to get to know someone before plunging into a relation-ship in future, but he could feel the pull of attraction to her. It was because he'd got caught up in her love for Christmas, and she had a good nature, that was all. He'd feel different once Lexi went home, with Ben.

As he walked along the street towards home, Joel saw a car parked outside Lloyd's house and a man walking up the path, away from the front door. It was unusual for Lloyd to have visitors. He frowned, the man looked a bit familiar . . . then, as the man opened the gate and he could see his face clearer, he realised who it was. Rocco! He must have considered what Joel said to him and come to visit Lloyd. Joel glanced at the closed front door. He would have thought that Lloyd would be standing on the doorstep waving him off. Had things gone wrong between them? He quickened his pace, hoping that maybe he could help patch things up.

'Hello! You came to visit your father. That's great!' he said as Rocco took his keys out of his pocket and pressed the button to open the door of his car.

'I did, but he's out. Which is probably a good thing. It was a stupid idea to drop by after all this time.' He opened the driver's door. 'Tell him I popped by.'

'No, don't go. Lloyd won't have gone far,' Joel said. 'Come and have a cup of tea with me, I'm sure he'll be back soon.'

Rocco hesitated. 'I haven't got much time . . .'

'Look, you've come all this way, please at least give him half an hour. I expect he's popped to the shop.'

Rocco nodded. 'Okay. Half an hour.' He closed the door and locked his car, then followed Joel down the path.

'So, how long have you known my dad?' Rocco asked, after Joel had made a cup of tea and they were both sitting in Joel's kitchen.

'Only a couple of weeks, I've just moved in. This is my sister's house.' Joel explained about his sister and partner moving to Dubai.

Rocco looked surprised. 'You've got friendly real quick then, haven't you?'

He had, hadn't he? Thanks to Lexi. He wasn't going to think about Lexi, she was probably engaged to Ben by now. 'I guess Christmas has brought us closer together. I invited Lloyd here for Christmas Day, and we both spent Boxing Day at a friend's house.'

'Blimey, this is a close community.'

'Close enough for me to know that he really wants to see you and would be devastated to know that you came to see him today when he was out. He misses you.'

'I miss him too, but there was a lot of bad stuff said. I was never that close to my dad when I was growing up, so when Mum died . . . Well, we had a few arguments and I left. Haven't been back since.'

'Until I said he wanted to see you? Is that what made you come today?'

Rocco looked thoughtful. 'I guess so. I've got a child, too, now, Erin. She's three, and a bit of a handful, but I adore her and I couldn't bear the thought of losing touch with her when she gets older. It made me realise that my dad might feel the same.'

They chatted for a while, then Rocco glanced at his watch. 'I really do have to go. Tell Dad I'm sorry I missed him, and I'll call back again.'

'Please make sure you do, and maybe you could bring your family with you? I think that would mean a lot to him, and it would help break the ice.'

Rocco nodded. 'I was wondering whether to, but I wanted to check how things were between us first. I don't want to introduce Erin to a grandfather if it's not going to be a long-term relationship.' He held out his hand. 'Good to meet you, Joel. Thanks for the tea and for the advice.'

'You're welcome.' Joel couldn't help feeling disappointed as they walked towards his front door, knowing that Lloyd would be upset that he'd missed his son. 'If he's out when you call next time, give me a knock. I'm happy for you to wait here. Or maybe I can give you my phone number and you could give me a ring when you're planning your next visit and I can see if he's in?' *And make sure he stays in!* 'I won't tell him that you're on the way.'

'That's kind of you.'

They were outside now. Joel reached in his pocket for his wallet and took out a business card, then handed it to Rocco.

'Thanks, mate.'

Joel watched as Rocco walked up the path. If only he could message Lexi and ask if she knew where Lloyd was, tell her what was happening, but if he did that now it might cause trouble between her and Ben, who had obviously thought she and Joel were having an affair. He should tell Lexi, though, getting in touch with Rocco had been her idea.

'Rocco!'

Joel and Rocco both turned at the shout.

Lloyd was walking towards them with Granny Mabe. 'Rocco, is that you?'

Rocco paused, as if wondering what to do next. Then his face broke into a smile and he almost sprinted towards his father, enveloping him in a big hug. 'Dad.'

'Oh my goodness, Rocco! I can't believe it's you.' Lloyd had tears in his eyes.

Joel swallowed a lump in his throat. Lexi should be here to see this, this had been her doing, she was the one who had insisted they try to find Rocco.

Granny Mabe would tell her. If Lexi hadn't already returned to Gloucester with her fiancé.

Chapter Thirty-three

Lexi's phone buzzed to announce an incoming call. *Not Ben again!* was her first thought. She really had to block him. She glanced apprehensively at the screen and saw that it was Lloyd. Although she had given him her number, this was the first time he'd phoned her. She answered the call, her pulse racing a bit – she hoped nothing was wrong. 'Hello, Lloyd.'

'Lexi, you'll never guess what happened ... Rocco came to see me today.'

'What?' She could hardly believe what he was saying. 'He did? How? That's amazing.' The words tumbled out of her mouth, she was so pleased and surprised. She knew that this would mean a lot to Lloyd. She could imagine his face when Rocco knocked on the door. He must have come because of what Joel had said to him. She wondered if Joel knew, or if Lloyd had phoned her first. Not that it mattered.

'It's marvellous, isn't it?' She could hear the delight in his voice. 'And I almost missed him. He turned up when I was out with your gran, would you believe? Thank goodness Joel saw him and persuaded him to have a cup of tea with him while he waited. In fact, Rocco had given up on me and was about to get in his car when I finally came home.'

So Joel does know.

'You were out with Gran?'

'Yes, I've joined the Bridge Club. They're a great bunch.'

Well, the day was full of surprises, Lexi thought as she listened to Lloyd talking about Rocco and how he was going to bring his wife and son to meet Lloyd on New Year's Day. 'I've got my family back, and friends, thanks to you and Joel. I can't thank you enough.'

'I'm so pleased.' Lexi promised to pop in and have a cup of tea with him in a little while, so he could tell her all about it, then finished the call. While she was pleased for Lloyd, she couldn't help feeling miffed that Joel hadn't told her about Rocco turning up. He knew how much she had wanted to reunite Lloyd with his son. He could have at least texted her.

Was he that annoyed with her for telling Ben that they were together, that he was freezing her out? She guessed it did sound bad, she'd have to explain when she saw him.

And actually, it was a good thing that Joel had walked off like that, or he wouldn't have been home in time to stop Rocco from driving off. Everything happens for a reason, her gran always said. Maybe this incident with Ben and Joel had happened to stop her getting too close to Joel. She needed to sort out her life, not get involved with another man, especially one that lived a two-hour drive away. She'd rushed into a relationship with Ben and look where that had got her. If she got together with anyone again, then she wanted it to be with someone who shared the same interests, who was a homebody like her, who adored Christmas and family times and animals. And that didn't seem like Joel. Although, he was a softie with Sweetie and he had saved their Christmas tree and worn the Christmas jumper she had knitted, she reminded herself. She grabbed her bag and car keys, not fancying another walk, and set off to see Lloyd.

'Lexi! Come in!' Lloyd gave her a big hug, a wide grin on his face. 'You have made my Christmas,' he told her. 'I can't thank you enough for bringing my son back into my life, and such good friends like Mabe and her Yarn Warriors. My life has been transformed.'

'You're more than welcome,' she told him, stepping inside. 'I'm so pleased that Rocco came to see you. And that he's bringing his family, too.'

'So am I. I was silly to let things carry on as they did. I should have apologised straight away, not let this distance grow between us. Family is far more important than a stupid argument.' He looked at Lexi, his eyes shining. 'I've got a little granddaughter, would you believe? Her name is Erin and she's only three. I can't wait to meet her.'

Lexi had never seen the old man look so happy.

'Will you stay for a cuppa?' Lloyd asked. 'I've not long boiled the kettle.'

'I'd love to. Tea please.'

'I'll only be a tick.' Lloyd disappeared into the kitchen. He really had a spring to his step today, Lexi thought. He was like a different man to the one she'd met last week. And such a lot had happened in that time. He'd met Granny Mabe, been reunited with his son, and got a whole new bunch of friends and interests, so it seemed.

'Here we are,' Lloyd came in with a tray set with two mugs, a teapot, sugar bowl and milk jug.

'Thank you.' Lexi looked up as there was a knock at the door.

'Do you want me to get that for you?' she asked as Lloyd was sitting comfortably, sipping his tea.

'Thanks. It's been like Piccadilly Circus here today.' He looked pleased, though, and was obviously enjoying so many visitors.

Lexi went to open the door and was surprised to see Joel standing there.

'Oh, hello.' He sounded awkward. So, he was annoyed with her.

'Hello. Lloyd messaged me about Rocco coming to see him, so I dropped by,' said Lexi. 'I was going to come and see you in a bit.'

He raised an eyebrow. 'To tell me your good news?' He looked at her left hand, as if expecting to see a ring there. 'Congratulations on your engagement, I'm very pleased for you. I presume you are going back home now.'

'I'm staying until the new year, my brothers are coming back then too so we can all see the new year in together.' She swallowed as his eyes held hers. 'And I'm not engaged.'

'But . . .'

'I turned him down. I told you that we'd split up. It seems that the woman Ben cheated on me with has kicked him out, so he's decided that I'm the love of his life after all. However, I've decided that I don't feel the same way.' She met his eyes. 'I'm sorry that I pretended me and you were together. I was a bit tipsy – too much of my dad's wine – and wanted Ben to leave me alone. He kept phoning and wouldn't take no for an answer.' She was gabbling now but couldn't seem to stop herself. 'I didn't think he would come down here. I didn't mean to embarrass you. I was hoping that if Ben thought I was with someone else he would leave me alone.'

'I see.' He gaze was still on her face. 'So, you had no idea he was going to turn up and propose.'

'Of course not.' She felt her cheeks flush. 'I feel awful about involving you in this.'

'Don't worry about it. I completely understand.' His face broke into a wide smile. 'I have to say that I'm pleased that you aren't going back home yet.'

Her heart skipped a beat. Did he want her to stay longer because he was going to miss her? As she would miss him. 'You are?'

He nodded and she held her breath, her eyes on his face. He was looking at her so solemnly, as if he was about to say something serious, but then he grinned. 'I need some help taking the lights and yarn-bombings from the tree tomorrow. I daren't keep them up any longer, I don't want to get on the wrong side of the council. We're hoping to get some more work from them.'

She pushed back her disappointment. 'And you want me to help?'

'Well, those woolly things are going to be very wet and dirty now.'

'So, I get the messy job?'

'Strictly speaking, it was your family who made the mess . . .'

His green eyes were twinkling as he bantered with her, and she was suddenly very pleased that she'd decided to stay until the new year.

'Well, if you put it like that . . .'

Joel's face broke into a grin.

'Are you two coming in, or are you just going to make out on the doorstep?' Lloyd shouted.

Make out?

They both spluttered with laughter.

'I think you'd better come in,' Lexi said.

'Anyone want cake?' Lloyd asked, appearing out of the kitchen with another mug of tea and a plate loaded with slices of fruit cake. 'Mabe brought this around earlier when she picked me up to take me to play bridge.'

So, her gran was visiting Lloyd and bringing him cake. It was wonderful that they had become such good friends.

'I'm going to have to go on a diet when I get home, with all the tea and coffee I'm drinking and cake I'm eating,' Lexi said, rubbing her stomach.

'Me too,' Joel agreed. 'Mind you, taking down the decorations from the tree tomorrow should get rid of any extra calories we've put on.'

'I heard you telling Joel that you're staying until New Year, Lexi? If you both have time perhaps you could pop in and meet Rocco and his family.' Lloyd put the plate down on the table. 'It's thanks to you two that he's back in my life.'

'It's Joel who found him . . .' said Lexi.

'And you who persuaded me to . . .' said Joel.

'I'd love to meet them, I'll definitely try to pop in, I could go home later on Sunday, it's only a couple of hours drive,' Lexi told Lloyd. It wouldn't take her long to sort out the remaining lesson plans. And to be honest, she wasn't looking forward to going back to her empty flat. Not after spending all this time with her family. The empty side of the bed, the empty side of the wardrobe, they were all reminders that Ben had gone.

And good riddance.

Yes, she knew that she was better off without Ben, and had realised as soon as she'd seen him today that she had no feelings for him. If she had loved him, and she seriously doubted it now, then she certainly didn't any longer. But it had been nice to live with someone, to have company, someone to share things with.

You don't need anyone. You're fine on your own. And you have friends you can share things with.

'So will I. What time are you expecting Rocco on New Year's Day?' asked Joel.

'After lunch. So, you've got time to recover if you have a wild New Year's Eve,' he said with a grin. 'About three be okay for you both?'

'Sounds good to me,' said Lexi.

'Me too,' Joel agreed. He winked at Lexi. 'Is there a wild New Year's Eve party we can go to?'

'Yep, there's one at the Olde Tavern,' she said, cutting off a bit of the cake with her fork. 'We're all planning on going to it. Join us if you want. Both of you.' She looked at Lloyd.

'Mabe's already asked me. I think I will pop along.'

Lexi and Joel exchanged a knowing glance. Granny Mabe was determined to get Lloyd out of his house and introduce him to the village social life.

'Don't look like that. Me and Mabe are merely good friends. Like you two,' he added mischievously. 'Now, it's good to see you, Joel, but did you pop around to see me or was there something you wanted?'

'Yes, I've come to drop off my spare key so that you can check on Sweetie tomorrow for me.'

Lloyd clapped his forehead with his hand. 'Ah, of course. She can stay with me for the afternoon, I've no plans to go back out again.'

'Thanks. I really appreciate it.' Joel turned to Lexi. 'Andy's arriving at ten with the platform. Would you be able to come and help get the yarn-bombing off the tree then?'

'No problem. Should we ask Gran and her friends, too, or do you prefer to do it ourselves?'

'I think we'd be quicker by ourselves. We can put it all in a bag and you can give it to your gran, perhaps?'

'Sure. I'll see you on the green at ten, then.' She finished her cake. She was ridiculously pleased to be spending more time with Joel. *He's a good friend, that's all*, she told herself.

'I shall miss you when you return home after the weekend,' Lloyd told her. 'I hope you call in to see me next time you visit your family.'

'I will, I promise,' she told him. She hadn't been able to come down and see her family often in the last year or so, not with the restrictions, but she intended to make up for that.

And maybe she'd even bump into Joel now and again. The thought made her feel warm and happy.

Chapter Thirty-four

They all went out for a family meal that evening to celebrate their wonderful Christmas. Jay and Sonia were
leaving early in the morning to do a bit of sightseeing, whilst
Ryan and Nell were going home in the afternoon as they had
to go to work the next day.

'I'm so glad that we managed to all get together,' Jay said. 'It's
been a brilliant Christmas. And I'm looking forward to us all
seeing in New Year together. Mum said that you're staying over
too, sis?' he said to Lexi.

'Yes. I've got nothing to rush back to and it would be good
to spend a few more days down here.'

'Mind, me and your dad don't fancy coming out to the pub,
so we'll look after Toby for you, Jay,' their mum offered. 'You
and Sonia have a good time.'

'That would be wonderful,' Sonia said. 'If you're sure you
don't mind.'

'Of course we don't, it's lovely to spend time with our little
grandson.'

'Are you going back Sunday or Monday?' Jay asked Lexi.

'Sunday, but not until later on the afternoon. I've still got a bit of work to prepare before school opens. I've got a knitting project to finish, too, but there's no rush for that.'

'Maybe you can start a yarn-bombing knitting group in Gloucester,' Granny Mabe suggested.

'I think one militant in the family is enough,' Craig retorted. 'Your gran's even got herself a new boyfriend, by the sound of it. Her and Lloyd are getting to be quite an item. Especially if they're seeing New Year in together.'

Granny Mabe rapped her spoon on his wrist. 'That's enough cheek, young man. I'm still your mother, you know.'

Everyone laughed.

It was a fun evening. Little Toby was exhausted by the time they got home, and Sonia took him straight up to bed. 'I think I'm going to turn in myself, we've got a long journey tomorrow,' she said, stifling a yawn.

'Me too,' Jay agreed, swigging the last of his coffee and standing up. 'Night, everyone. See you in the morning.'

Lexi had to admit that she was tired, too. She was glad she'd decided not to go home yet. It would be good to see New Year in with her family. And to spend a bit more time with Joel, now they had sorted things out. He was turning out to be a good friend.

She switched off the light and settled down to sleep, but her mind kept replaying that Boxing Day kiss, and the warmth in Joel's eyes when she had told him she was staying until New Year. She was going to miss him. Would he miss her?

Jay, Sonia and Toby were gone by nine the next morning, and shortly afterwards Lexi headed straight for the green. Joel and

Andy were already there, and the lights had been taken off the tree. 'Did you two get here at the crack of dawn?' Lexi asked, suppressing a yawn. Despite being exhausted when she went to bed, she hadn't slept very well, thoughts of Joel occupying her mind far too much. 'I thought you said to be here for ten.'

'For you, yes, but we got here at nine,' Joel told her. 'I wanted to get the lights down before you arrived. Then I could take the yarn-bombs down from higher up the tree, and you and Andy can do the bottom.'

Lexi knew that a lot of people were back at work today. 'Do you think someone from the council might check on the tree today?' she asked.

'I wouldn't put it past them. There's been some pictures on social media, and the local paper has run a report about the carol service, so the council will be aware we decorated the tree. If I can get it down today, I think they might be okay about it. I don't want any bad feeling that could affect us working with them again.'

Lexi remembered how disapproving of the yarn-bombings the man and the woman she'd seen when she first arrived had been. Would they inform the council? She didn't want Andy and Joel to get into trouble when they'd been so kind as to decorate the tree for them.

'We'll have it all down in no time,' she said and immediately set to work taking off the festive woollen baubles from the bottom branches of the tree. They were wet, because of the snow, and difficult to take off, she could understand what Joel meant when he said that yarn-bombing tree trunks could damage them. Andy was taking the knitted baubles off the other side of the tree, while Joel was on the platform taking them off the higher branches. It was a slow process.

'Here, let me give you a hand with that. After all, we're responsible for it.' It was Granny Mabe, walking across the green towards them. 'I'll get some more help, too.' She took her phone from her bag and made a couple of phone calls. Then she marched over to the tree and started taking off some of the knitted baubles on the opposite side of the tree to Lexi whilst Andy joined Joel on the platform.

Within ten minutes, half a dozen of the Yarn Warriors arrived, carrying big plastic boxes. 'We can put the baubles in here,' one of them said. They all set to work, and soon the tree was bare again. Lexi was pleased to see that they had also taken the yarn-wrappings off the lamp posts.

'Thanks again for putting lights on the tree for us, and helping us to decorate it,' one of the women said to Joel and Andy. Then they picked up the boxes of grubby, wet knitted baubles and carried them away.

'I've got to be off, too, mate. See you again soon.' Andy hitched the platform to the back of his truck and was off.

Lexi put her hands in her pockets and studied the now-bare Christmas tree. She always hated this part, when the Christmas decorations were taken down and everything looked dull again. 'Do you think the council will still chop the tree down?' she asked.

'I've no idea. It depends how much they want to build the houses here,' Joel replied. 'Maybe now the council have seen how much the tree means to the villagers, they might reconsider.'

'We have to keep fighting it. I'll still continue with my petition, even when I go back home. And I'm sure my parents and other folk will, too,' Lexi said.

'Are other village events held on the green?' Joel asked. 'It would help if we could show the council that it's an important part of village life.'

That was a good idea, Lexi thought. 'There was when I was a child. I remember the summer fayre, and picnics. I'll ask my parents tonight – they'll know. I've lost touch a bit.'

'Has it been good to be in the village again? Do you miss living here?' Joel asked.

Lexi thought about it. She had loved living in Lystone as a child, although, as a teenager, she had found it boring and couldn't wait to get away. She'd enjoyed being with her family again this past week or so, being involved in the village community and meeting Joel. However, she loved her life in Gloucester, too, and the school she taught in. 'I don't think I'd like to live here again' she said finally. 'I've really enjoyed my visit, though, and intend to come down and see my folks more often. What about you?' she asked, suddenly remembering about his parents in Scotland. 'Do you visit your parents much?'

'No, they're busy, working all hours in A&E,' he told her. 'They're doctors so they're usually working all over Christmas too,' he added.

That could explain why Joel wasn't so big on Christmas. She had dismissed him as a grouch, when really he had probably had his childhood Christmases overshadowed by his parents working flat out at the hospital.

'Then I think I owe you an apology,' she said.

Joel raised an eyebrow. 'For what?'

'For lambasting you for not having enough Christmas spirit when your Christmases were probably ruined by people who had too much Christmas spirit – as in alcohol!'

He grinned. 'Yes, my folk were always on duty Christmas Day, so Hazel and I were sent to my grandparents. They gave us a wonderful Christmas, but I did resent my parents not being there when I was younger. As I grew older, I just didn't think it worth bothering about. I've enjoyed Christmas this year, thanks to you. Although, I don't think I will ever be as –' he paused as if searching for the correct word – 'enthusiastic about it as your parents.'

'Fanatical, you mean.' Lexi laughed. 'I guess they are over the top.'

'Anyway, if you really are sorry, you can make amends by joining me in the Olde Tavern for lunch,' Joel told her. 'The job I was going to do this afternoon has been postponed until next week.'

'I'd love that,' Lexi replied.

'One thirty be okay?' he asked. 'I need to get this equipment home and take a shower.'

'Perfect,' Lexi told him. She could do with another shower, too, she felt a bit mucky after handling all those wet woolly baubles and wanted to change into something a bit prettier than the chunky jumper and jeans she was wearing.

When she got back home, Ryan and Nell were about to leave. 'We were going to stop off at the green and say goodbye to you,' Ryan said, holding out his arms to hug her.

'I'm a bit grubby,' she warned him.

He put his arm around her shoulder and kissed her on the cheek. 'I don't care. See you on Friday.'

Nell obviously did care, as she stepped back and blew Lexi a kiss instead.

'See you on Friday,' Lexi told them.

The house felt empty when they had gone. Their parents

were at work and Granny Mabe was out. Funny how quickly she'd got used to a houseful of people, she thought, as she went upstairs to have a shower and get changed. Her little flat would seem so quiet when she went home.. Well, she'd get used to it. Her days would be full once school reopened on Tuesday, and there would be lesson planning and marking to do in the evenings, plus her knitting. Ben had hardly been home the past couple of months anyway.

You're better off without him, she told herself as she stripped off and got into the shower.

When she came back into the bedroom, she saw a message on her phone. It was from Fern. She quickly read it. 'How's things, hun?' Gosh, she hadn't even told Fern about Ben showing up yesterday and proposing to her! And she didn't have time to chat now. She was meeting Joel in half an hour. She sent a quick reply saying everything was fine and she would phone Fern later, then she selected a long cream V-neck sweater with three buttons on the sleeves and a scalloped edge, which she had knitted and designed herself, and a pair of port-wine-coloured skinnies, which she tucked into black-suede thigh-high boots. She pulled on a port-wine fedora and studied her reflection. *Edgy but casual,* she thought approvingly. Grabbing a black suede shoulder bag she shoved her purse, phone, tissues, lipstick and car keys inside it and set off.

A message pinged in and she saw it was from Joel.

Just arrived. Want me to get you a drink in?

Shandy, please. Leaving now, she texted back.

Joel was already sitting at a table by the window when she arrived. He waved and stood up, so she went over to join him, and pulled up the chair opposite. 'How's Sweetie?'

'Brilliant. I actually got to sleep in bed by myself last night. She never disturbed me once,' he told her. 'She's with Lloyd now.'

'That's great.' Lexi took a sip of her shandy. 'I think you're getting fond of her, aren't you?'

'I am,' he admitted. 'I like dogs, but I've never had one – my grandparents had a few on the farm, but my parents were always too busy, and so was I. I think I'd quite like one when I get my own place. A lot of the time, I could take a dog to work with me, if it was well-trained. I'm not always chopping down trees,' he added.

'I was thinking of getting a cat. Like you, I'm out all day so it wouldn't be fair to leave a dog cooped up in the flat, but a cat's different and I could get a litter tray. The trouble is, I was thinking of coming down to spend the weekend with my parents more often, and that would be awkward with a cat.'

Joel nodded. 'It's a problem, isn't it?' He cradled his glass thoughtfully. 'I guess you're going to miss your family when you go back.'

'I am. And I'm hoping that Ben doesn't make a pest of himself. That's one of the reasons I stayed down here a bit longer, to make sure he gets the message that I don't want anything more to do with him.'

Joel looked concerned. 'Are you worried that he'll harass you?'

She bit her lip. 'A bit. He'd been messaging me a lot, and I can't believe he came down like that and proposed.' She shook her head. 'I've blocked him now, and as I rejected his proposal he's hopefully finally accepted that we're over.'

'I had the same with Toni,' Joel told her. 'Our Decree Absolute is due to come through any day, but last week she asked me to meet her urgently. I thought it was something to do with the divorce, but she said she wanted me back. It had all been a mistake, she said, and she still loved me.'

Lexi felt her heart skip a beat. Was he getting back with his ex? 'What did you say?'

'I told her we were over, and there was no going back. Then she confessed the guy she'd left me for had dumped her.' His eyes met hers and she could see the empathy in them. 'Seems like our exes both think we're mugs.'

She nodded. 'Well, if it's taught me one thing, it's that I'm not putting anyone else first again. From now on, I'm going to live my life for me.'

Joel raised his glass. 'I'll drink to that.'

Chapter Thirty-five

Wednesday

'Come on, Sweetie. We're going out!' Joel called, holding out the lead. The little dog wagged her tail happily and trotted over to him. It was good to be able to take her with him today instead of leaving her at home. Last night, Lexi had suggested a sightseeing trip, and as he had no work lined up, he'd taken her up on it, seizing the chance to find out more about the area he was thinking of making his permanent home. Lexi had offered to do the driving, pointing out that her car was more comfortable than his van, and that Sweetie would be fine on the back seat in a restraint. He was looking forward to it. Although, if he was truthful, he'd rather be doing the driving; he'd heard too many tales of fatal driving accidents from his parents to be comfortable with anyone else driving him around – and he'd had a frightening near miss when he'd been in the car with Toni and she was arguing at him. He'd taken his mind off the road for a split second as she railed at him, but luckily had turned back in time to see the car that had spun around the bend out of nowhere and had taken action. The memory still made him shudder. If Toni had been driving, he knew that they would have crashed and there would have been nothing he could have done to avoid it. Which is why he had always insisted on doing the driving when they both went anywhere after that, but that suited Toni, though, as she could then have a drink. *Lexi isn't Toni*, he reminded himself, and anyway, most of the snow and ice had gone now, so the roads were perfectly safe.

Lexi arrived, dressed in her usual outfit of jumper and skinny jeans. Today, she was wearing a chunky cream cowl-neck and black skinnies with black boots. 'Did you knit that jumper too?' he asked. He'd complimented her on her jumper yesterday, and she'd told him she'd knitted it herself. He'd been impressed.

She nodded. 'I rarely buy jumpers, I usually knit them.' She bent down to make a fuss of Sweetie. 'Are you excited to be coming out with us?'

'I presume you have a coat in the car?' Joel asked, reaching for his parka.

'Yep. I can't drive in a coat, makes me feel all stuffed up.'

'Me too,' he agreed. 'And any time you get tired of driving and want me to take over, do say.'

'Will do,' she promised.

Joel put Sweetie's blanket on the back seat, then strapped the little dog in before slipping into the passenger seat and fastening his seat belt. Then they set off.

Lexi was a calm, steady driver, negotiating the bends in the narrow country lanes with ease, and Joel felt himself relaxing as he took the opportunity to study the scenery. Huge fields hosting cows or sheep and the occasional horse, and trees bare of their leaves but still hauntingly beautiful with their spindly branches reaching up to the winter-blue sky, lined the lanes. The frosted snow-spattered landscape was stunning, and he imagined it in all its summery glory, when the trees would be bursting with vibrant green leaves, the fields would be full of corn and other crops, and the sun would be shining down on lambs frisking in the grass and calves snuggling up to their mothers.

'It's amazing, isn't it?' Lexi said. 'Although, I'm sure the scenery is more dramatic in Scotland.'

'I don't think you can compare, they're both spectacular in their own way,' Joel replied, his mind going to the remote farm where his grandparents had lived, surrounded by miles of undulating countryside, broken only by hills and lakes and the magnificent forests where he had worked, full of willows, birch and tall pines reaching up to the sky.

They were driving through a quaint village now; thatched cottages lined cobbled streets. 'Do you fancy stopping off and having a look around?' Lexi asked. 'Give Sweetie chance to stretch her legs?'

'Sure. I wouldn't mind a coffee and snack, too, if you fancy it?'

'Sounds good to me.' She located the car park, found a parking space, and got a ticket, then they got out to explore the village. Sweetie trotted alongside Joel, sniffing everywhere, and stretching the lead to its full extent as she tried to explore. Lexi smiled as she watched her. 'She's enjoying all the different smells, I think.'

They soon found a tearoom, which was luckily dog-friendly, and ordered two coffees and a chicken salad sandwich each. When they'd finished, they took a slow walk around the village, then got back into the car and headed off again.

When they finally arrived back in Lystone, it was already dark.

'Thanks so much, I've really enjoyed today,' Joel said as Lexi pulled up outside his house. 'Do you fancy coming in for a drink?'

Lexi hesitated, she did but she was sure that if she stopped to have a coffee – or wine – with Joel they would get chatting and she would end up staying all evening. 'I'd love to but I've still got some lesson plans to do so I'd better get back,' she said. 'We can go sightseeing again tomorrow though, if you fancy it.'

Joel's eyes lit up. 'I'd love to, thank you.'

'I'll pick you up about ten,' Lexi said as Joel got out, then opened the back door and scooped Sweetie up.

'Look forward to it.'

She couldn't remember when she had enjoyed herself so much, Lexi thought the next afternoon, as she drove them back home after another day sightseeing. Joel was easy company and Sweetie was a darling. Today, wrapped up in coats, hats and scarves, and wearing trainers, they had taken a trip to nearby Dartmoor and spent a couple of hours walking around. They had taken a map with them, and followed one of the guided routes, not wanting to get lost on the moors. As they'd walked side by side, admiring the beauty of it all, she'd had an almost irresistible urge to reach out and take Joel's hand in hers, but she'd thrust her hand in her pocket instead. *Don't get carried away with the moment, you're just friends*, she'd told herself.

Sweetie had enjoyed herself, too, exploring the new sights and smells excitedly, tiring herself out so much she fell asleep on the back seat of the car on the way home. This time, Lexi accepted Joel's invitation to stop for a drink, choosing wine rather than coffee, and they chatted and laughed as they talked about their trip out. It had been nostalgic for her, too, and she felt a tug to return to the village of her childhood.

'I'd forgotten just how beautiful it is down here,' Lexi said as Joel refilled her glass.

'I have to admit that I've fallen in love with Lystone,' Joel told her. 'I love it that it's so close to Dartmoor, but not that far from the coast, either. I shall take a drive there one of the days.'

'My parents used to drive us over to the coast sometimes on a Sunday in the summer, and we'd spend the day there. It's only just over an hour away. I wish I could come with you, but I'm going back Sunday,' she told him. 'I've got such a lot to do before the school opens on Tuesday.'

'Maybe next time you come down?'

'Sure. I'd love to.' She would, too. She had never really spent time like this with Ben, and Joel was such good company. They'd got a lot more in common than she had originally thought.

'I'll hold you to that. I've enjoyed today.' Joel's voice was soft, and she glanced quickly at him, wondering if he was feeling a connection with her as she was with him, but Sweetie chose that moment to bark at the door, wanting to go out, and Joel stood up. 'Back in a sec.'

She'd finished her wine by the time he returned and decided to set off back home, after arranging to meet Joel in the Old Tavern the following evening. She was looking forward to seeing the new year in with her family and friends.

Her parents and Granny Mabe were in the lounge, watching the TV, and all turned to look at her when she walked in. *Uh-oh.* Had they been chatting about her?

'Have you had a nice day?' her mum asked, adding, 'I didn't do you anything to eat because I wasn't sure if you'd eat out, but there's plenty in the fridge if you want to help yourself.'

'Don't worry, Mum, we had a meal out. And, yes, it was lovely. We went to Dartmoor.'

'You two seem to be getting on well . . .' her mum said.

Thankfully, before they could question her any further, Lexi's phone rang. She took it out of her pocket. Fern. Heck, she hadn't phoned her back, or told her about Ben's proposal yet.

She answered. 'I'll make myself a hot chocolate and phone you back. Promise,' she said. Then she ended her call and gave her mum an apologetic look. 'Sorry, but I need to speak to Fern, then I think I'll go to bed. It'll be a late night tomorrow.'

'You go ahead,' her dad said. 'We'll be turning in ourselves soon.'

'Does anyone want a drink? Coffee, tea, hot chocolate?' Lexi asked.

No one did, so she made a hot chocolate for herself, popped a couple of marshmallows in it, and took it up to her room. Then she dialled Fern's number.

'You'll never guess what happened . . .' She filled her in about Ben turning up and proposing.

'OMG! And you've waited until now to tell me!' said Fern.

'Sorry, I've been out.' Lexi told her about her day trips with Joel.

'Well, you two seem to be hitting it off. Good. I'm glad you've got over Ben.'

'Joel's very nice and we're just friends, but, yes, I am definitely over Ben,' she replied. And, hopefully, Ben was over her, too, as she hadn't heard from him since she'd rejected his proposal. 'Now, that's enough about me. I want to hear all about your Christmas.'

She settled down on her bed to sip her hot chocolate and listen to Fern tell her all about Polly's latest escapades and how Phil, her partner, had turned the spare room into an office for them both. Fern and Phil both worked a couple of days in the office, and a couple at home, alternating the days so that they could look after Polly.

'Make sure you come by and see us when you come back,' Fern told her. 'I've still got your present here.' She paused, then added. 'You've not fallen in love with Lystone – and Joel – and decided to stay down there, have you?'

'No, of course not, although I've enjoyed seeing my family again, and Joel is good company. I'll be back home on Sunday and will see you one of the evenings next week, I promise. I've got presents for you all, too.'

After the call had ended, Fern's words repeated in her mind. She had to admit that part of her wished she could stay in Lystone, and she wasn't looking forward to going home. *It's only because it's Christmas and you've had such a good time with your family,* she reminded herself. *And Joel. You'll be fine when you settle back into your normal routine again.*

Chapter Thirty-six

New Year's Eve

New Year's Eve already. She'd been here two weeks and the time had flown, Lexi thought, as she rummaged through her clothes, wondering what to wear. She had only intended to come down for a week, so hadn't brought that many clothes with her, mainly jumpers, jeans and leggings, throwing one dress in the suitcase 'just in case'. She looked at it, it was red lace, with three-quarter sleeves, and finished just above her knee. It was a nice dress, and fitted her perfectly, and she'd popped some strappy silver sandals in her case, too, to wear with it. Should she wear that? Or stick to a pair of skinnies with the floaty silver top?

She looked around as there was a knock on the door. 'Are you decent?' Nell called.

'Yep, come in!' she shouted.

The door opened and both Nell and Sonia came in, dressed to cause a stir. Nell was wearing a short, sparkly silver dress that looked like she had been poured into it, with flesh-coloured tights and silver stilettos which emphasised her long, slender legs. Sonia was wearing a white, slightly longer floaty dress with strappy gold sandals that matched the gold braiding across the bodice of the dress.

Okay, not a good idea to wear her skinnies and silver top then.

'Wow! You both look incredible!' she said. 'And now I'm going to feel like Cinderella. I've only bought the one dress with me.'

'Let's take a look, we'll sort you out,' Nell said. And before she could stop them, both women were rummaging through her wardrobe.

'Hmm, it's pretty,' Nell said, holding up the red-lace dress. 'But it's a bit sort of "family party-ish".'

'Which is exactly why I brought it with me. I thought I might wear it on Christmas Day or Boxing Day, but decided against it as no one else dressed up.'

'What about the dress you bought when you were out shopping with us?' Sonia asked.

'I'd forgotten all about that,' Lexi said. The ankle-length peacock-blue dress with its thin straps, fitted bodice and long slit up the left side had caught her attention straight away. Sonia had encouraged Lexi to try it on, and when she'd seen how it hugged her figure, and left an expanse of leg tantalisingly exposed, she'd decided to buy it. It was an ideal fallback for a party, dinner dance or even a wedding. She had put it in her case, still in the carrier bag. She put her case on her bed, opened it up and took the dress out of the bag, then held it up. 'What do you think? Is it too dressy?'

'It's perfect.' Both women nodded approvingly.

'Put it on, then come and show us,' Nell said as she and Sonia both left the room to finish doing their make-up. They were both using Nell's room, as Toby was fast asleep in bed.

Lexi changed into the dress and studied her reflection in the mirror. It was sexy, but not too revealing, and suddenly she really wanted to look sexy tonight. Like Sonia and Nell did. Joel had only ever seen her wearing skinny jeans and jumpers, and just for once, she wanted him to see how good she could look, to see her as a sexy woman rather than a friend, to be attracted to her. Because, she admitted, she was attracted to him. She pulled on her silver sandals, turning this way and that so she could see her reflection. Was it too much for the local pub, even if it was New Year's Eve?

The door to Nell's room was open and both women were putting on lipstick. They turned as Lexi poked her head around the door and asked, 'What do you think?'

'You look amazing!' Nell said, clapping her hands in delight.

'You do!' Sonia nodded. 'Joel's eyes will pop out on stalks when you walk in.'

'I keep telling you, we're just friends,' she said, although, she was secretly pleased with Sonia's remark. That was exactly the reaction she was hoping to get from Joel.

Nell studied her face. 'You could do with a bit more make-up on.'

'I like the natural look,' Lexi protested, not wanting Nell to do her up like a painted doll.

'You don't have to go mad, some lash-lengthening mascara and a red lipstick would do it. Here, I've got a tube of mascara I haven't opened yet.' She handed it to her.

'Thanks. Let me pay you for it ...'

'Nah, it's not expensive. Call it a present. Do you have red lipstick?'

277

Lexi nodded. 'I'll go and put some on.'

She applied two coats of the lash-lengthening mascara and the red lipstick, then studied her reflection again. She used to wear mascara a lot in her late teens and early twenties when she went out with her friends, and had forgotten the difference it made. Her eyes looked wider and brighter, and the red lipstick made her lips look fuller.

Wolf-whistles from Nell and Sonia, who were now standing at the doorway behind her, made her turn and smile. 'I'm nothing compared with you two,' she told them.

'Rubbish. You're gorgeous. Come on, sis, let's knock the men dead.' Nell winked.

When they all went into the lounge, Jay and Ryan grinned appreciatively.

'We're going to be the envy of the pub tonight, walking in with three stunning ladies,' Ryan said.

Thank goodness I bought this dress, Lexi thought. She'd have felt a bit dowdy next to Nell and Sonia otherwise.

'Now, you all go and have a good time, and don't worry about Toby, he'll be absolutely fine. Me and your dad are happy to have a quiet evening, aren't we Craig?' said Paula.

'You bet we are,' Craig agreed. He was sitting on the sofa, feet up on the footstool. 'And keep an eye on your gran, make sure she gets home safe, will you?'

'Where is she? She can come with us,' Lexi said.

'She went out half an hour ago, while you were all getting ready. Said she was picking up Lloyd,' Paula told them.

'I don't think Granny M needs looking after, it's Lloyd we need to take care of,' Ryan quipped.

Lexi thought that he was probably right!

'Come on, then, let's see if we can get you there before your gran,' Craig said, getting up. He'd said he'd drop them all off at the pub, and then they would get a taxi back afterwards.

'Thanks, Dad! See you later, Mum,' they all called, grabbing their coats and setting off.

'Mind what I said about keeping an eye on your gran,' Craig said as he dropped them off in the pub car park.

'Your gran is hilarious. I hope I'm like her when I'm in my eighties,' Nell said as they all walked over to the pub.

'I wouldn't mind being like her now,' Sonia said. 'Most nights I'm that exhausted all I want to do is sleep.'

The pub was crowded when they walked in and the atmosphere buzzing. The landlord had laid on free nibbles of crisps and peanuts, and music was playing from the jukebox, whilst two singers were setting up in the corner – they were going to be the entertainment for the night. As she looked around Lexi felt a bit sad. This was the last night they would all be together. Tomorrow, her brothers were leaving, and so was she. She'd miss Lystone. And Joel.

Joel finished the video call to Hazel and Al, and glanced at the clock. Just gone nine, which made it just gone midnight in Dubai, so he had been able to see New Year in with his sister and her husband, who had both been delighted to see Sweetie, too, and now he could go and see New Year in with Lexi and her family. He let Sweetie out for a few minutes, then she settled into her basket, ready for sleep.

'Good girl. I won't be long,' he told her. He intended to stay till midnight, then come straight home. He was pretty tired himself.

He picked up his coat, choosing his black-leather jacket rather than his parka, even though it was chilly. It had stopped snowing, and was only a ten-minute walk to the pub. It had taken him a while to decide what to wear – he'd wondered how much people in the village dressed up to go to the local pub on New Year's Eve – but he had finally decided on a pair of black slim-leg jeans and a pale-blue, collarless, slim-fitting shirt, the top two buttons of which he left undone, and black boots. He pulled on his jacket, and turned to look at Sweetie, who opened one eye and wagged her tail at him. She'd be fine for a few hours, he thought, as he set off.

The Old Tavern was bustling, and more people were piling in. It certainly was a popular venue, he thought, as he stood by the doorway, scanning the crowd for Lexi's honey-brown hair. A place had been cleared to the left of the bar, and a man and woman were setting up a microphone and a deck. A guitar had been placed against a chair. He hadn't realised that there would be entertainment tonight. Several people glanced over and waved at him, he recognised them from the carol service on Christmas Eve. Suddenly, it seemed like most of the village knew him! He stopped to chat to a few people, including Lloyd and Granny Mabe, who were sitting with a bunch of friends, then weaved his way through to the bar. Suddenly he felt a pat on the back.

'Okay, Joel?'

It was Ryan. 'We're over in the far corner if you want to join us. Me and Jay are getting the drinks. What you having?'

He was tempted to say that he'd get his own, not really wanting to get into a round as he only wanted a couple of drinks, but it sounded churlish so he said, 'I'll have a shandy, thanks. Want me to help you both take the drinks over?'

'We're good. You carry on over to the table.'

There was such a crowd by the bar, it took him a while to inch through and spot the table where Lexi, Sonia and Nell were sitting. Lexi had her back to him and was wearing a peacock-blue backless top or dress that exposed an enticing amount of creamy skin. Nice. Then she stood up and turned around and he did a double take as he saw that it was a figure-hugging dress – the bodice plunged into a deep V that hinted at even more creamy skin, then the fabric nipped in at her slender waist, before flowing over her hips. As she stepped away from the table, he saw that the dress had a split on the left side that went almost up to her hips – and wow, she had long legs. He couldn't take his eyes off her as she leant over to talk to Nell. Then Nell spotted him and waved, and Lexi turned, too. Their eyes met and their gaze held for a second, he tried to steady his heartbeat as Lexi's bright-red lips formed a smile, and she waved cheerily at him, before walking away, over to the Ladies.

'You all right, mate?' Ryan and Jay were standing by him, each holding a tray of drinks.

Joel pulled himself together. 'Bit crowded, isn't it?' He looked at the two trays. 'Stocking up?'

'Thought it best to get two rounds in. It's manic at the bar,' Jay told him.

They all walked over to the table, and both women greeted him with a smile and a 'Hi, Joel!' then Jay and Ryan sat opposite Sonia and Nell, leaving the empty seat next to Lexi for him. Feeling a little awkward, as if he was interrupting a family get-together, he sat down.

'I hear you're all off tomorrow,' he said, then added, 'Thanks,' as Ryan placed his drinks in front of him.

'Yeah, we've got work,' Ryan said.

'And we're going travelling a bit. I want to show Sonia some more of England before we go back to Canada,' Jay told him.

'Lexi's going home, too. Our folks won't know what to do with themselves after having us all around for a couple of weeks,' added Ryan.

'I should think they have plenty to do with work – and your gran keeps them on their toes,' Nell said.

As he chatted to them, Joel's senses were on high alert, waiting for Lexi to come back. Then a wave of heady perfume wafted over, and he looked up, and she was there, looking absolutely stunning with those dark-lashed eyes and ruby-red lips – and that sensational dress . . .

'Hi, Joel.' She pulled out the chair next to him and sat down, her leg so close to his that it was all he could do not to reach out and stroke it.

Bloody hell, Joel, get a grip. Anyone would think you were a hormone-riddled teenager!

'How's Sweetie?' Lexi asked, and Joel realised that he hadn't returned her greeting.

'She was fast asleep when I left her,' he said.

Suddenly, the microphone crackled. 'Testing. Testing. Can you all hear me?' the man called.

'Yes!' a chorus of shouts told him.

'Who are they?' Joel asked, pointing at the musicians.

'No idea. They must be local. Good to have a bit of entertainment, isn't it?' Lexi replied.

The man picked up his guitar and the woman stepped forward, holding a mike, and they broke into song.

Joel picked up his shandy and took a long sip. This was going to be an enjoyable evening.

Lexi glanced at her brothers and their partners sitting around the table, and at Joel sitting next to her, and thought how happy she was. And how glad she was that she hadn't gone back home earlier. It was good to see New Year in with her family. And Joel.

She didn't know whether it was because Joel looked so different in that opened-necked shirt and tight jeans, with his hair gelled up like that, or whether it was the party atmosphere, with everyone joining in with the singers, or the knowledge that she was going home tomorrow, that made her so acutely aware of him. She could smell the tang of his aftershave, feel his leg briefly touching hers whenever he moved, sending tingles up her spine. His hand had briefly brushed against hers when he'd reached for his glass, and a shiver had run through her. Maybe she'd better watch how much she had to drink tonight, she didn't want to make a fool of herself.

'This reminds me of when we were younger and all used to gather here for New Year's Eve,' Ryan said. 'Do you remember that time when the singer called you up to do a duet with him, Lexi?'

'As if I'd ever forget!' Lexi said.

'Can you sing?' Sonia asked.

'Haven't got a tune in my head,' Lexi admitted, laughing. 'I think he regretted it as soon as I opened my mouth!'

Old friends came over to reintroduce themselves, and everyone moved up to make room for them. Soon there were more and more people around the table, all joining in with the singers. It was a fun atmosphere.

The nearer to midnight it got, the more packed the pub became, with people piling in for the final hour. Finally, the landlord rang the bell. 'Get ready for the countdown!' he shouted.

'Ten, nine, eight, seven, six, five, four, three, two, one! Happy New Year!'

Everyone was standing up now, cheering, shaking hands, kissing each other.

Lexi was caught up in the elation of it all. 'Happy New Year! Happy New Year!'

Then she felt an arm go around her and Joel was whispering, 'Happy New Year!' as he wrapped her in his arms. She snuggled into the warmth of his body, turning her face towards him, then his lips found hers and a tremble coursed through her as his kiss deepened, and she returned it, revelled in it, in the feel of his body close to hers.

'Want to come back to mine?' he asked.

She nodded, knowing that there was nothing she wanted more.

Chapter Thirty-seven

Sweetie was fast asleep in her basket when they walked in. She opened her eyes, wagged her tail at them both, then went straight back to sleep.

'She looks like she's happy to sleep down here,' Lexi remarked.

'Yep, I get the bed to myself at last.' Joel turned to Lexi and wound his arms around her waist. 'Except tonight, I would very much like you to share it with me.'

She wrapped her arms around his neck. 'I would very much like that, too.'

Hand in hand they went upstairs. Joel opened the bedroom door, his hand still holding Lexi's, and closed it behind them as soon as they were inside. He turned and pulled her gently into his arms, his lips seeking hers. Then he trailed butterfly kisses down her neck, and her shoulders, his fingers undoing the clasp at the back of her neck so that the top of her dress fell down, exposing her breasts. Joel groaned and cupped them in his hands. 'You're beautiful,' he murmured, thickly.

Lexi's breath quickened, her desire rising. She tugged his shirt out of his trousers and ran her hands up his back, pulling his body closer to her. She heard Joel draw in his breath, then he raised his head, his eyes seeking hers. 'Are you sure about this?'

'Absolutely sure,' she said, unbuttoning his shirt.

They undressed each other wildly, leaving their clothes in a heap on the carpet, and still kissing, caressing, touching, they sank to the floor and then Joel was on top of her, and inside her, and it was just as wonderful as she had dreamt it would be.

They reached a crescendo together, then lay in each other's arms for a while, before moving to the bed and doing it all over again. And again. Finally, exhausted, they fell into a deep sleep. Lexi woke at dawn, conscious of someone's arm around her waist. It took her a couple of seconds to remember that she'd gone to bed with Joel, he was spooned against her, snoring very softly, and it felt so right. She lay there, revelling in the nearness of him.

This is exactly where I want to be.

She registered the truth in her thought, then fell back asleep and only woke up when Sweetie yapped outside the door, wanting to go outside for a wee. Light was streaming into the room. Lexi glanced at the clock. Almost ten.

'Do you have time to stay for breakfast?' Joel asked, noticing her glance at the clock and knowing that her brothers were both leaving today. And she was meant to be too.

'I do. And thank you, that would be very nice.'

'Coffee and croissants?'

'Perfect.'

He leant over and kissed her tenderly. 'You stay here and I'll bring it up in just a few minutes.'

'Thank you.' She wound her arms around his neck and kissed him.

When he'd left the room, she lay there for a moment reliving the previous night's events. She could hardly believe that she'd come back with Joel, but it was what they had both wanted. And now her body was tingling with the effects of their love-making. She felt her cheeks glow as she recalled just how adventurous they had been.

She jumped out of bed to go to the bathroom, and decided to have a quick shower while she was there. Afterwards, wrapped in a towel, she stepped back into the bedroom, just as Joel opened the door, carrying breakfast on a tray.

'That looks delicious, thank you,' she said, sitting down on the bed and looking hungrily at the two croissants and the milky coffee. A small pot of jam, butter, a spoon and a knife were on the tray, too.

'I've warmed them up for you,' he said, sitting down beside her.

'Perfect.' She spread the warm croissant with butter, then jam, and bit into it. It was delicious. Joel took the other croissant and tucked into that. They both ate in companionable silence for a while.

When breakfast was finally finished, Lexi suddenly felt awkward. She was going home in a few hours, and hadn't planned for this new development with Joel. Not that she regretted sleeping with him, it had been fantastic, but where did that leave them now? Was it just a one-off as far as he was concerned, a sort of 'Goodbye', or did it mean something more? Because it certainly meant something more to her.

'Any regrets?' said Joel.

She raised her eyes to his.

'None at all,' she said truthfully. 'What about you?'

'Absolutely none.' He reached out and took her hand. 'What time are you planning on going home?'

'About two,' she said.

'Then I'd better say goodbye properly,' he said, leaning forward and kissing her on the nose. Then the lips. And somehow, her towel had slipped down, and he was kissing her breasts, then his mouth moved lower ...

It was much later when she had another shower, then dressed and went home to say goodbye to her family.

Her brothers were all packed and ready to go.

'We were just going to text you, we decided to leave earlier,' Ryan said.

'Sorry, I ... err ... overslept,' she stammered.

'Or maybe never slept,' Nell said with a grin.

Lexi grinned back, glad her parents weren't in the room to hear that remark, although, she was sure they had guessed where she was last night.

The door opened and her mum came out of the kitchen. 'Oh, hello, Lexi. Did you have a good night last night?'

Nell sniggered and Lexi gave her a slight kick. 'It was great, Mum. We all had a good time, didn't we?'

They all chorused their agreement.

Craig came in then, and Granny Mabe. 'It's been so lovely to see you all,' she said. 'It's really made my Christmas.'

'It certainly has,' Paula agreed. 'There's nothing like a Forde family Christmas.' Her eyes went a bit teary. 'And this is the bit I hate the most. Saying goodbye.'

She wiped away a tear as she hugged Jay, Sonia and Toby. 'Don't leave it too long before you come again,' she said.

'We won't, we'll be back over as soon as we can,' Jay promised, giving his mum a big hug. 'And remember that you can come and see us too.' He turned to Lexi. 'And you. Bring Joel, too.'

'Are you two . . . ?' Paula asked, turning to look at Lexi.

'No, we're just friends . . .' Although, last night had changed that for her. Had it for Joel?

'What about me and Lloyd? Can we come?' Granny Mabe asked. 'And before you ask, we're just friends, too.'

'You can all come. We'd love to see you and we have plenty of room,' Sonia told them. 'We could even put you all up at the same time if someone is happy to sleep on the sofa in the lounge.'

'We don't mind doing that, do we, Nell?' asked Ryan.

'No problem,' Nell agreed. 'Let's all see if we can go over together.'

It would be lovely to go to Canada, thought Lexi, and doable now she had only herself to think about. She could save up and maybe visit Jay and Sonia later in the year. It would do her good to plan a life without Ben. Maybe she would even move from her flat, too. A new start was what she needed.

Everyone hugged and said goodbye again. Ryan and Nell were going, too.

'We'll be back down soon,' they promised.

'Make sure you are,' Paula told them.

'Look after yourself, sis.' Ryan gave Lexi a hug. 'Come and see us, you're welcome any time.'

'And don't let Joel get away, you two are made for each other,' Nell whispered as she hugged Lexi, too.

There was more hugging and waving and then they were gone.

The house suddenly seemed quiet and empty. Lexi looked at her parents, feeling sorry for them. The house had been so full of life. They must miss everyone already.

'I could go back tomorrow,' she told them.

Her mum shook her head. 'It's very kind of you, love, but I know you've got lessons to prepare for Tuesday. And we're at work tomorrow. It would be lovely if you could stay another hour or so though.'

'Of course I will,' she agreed.

It was two hours later when she packed her things and loaded them in the car, then went to say goodbye to Lloyd, promising to come and say hello when she was next down. He looked so much happier. Rocco had been with his daughter and wife; Lloyd showed her a photo of them all, his face brimming with happiness. 'Oh gosh, I'm sorry, I said I'd come to meet them,' she said, clapping her hand to her mouth. 'Did Joel pop around?'

'No he didn't but it doesn't matter. They didn't stay long and it was probably best for us to chat together and clear the air. Rocco's going to pick me up next Sunday and take me over to his for lunch,' he said. 'And it's all thanks to you and Joel. You've both given me my family back.'

'I'm glad.' She gave him a big hug and promised to drop in and see him when she came down to visit her parents again.

Now it was time to say goodbye to Joel.

She took a deep breath, walked up his path and pressed the bell. Sweetie immediately started barking. As soon as Joel opened the door, the white fur ball ducked around his legs, ran out and jumped up at Lexi.

'Hello, girl.' Lexi bent down to stroke her, appreciating the chance to compose herself.

'Are you leaving now?' Joel asked.

She took a deep breath, stood up and forced a smile onto her face. 'Yes. I don't want to be back too late.' She stepped forward and kissed him on the cheek. 'Thank you. For everything. Saving the tree and . . .' Damn, she was going to cry any minute.

'So, it's goodbye, then?' he said, his eyes still holding hers.

She nodded. 'I'm heading off now.' She felt like her heart was aching, she was going to miss him so much.

'I'll miss you.'

Her eyes went to his face at his words. Miss her how? As a friend?

'I'll miss you, too,' she admitted.

'Will it take you long to get home?' he asked.

'A couple of hours.'

He nodded. 'When do you think you'll be down again?'

'I'm not sure, but I'll definitely come down for Granny Mabe's birthday at the end of May.'

'That's five whole months away.'

'I know.' She swallowed, waiting to see if he would ask her to come and see him, say he didn't want her to go. That he couldn't bear to not see her again, that his heart was breaking as hers was. He was staring at her intently, but was silent. *Okay, time to go before you make a fool of yourself. It's clear it was just a one-night stand.* 'Goodbye, Joel.'

She turned and walked quickly down the path.

'Lexi, come back!'

She wanted to turn around but she didn't dare. She knew that if she did, she would confess her feelings for him and make a fool of herself. What she felt for Joel was because she was on the rebound. And she was sure it was the same for him.

He was recently divorced, and Christmas was such a special time, it was no wonder they'd both drifted towards each other, sought solace in each other's friendship. It had been a good Christmas. The best Christmas ever. But it was over. Time to go home.

Chapter Thirty-eight

'Lexi! Please come back!'

She could hear Joel's footsteps racing after her. She turned to him, blinking back the tears from her eyes.

He moved a little closer. 'How do you feel about me coming to visit?'

Her heart grew wings. 'That would be nice.' Did he mean as a friend? 'You can bring Sweetie too.'

'How about next weekend?'

She paused. That soon? Did that mean he was going to miss her as much as she would miss him? 'Sure.'

Suddenly Sweetie jumped up at her and she fell forward. Joel caught her in his arms, steadied her, and wrapped his arms around her. His face was so close she could feel his breath on her cheek, smell the male scent of him, feel the warmth of his body. She saw the question in his eyes as he held her against him and slowly nodded her head. Then his lips were on hers and they were both lost in a passionate embrace, the kissing getting deeper and deeper, their bodies pressing closer and closer.

She almost moaned as Joel pulled his head away and looked at her. 'I want to be more than friends. Do you?'

'Yes,' she groaned, pulling him closer to her. 'Much more.' Then their lips found each other again.

'Do you have to go now?' he asked. 'Could you go a little later? So we can say goodbye properly?'

She nodded and, arms wrapped around each other, they walked back into Joel's house.

Much later, as she lay in Joel's arms in his big double bed, Sweetie fast asleep downstairs, Lexi said. 'I guess I could go home in the morning.'

'I wish you didn't have to go home at all.' Joel sighed. Then, seeing the look that crossed Lexi's face, he added. 'But I'm grown up enough to deal with it.' He pulled her closer to him and kissed the top of her head. 'We can make this work, Lexi. Lots of people have long-distance relationships. That is, if you want to?'

'I do,' she nodded.

'I really like you, Lexi.' He was propped up on his elbow now, looking down at her, his eyes searching her face. 'And I think you feel the same about me, too.'

She bit her lip. She hadn't felt this way about anyone before, not even Ben, but was it too soon? They were both fresh out of relationships. They needed time to move on before they got involved with someone else.

'I know we've only just met, and it's sudden and unexpected, but that doesn't matter. What matters is how we feel about each other. Do you feel it too?'

His eyes were holding hers. As if he was looking deep into her soul. How could she deny it?

'Yes.' Her reply was almost a whisper.

'Then let's see where this goes. You live a couple of hours away. Okay, it's not ideal, but it's not that difficult either. We can keep in touch, see each other at the weekends – not every one, if you don't want to. We can take it as slow – or as fast – as you want.'

It would be good to know that Joel was there, on the other end of the phone, to see him again. To know that she didn't have to say goodbye.

'I'd like that,' she agreed.

He leant down and kissed her, and she kissed him back, wishing she didn't have to go.

I could stay one more night.

But then she would have to say goodbye all over again tomorrow.

'Will you stay overnight again?' he asked, his voice husky with desire. 'It's dark already now, and I have to go to work tomorrow, we could leave at the same time. Saying goodbye wouldn't be so hard then.'

'I'd love to.'

His face broke into a huge smile, and his eyes crinkled at the corners. He pulled her to him. 'Now, tempting as it is to spend the rest of the day in bed, let's get up and have something to eat.'

That sounded good to Lexi, her tummy was rumbling.

They showered and dressed, then Joel rustled up a tuna pasta bake and Lexi found a tin of fruit and cream in his cupboard, and they sat and ate it as if it was a feast.

'This calls for a celebration, but as we're both driving early in the morning, perhaps we should restrict the alcohol and celebrate with hot chocolate and a shot of brandy instead?' Joel suggested.

'That sounds good to me. Do you have marshmallows?'

'Of course.'

A few minutes later, armed with a mug of hot chocolate with a shot of brandy in each, they sat in Joel's lounge and talked. It was as if they wanted to tell each other everything. Joel told her more about his childhood, and she understood why he had never bothered much about Christmas as he grew up. 'You showed me the true spirit of Christmas, and I'm grateful to you for that,' he said.

'Does that mean you're going to put up a Christmas tree and wear a Christmas jumper every year?' she teased.

'Yes, and when the jumper you knitted me wears out, you'll have to knit me another one,' he said with a grin.

They talked all evening, before saying goodnight to Sweetie and going up to bed together. This time their lovemaking was slower, gentler, like the merging of two souls.

Joel stirred and opened his eyes. Lexi was facing him, her arm wrapped around his chest, her eyes still closed, her breathing soft. She looked so peaceful. And beautiful. He lay watching her sleep for a while, hardly believing how things had turned out. He'd come down to Devon to make a new start and recover from his marriage break-up, and here he was involved with someone he'd only just met, and who was going back home today. Not that Gloucester was the other side of the world, but it was far enough away for them not to be able to see each other regularly, to spend evenings going for a walk, or a meal, or share a bottle of wine in front of the TV and go to bed wrapped in each other's arms. But then perhaps they both needed this time to be themselves, to pick up the threads of their lives and decide what they wanted to do with the rest of them. He hadn't planned to get involved with anyone else, but Lexi had snuck into his heart and he didn't want to let her go.

'Yap! Yap!'

Lexi's eyes flew open. Then they rested on his face and she smiled. 'Hello.'

'Hello.' He leant forward and kissed her on the mouth.

'Yap! Yap!'

'I think Sweetie wants to go out.'

'I know. I'm going to let her out now. Fancy a cuppa?'

'Yes please.'

He kissed her again, then got out of bed and went down to make coffee for them both, after opening the back door for Sweetie to go out first.

He didn't want Lexi to go.

He had to be adult about this. She had her life, and he had his, but at least they could see each other now and again, see where it went.

Sweetie came back in and stood by her bowl, wagging her tail, indicating that she wanted something to eat. He took a tin of dog food out of the fridge and scooped some into the bowl, then gave her a fuss. Then he picked up the two coffee mugs and took them upstairs.

Lexi was in the bathroom, he could hear the shower running. He put her mug down on the bedside table on her side of the bed, and his on the other one. Then the bathroom door opened and Lexi walked out, rubbing her hair. His eyes rested on her naked body. God, he really didn't want her to go.

'Hiya, I thought I'd freshen up. How's Sweetie?'

'Absolutely fine.' He walked over to her and gently took the towel out of her hands, put it on the chair, and cupped her face with his hands. Then he kissed her gently on the lips. She wrapped her arms around him and kissed him soundly back.

'Fancy coming back to bed? One last swansong?'

'Sounds good to me,' she murmured.

It was over an hour later, and the coffee had gone cold before they got out of bed again.

'I really need to go now,' Lexi told him. 'I don't want to get home too late.'

Joel pulled her closer to him. 'I can't wait until next weekend. Can I come up on Saturday afternoon? And maybe stay overnight?'

She kissed him. 'That sounds a very good idea.'

It was strange being home. She'd spent two weeks surrounded by her family, and now the flat was silent, empty. And bare. She'd left her flat, heartbroken, just a fortnight ago, and such a lot had happened in that time. How had she met someone else, and fallen so head over heels, in only two weeks?

Maybe it was the equivalent of a holiday romance. It was Christmas, the season of goodwill, and friendship, and she and Joel had been thrown together. Perhaps when they both returned to their normal lives, they would realise that it had all been in the heat of the moment, that they didn't actually have anything in common after all.

A text pinged in. Her heart skipped a beat when she saw that it was from Joel.

Missing you already. Are you home yet? Can I video call you?

She immediately pressed the video-call button and Joel's face appeared on the screen.

'Hello,' he said softly.

She touched his face with her finger. 'Hello.'

'How was the journey?'

They talked for a while, and she felt herself wishing she was still down in Devon, cuddled up to him on the sofa. Or in bed.

'Sweetie wants to say hello, too.' Joel placed the phone so Lexi could see the little fur ball, who barked when she saw her image.

Lexi swallowed a lump in her throat. She missed them both so much. Especially Joel.

They finally said goodbye, and Lexi set about unpacking her case, then had a shower, and got into bed. It was strange being in the bed by herself, but it wasn't Ben she was missing, it was Joel. She lay there for a while, memories of their two nights together flashing across her mind. Joel had raised feelings in her that she never knew she had. She had thought she loved Ben, but it had felt nothing like this.

As she drifted off to sleep, images of their lovemaking flitted across her mind, how he'd kissed her, every part of her, and she felt that she could still feel his hands on her body, his kisses on her lips.

Chapter Thirty-nine

Saturday, 8 January

Lexi glanced at her watch. Joel would be here any moment. She couldn't wait to see him again. They'd exchanged texts over the past week and video-called at least once a day on the phone, but she was missing him like mad. Lloyd had offered to look after Sweetie for the weekend, as Lexi lived in a flat. She was really looking forward to spending time together again.

It had been less than a month since Ben had left, but already it felt as if he had never lived with her. She realised now what little input Ben had had in her life, he'd just been there, someone to come home too, wake up with, occasionally share things with, whereas Joel was ever there, even at a distance. He sent her texts asking her how her day had gone, genuinely interested in her life, as she was in his. And now, they had two whole days together.

A message pinged in. *I'm outside! J xxx*

She pressed the buzzer to let him in, and went to open the door to her flat. A couple of minutes later, there he was, holdall in one hand, a big bunch of flowers in the other, and a huge smile on his face.

He put the holdall down, then the flowers on top of it, and held out his arms. She went straight into them, and felt the warmth of his hug enveloping her. They kissed, long and deeply, then she pulled herself away. 'Would you like a drink? I've got some beer in the fridge, and wine.'

They'd agreed to order a takeaway that night, and go out for a meal the following night. She was pleased, much as she enjoyed the physical side of things with Joel, she didn't want that to be all their relationship was about. She wanted them to go out together, and share experiences, as they had done in Lystone.

'I hope this doesn't sound boring, but a cup of coffee would be great,' he told her, picking up the flowers and handing them to her. 'I wasn't sure what ones were your favourite, so got a mixed bunch.'

'They're gorgeous. I don't have a favourite, I love all flowers. Thanks so much, I'll go and put them in water.'

Joel followed her into the open-plan lounge and kitchen, and watched as she took a vase out of the cupboard. 'Want me to make the coffee?'

She was about to say no, when she stopped herself. She wasn't going to be the one who did all the chores, as she had with Ben. 'Please. The coffee pods are on the rack by the wall.'

Joel selected two pods and put one in the machine, and turned it on, then took two mugs off the mug stand.

'How's Sweetie?' Lexi asked him when the flowers were in water, and they were both sitting down on the sofa, mug of coffee in hand.

'Great. I can actually leave her to go to work, and she's happy to settle in her basket at night. I've given Lloyd a spare key and he pops in and lets her out for a run around. Sometimes he takes her back to his house, but to be honest, most times he's out. He's got a full social life now, thanks to your gran.'

'I'm glad.'

'And how's your work going? Are the kids giving you grief?' Joel asked.

She amused him with a couple of incidents at school, then they ordered a Chinese takeaway. By the time they'd eaten that, while listening to music, it was time to go to bed.

'I've missed you,' Joel said as he climbed into bed beside her, and wrapped his arms around her.

'I've missed you, too,' she murmured, snuggling up to him.

Later, when they had made love and settled down to sleep, Lexi thought how wonderful it was to be with Joel again. If only she could wake up with him every day.

But how could she do that when he lived two hours' drive away?

Just make the most of the time you have together, she told herself as her eyes closed wearily.

Joel woke up the next morning wondering where he was for a moment, then remembered that he was in Lexi's flat.

And Lexi had gone. The other side of the bed was empty.

The bedroom door opened and Lexi came in carrying a tray laden with scrambled eggs on toast and two glasses of orange juice.

'I thought I'd make us breakfast. I hope this is okay.' She put the tray down on the bed.

'It's perfect,' Joel told her as she pulled the duvet back and got into bed beside him.

'Mind you don't spill the egg all over the sheets,' she said as he kissed her.

They chatted away as they ate their breakfast, then made love again, showered and got up. Lexi had promised him a sightseeing trip today – Gloucester Docks and the shopping centre. He was looking forward to it, Gloucester was a historical town and he was sure there would be plenty to see there.

'You must come up in June, when the tall ships festival is on,' Lexi told him as they walked along the dockside. 'I always like to go and see them. I find them fascinating.'

Joel's heart soared. So, she was still expecting them to be together in five months' time. Well, that was fine by him.

After the docks, Lexi suggested that they went to take a look at Rainbow Street. 'It's only ten minutes or so from the shopping centre, so we can go to the shops and grab something for lunch. I've been meaning to see it myself, but not got around to it.'

'Sure. Is there a rainbow painted on every house or something?' he asked.

'It's called St Mark Street really, but the locals call it Rainbow Street. You'll see why.'

They got back into the car and set off.

He soon discovered that it was so named because so many of the houses were painted in different colours: red, orange, vibrant lime green, blue, yellow. 'Wow, it's colourful,' he said. 'Who did this?'

'A local landlady. She wanted to bring a bit of colour into the street and improve the desirability of the houses, so she arranged for them to be painted in different colours. They're now quite a tourist attraction.'

'I'm not surprised,' he replied.

Later, after lunch in a pub at the nearby shopping centre, they took a look around the shops then returned home to get changed before going for a meal at a local Italian.

The next day, they set off to have a walk around the Forest of Dean, then a drive over to Symonds Yat Rock. He hadn't expected Gloucester and the surrounding area to be so beautiful and interesting, Joel thought, as he drove home later that evening. He could understand why Lexi liked living there, it was a good mix of shops and countryside. He'd been hoping that she might want to move back down to Devon, but she seemed so happy there, he thought it was unlikely.

Showing Joel around had reminded Lexi just how much she loved Gloucester. While she'd been staying with her parents she'd been drawn back into life in Lystone again and wondered if she should move back down there, but now she realised that her life was here and, much as she loved the little Devon village where she grew up, she didn't want to live there. But Joel had been talking about buying a place there to move into when his sister and her partner returned. How could they continue with a long-term relationship when they both lived so far apart? And she did want a relationship with him, she'd really enjoyed this weekend.

Just take it as it is, she told herself, *you can be in a relationship with someone without living in their pocket.*

'We can make this work,' Joel had told her when he left.

He was right. They could.

Chapter Forty

Five months later

S he was almost there. Lexi couldn't wait to see her family
again. Joel. Ryan and Nell would be there, too, although,
unfortunately, Jay, Sonia and Toby couldn't come. Canada was a
bit far for them to travel over twice in one year, even if it was
Granny Mabe's eighty-fifth birthday. Her gran's party was
tomorrow night, Saturday, so Lexi had travelled down on the
Friday after work, planning on spending two nights with Joel.

A smile came to her lips as she thought of her gran, they'd
chatted a bit over the last few months – when she could catch
her gran in that was – and Granny Mabe had mentioned Lloyd
a few times. It seemed that they'd become very friendly and
that Lloyd was really involved in village life now, which was
great.

Joel and Andy had been offered more work with the council
over the past few months. And the green had been declared an
area of outstanding beauty, so all plans to cut down the tree had
been shelved. Things had worked out well.

As she drove into the village, Lexi tried to imagine living here again. Hazel and Al were coming back next month so Joel would be getting his own place and last weekend he had asked Lexi if she would live with him. Of course Lexi had agreed. They'd become so close over the last few months and she really loved Joel. She wanted to wake up to him in the morning, to come home to him at night, but she had worried all week about where they would live. Joel had settled in Lystone and was building his business again while she loved her job and living in Gloucester. Devon seemed too quiet and far away for her now. Joel was happy here though so after a lot of thought she had decided to tell him that she would move to Lystone. She could get a job in another school and she'd be near her family. She'd soon adjust again.

Joel greeted her with a big hug and, as she stepped into the house, she felt as if she'd never been away. Sweetie came rushing to greet her, tail wagging like mad.

'I've missed you.' Lexi knelt down so that she could give the little dog a big fuss. 'She looks so happy, I can see how close you've both got,' she told Joel.

'Yes, but not for much longer. Hazel and Al are coming home next month,' he told her. 'So we need to decide where we're going to live.' He reached out and touched her cheek. 'You still want us to live together, don't you?'

She nodded. 'I can't wait. Maybe we can go online over the weekend and look at some houses? Then you can check them out in the week and let me know what you think.'

'Well I was hoping I could move in with you and we could choose somewhere together.'

'What?' Her eyes met his, startled.

A broad grin spread over his face and he placed his hands on her shoulders, his gaze holding hers intently. 'I'd like to move to Gloucester. I love spending weekends there and think it's a great place to live. Unless you prefer to move down here, to be by your parents? If so, I don't mind. Whatever makes you happy.'

He was studying her face, waiting for her reaction, and she saw him relax when she grinned in delight. This was amazing! 'I want to stay in Gloucester, too. But are you sure? What about your job?'

'Andy lives in Exeter, there's not that much difference in the travel time, but actually, I've been offered a job working in the Forest of Dean. It sounds perfect but I haven't agreed to take it yet, I wanted to talk it over with you first. What do you think? Am I okay to move in with you while we look for a house together?'

She nodded emphatically. 'Yes. Yes, please!' She threw her arms around his neck and kissed him.

'We'll tell your folks on Sunday, after your gran's party,' he said. 'Do you think they'll mind? I wondered if they were hoping we'd find a home down here.'

'They won't mind at all. And we can visit regularly at weekends,' Lexi assured him. She snuggled into him. 'Have I told you how much I love you?'

'Once or twice,' he whispered, his breath tickling her ear. 'Why don't you show me instead?'

So she did.

The Olde Tavern was full. People kept dropping in to wish Granny Mabe a happy birthday, bringing her cards and gifts.

She sat with a big smile on her face all night, and now and again Lexi was sure she saw a tear in her eye as she turned to show another present or card to Lloyd, who was sitting next to her.

When everyone had sung 'Happy Birthday' and the cake, with two candles, an eight and a five, on it, had been brought in, Granny Mabe blew them out and thanked everyone for coming.

'This has been such a special day for me, and I'm so pleased to have so many members of my family, and friends, to share it with,' she said, her voice wobbling a little.

Everyone clapped and cheered.

'And now I want to share with you some news that has made my day even more special.' She held out her hand to Lloyd and he stood up beside her.

'Lloyd has asked me to marry him, and I've accepted,' she said.

This announcement was greeted by even more claps and cheers.

Joel put his arm around Lexi's shoulder and hugged her as she clapped excitedly. This was the best news.

'Fancy Granny getting married again,' Ryan said with a grin. He winked at Lexi. 'If anyone was going to make an announcement like that, I thought it would be you two.'

Joel looked into Lexi's eyes and smiled. 'Maybe next year,' he said.

And, as Lexi snuggled into him, she thought that next year would be perfect.

Acknowledgements

I love writing Christmas books. Christmas is such a warm, fun, heart-warming time and the stories are so uplifting to write with the themes of love, friendship, family and goodwill. It's not easy though to set the scene for snow and Christmas festivities when it's summer and you're basking in over 40 degrees in southern Spain! I find that having some Christmas carols playing in the background and cinnamon and apple candles burning helps set the mood a little. :)

A writer needs a support system when writing a book. I'm grateful for the expertise of my publishers, Headline, and would especially like to thank my fabulous editor Katie Sunley, copy editor Eloise Wood and proof-reader Kay Gale for their expertise and support. Thanks also to talented artist Emily Courdelle for designing another beautiful cover.

As always, I am indebted to the bloggers and authors who support me by hosting me on their blogs, reviewing my books and sharing my posts. Particular thanks to the members of the Romantic Novelists' Association who are always willing to share their writing experience and advice. Also thanks to Nick

Organ, Arboricultural Consultant at Tree Maintenance Limited and Miles Hamilton, tree surgeon, both of whom I consulted regarding tree diseases and maintenance. Their advice was invaluable and any mistakes are my own. Also heartfelt thanks to Annette Burton for being the sort of friend you can message late at night for information on whether a primary school teacher has to do any work during the Christmas holidays (they do!) and replying to my message even though she was in bed. You are a super star.

Last but not least, massive thanks to my husband Dave, the wind beneath my wings, for being my biggest champion and for spending hours checking proofs and helping me spot those elusive typos. And to all my family and friends for their encouragement and support. I love you all. xx